Elizabeth Parmer
Caren Penland

The Poison of Life

"Feeling without judgement is a washy draught indeed;
but judgement untempered by feeling is too bitter and
husky a morsel for human deglutition."

— Charlotte Brontë, *Jane Eyre*

[handwritten inscription:] Chris— So nice to meet you! Hope you enjoy the book. *Caren Penland*

[handwritten inscription:] C— You too! msn. Thank U *Elizabeth Parmer* 2016

THE POISON OF LIFE
COPYRIGHT © 2016 BY ELIZABETH PARMER
AND CAREN PENLAND

First Printing: April 2016

This is a work of fiction. Names, characters, places, and incidents are the product of the authors' imaginations or are used fictitiously, and any resemblance to actual persons, living or dead, businesses, companies, events, or locales is entirely coincidental.

www.betsyandcaren.com

PO Box 471264
Fort Worth, Texas 76107-2778

ISBN-13: 978-1523876785
ISBN-10: 1523876786

CREDITS

PUBLISHERS: ELIZABETH PARMER AND CAREN PENLAND
EXECUTIVE EDITOR: TARA YOUNG
COVER DESIGN: SARAH HUFFSTETLER
COVER ARTWORK: JAMES HINKLE
AUTHOR PHOTO: ROSS HAILEY

Dedication

We accidentally made a washed-up forty-something queen cry at Good Friends Bar in New Orleans. He was upset because his nineteen-year-old boyfriend ditched him. We were just trying to make him feel better about life in general. He bit Betsy and called her a "sexy Leo bitch" and tried to make out with Caren. Thank you, random drunk stranger, for inspiring many scenes of French Quarter debauchery in this novel.

This book is for Sarah, James, and Claire, all of whom had to hear about this sort of nonsense over and over. Thank you for putting up with our writing adventure.

Acknowledgments

As with anything worth doing, this book started out as a thought and a dream over a glass of wine with good company. To make that dream a reality, we needed support and help. We got more of both than we could have ever desired.

Lee and Helen Williams and Victoria des Rosiers opened up their homes to us, making it possible to actually walk the streets of New Orleans and Chicago. Their hospitality was incredibly generous.

The bartenders and drunken strangers we met along the way provided the kind of color you just can't make up. It took meeting people like Reggie, our train attendant on the Texas Eagle route from Fort Worth to Chicago, to make our characters come alive.

Behind every good writer is a better editor. Your comments are always amusing, Tara Young, even when you're wrong. So very wrong. There is such a thing as bad eighties music. Thank you for keeping us on track and cleaning up our copy. The whole project feels more legit with you on board.

James Hinkle, your artwork is stunning. We are honored to have the original painting "Mardi Gras Girl" grace our cover. Sarah Huffstetler, thank you for knowing what to do with it. Your design skills aren't nearly as rusty as you thought.

Thank you to our families, particularly Claire Bear, and to an amazing group of friends. Your enthusiasm and encouragement kept us going. You bitches are going to die when you read this book!

Most of all, thank you, New Orleans. There is no other city that breathes with more life, filth, and desire. The late nights we spent staggering home arm-in-arm were not wasted. We couldn't have scraped the experiences off with more joy. We adore you.

Chapter One

Greyson Chesterfield screwed her face up into the deepest, meanest scowl she could muster—her cheeks blushing madly, her green eyes watering in the effort to make herself appear more menacing than was possible. She was out of breath from giggling and gasped with indignation when Bradley reached out and playfully swatted at her jet-black bangs.

"Then," he continued, hoarse laughter bubbling up around each word, "we can go check out girls together at the mall." He coughed and cleared his throat, the fit subsiding quickly. "You'll be all like, 'Check out that one,' and I'll say, 'Nah, man, she's got ten boyfriends already.'"

"Shut up, Bradley," Grey hissed. "Not funny. I'm being serious."

"Oh, okay, killjoy."

Bradley sighed and touched her bangs again, this time brushing them back in place with trembling fingers. He cupped her cheek and grinned at her. "Can't say I'm all that surprised. Who would have thought that the girl who wanted to play G.I. Joe and hated My Little Pony would turn out to be a lesbian?"

"Don't be ridiculous. This is a *big* deal." She pouted, turning away angrily, annoyed at how her older brother always managed to make her most monumental announcements seem silly. "You will never understand."

"Really? I will never understand?" He smiled smugly from the bed. "Sister, I plowed this ground well in advance of you, remember? It's okay. It's not easy. And Dad, well, let's just say Dad doesn't exactly 'get it,' but as coming out goes in Catholic families, it ain't that bad."

Bradley smiled gently, but his eyes creased a little at the edges. It was an indication of a pain that Grey had grown used to over the last several months. She was instantly aware of her own selfishness and leaned in to her only sibling.

He was so pale. The age gap between them appeared far more than fourteen years. More like thirty. She laid a concerned hand across his damp forehead, just as she remembered her mother doing when she was much smaller. He felt cold and frail, his hazel eyes sunken and glassy, his cheeks sharp and prominent. It was strange, seeing him without hair again. She had loved it when he had grown it longer, waves of silky black draped over his shoulders—sparkling blue highlights in the sun.

Grey hated this room with its fluorescent lights and vanilla ice cream walls, its slick floors that made her designer sneakers squeak, the smell of disinfectant that for years to come would inspire nausea rather than elicit a feeling of security in its cleanliness. It felt like a prison. Or a mental institution. It was sterile, harsh, and too quiet.

An adjustable bed. A mounted flat-screen television, currently on but muted. Two identical gray plastic chairs. Machines she didn't understand. Mauve curtains that were probably supposed to be perceived as soothing. At least this room was a little better than the last. It had a window facing a small park instead of an expansive parking lot.

Grey couldn't remember Bradley ever having to stay away from home for so long. She was ready for this to be over so things could return to normal. They had video games and movies to catch up on. He had missed their date to see the midnight release of *Harry Potter and the Order of the Phoenix*, which was nearly unforgivable.

"Well, anyway, it's you and me together again, isn't it?" She smiled, then giggled and whispered fiercely, "I'm going to get you out of here. I'll bust you out."

"Yeah, kiddo. Always. And please do. I could go for a burger and a beer. For real." And with that, he sat up and kissed her softly on the top of the head, struggled to pull the pillow out from behind him, and smacked her across the butt with as much force as he could muster before she even knew what hit her.

"Bradley Tyrone Chesterfield, I'm gonna kick your ass!"

Grey squealed and scrambled out of reach, nearly tripping over a collapsed wheelchair. She resumed her scowl and vowed revenge. Her gaze darted about the tiny room desperately. She needed something, anything to get back at him. She found her solution in the form of a plush gift bear plopped on one of the gray plastic chairs. She grabbed it and hurled it at him.

"Whoa! Easy with the gifts!" He growled at her, shaking his bone-thin finger. "You watch out, young lady," he gasped, "or I'll have to call for help."

Grey ignored him. She snatched the remote from his hand and tossed it aside, giggling maniacally. "Now you can't call shit."

"Okay, okay, okay!" he shouted, wheezing. "Touchy thing, aren't you?"

They grinned at each other, smiles nearly identical except for the thin, chapped, and pale lips of the one. In the sudden quiet, Grey felt the need to fill the silence.

"This is okay, right? I mean, you don't think this is just something I came up with to, you know," she rolled her eyes, "be like you, right? Because it's not. I know what I know."

"Yeah, I know." He beckoned her back over and took her hand. He squeezed it, and she let him. "I get it. You'll be okay. It'll suck, but it'll be okay. I promise."

She crawled into the narrow bed and tucked her head down under his pointy chin, the way she had when she was a toddler, and he wrapped his thin arms around her. It was her comfort position. She was thirteen, embarrassed of all forms of affection, but this she didn't mind. She could make an exception for her beloved older brother.

"I love you, Greyby-baby," Bradley whispered, his eyes inexplicably filling with tears. "And anything you are is fine with me and Dad, okay?"

"Okay," she said, biting her lip, breaking away before tears overcame her, as well.

They both looked up at the sound of voices behind them. The door opened to reveal a copy of what Bradley should one day grow into. The man looked like a movie star at the very least, broad shoulders and a barrel chest straining against a crisp, blue Armani shirt, his head topped with a mop of thick, jet-black wavy hair with the barest hints of gray, slicked back and grazing the edges of the collar, framing a hard, angular, and strong face—one with the distinctive features and creases typical of those accustomed to issuing directives more than displaying a rare but charming smile. He was a testament to their Italian and British heritage, however many generations removed.

He was tall, like Bradley, but fit and tan, not pale and wasted. Striking in his midfifties. Like his own father, Wilson Chesterfield had aged well.

At that moment, the face was more stern than charming, thick eyebrows furrowed, lost in thought. He

4

cleared his throat and checked his Rolex impatiently, distracted.

"Grey, honey," her father grumbled from miles away, his dark eyes not meeting hers. "Let Bradley get some rest and spend a little time with Jonathan. Go on now."

Grey wasn't even hurt by the gruff dismissal. It had happened too often lately to be upset by it. She knew he'd come back around unexpectedly and sweep her up in those strong arms with a thousand-watt smile, reserved just for her, his baby girl.

Another man stepped out from behind her father's shadow. Good-looking and tall in a completely opposite way. Slender, soft, and, Grey had always thought, more beautiful than handsome. Jonathan smiled at her through bloodshot and sky blue eyes. She did not miss the furtive glance between him and her father, but she wasn't sure what it meant.

She ran over and jumped into Jonathan's arms for another bear hug before leaving the room. Whatever was troubling them so—perhaps they had had another work-related argument, it happened not infrequently—Jonathan, at least, would shrug it off quickly for her benefit. She had always liked her brother's suitor from the beginning. He had won her easily with his dark humor and quick, snarky comebacks.

Looking over her shoulder, she saw Bradley give her the thumbs-up and mouth the words "You're my Greyby-baby forever."

Jonathan took her from the room, his lips pressed tightly together, his jaw clenching as he ground his teeth with the effort to keep his mouth shut, apparently unable to find an appropriately sarcastic comment.

Grey didn't know it then, and she might have done many things differently, might have said so many things to her beloved Bradley, but that afternoon was the last time they shared words. And no matter how much time passed, she couldn't help but repeatedly go over this conversation in her head.

Yes, he supported her. No, she didn't discuss his illness, didn't know how bad it was, didn't know how to support him. His illness had been an incomprehensible abstract. All she knew was that her brother was a fighter, that was what everybody said. The doctors would fix it. Somehow. Like they had before many times. And Bradley would fight. And win.

Except that time it wasn't fixable. He was defeated.

Grey was disoriented. It wasn't often that this particular memory troubled her into full alertness, like it was yesterday that she had lost him, like eight years hadn't passed in the blink of an eye. But she was suddenly wide awake and in tears, remembering this last bit of her Bradley that she would never get back. Twenty-one was not too old to miss her brother. If she had ever needed a champion, and this he had been all her young life, it was in that moment.

Distracted, she wiped her eyes and stretched, rolling her shoulders knotted with stress. She ignored the older passenger across the aisle from her, who was staring agape. There was no explanation she could give that would be sufficient. Instead, she straightened in her seat and took a deep breath, firmly putting the stranger out of her mind, her gaze sliding away and toward the window.

The tears on her cheeks fell in perfect unison with the Louisiana humidity, which had condensed at the top of the bus window and was now idly rolling down the inside of the glass. Listlessly, Grey wiped her hand across the pane, clearing her view of the countryside.

So this was the Deep South. There hadn't been much to look at since she left Chicago. Faulkner was clearly delusional. She couldn't see any romance in the abandoned farmhouses and endless gas stations she'd passed. Hell, she still had hours to travel before any real sleep was possible. Grey blew her nose into the napkin she got from a hotdog purchased an hour earlier during a brief pit stop and tried to get her bearings. She fought the urge to think, again, that she was better than a bus ticket—that she shouldn't be traveling "like this."

"You all right, honey?" the elderly woman to her left asked, clearly concerned by the mascara trails left on Grey's face. It was the stranger she had firmly ignored. She reluctantly awarded the woman a fraction of attention, trying not to judge the thinning, permed, purple-gray hair, clearly a product of too much Shimmering Lights shampoo, and the dated, frayed, and wrinkled Kmart old lady suit in a lurid shade of pink.

Grey forced a small smile. "Oh, yes, ma'am. I think I just had a bad dream."

"Well, if you need to talk, honey, I'm right here," she said, her warm Southern accent punctuated by a kind squeeze of Grey's left hand. The older woman's eyes held Grey's own a bit longer, the shear authority of age demanding that she verify her statement with a nod.

The stranger's kindness touched Grey in a way she hadn't anticipated. She was instantly ashamed of her snobbery. It wasn't as though she hadn't experienced kindness, but it had been a while since a person had shown her any without some sort of agenda. Everyone always wanted something from her. Or more accurately, from her father.

Lost in thought, she stared bleakly out the window, the landscape streaking by in a blur of luscious greens. It was almost as though the bus was standing still and the landscape was rushing away from her. But then the road jostled her slightly, and she remembered her manners.

"Thank you," she said absently. "I was just dreaming about something that happened a while ago. I'll be fine. I appreciate your concern."

The woman nodded politely, adjusted her thick black glasses, and resumed her knitting.

Grey's gaze returned to the window. It was so different outside from what she was accustomed to—so much less industrial. The bus rolled on through sprawling towns and drew up occasionally beside old forgotten state highways. Grey tried to imagine where the passengers of those cars were headed. But these fantasies were interrupted by the flood of problems and concerns surrounding her current dilemma: the complete and total desecration of her life, planned and otherwise.

Remembering Bradley shook her deeper than she would like to admit, especially considering what had happened after he was gone.

Wordlessly, as so often, she mouthed the words, "But you promised it would be okay."

You promised it would be okay. Those were a child's words.

You're no child now, Grey, she thought with self-reproach and leaned her forehead against the window, closing her eyes, hoping the five remaining hours to New Orleans would pass with less emotion. She didn't have the luxury to do much of anything anymore, much less feel. She drew her arms tightly around her own waist, as if acknowledging that she only had herself for comfort. Alone.

I'm a freaking orphan, she thought, intending it to be sardonic. It wasn't. It was sad. She shut her thoughts to the pain and loss of the last three weeks and tried to focus on something good. But even her happiest memories were costly to her now because they came with the acknowledgment that she would never have that security again. Or at least not for a long while.

It didn't matter. All she had now were memories.

"Oh, Sarah," Grey said in a voice so quiet she could barely hear it herself.

Chapter Two

Three weeks was not enough time. Twenty-one days before, they had been lying in each other's arms in Grey's dorm room laughing hysterically, exchanging small kisses, with tears running down their cheeks as they reminisced about the party the night before.

Wellesley College seemed a thousand miles away to Grey now—long runs together before class, sucking crisp September air, their tongues coated with a hint of damp earth and falling leaves, left behind by the Massachusetts breeze after its travels along red-golden fall foliage. The damp air sank into their skin and hair, mingling with sweat and determination.

Two twin beds pushed together against regulation in Beebe Hall. Her room decorated just so, simple, eclectic, with just the right amount of literary snobbery and pop culture novels on the narrow bookshelf to confuse visitors as to what exactly her major could be. No reason the Brontë sisters and Joyce couldn't mingle with graphic novels and vampire tales. A picture of her late brother and another of her handsome father rounded out the extent of personal touches, aside from the sloppy heap of textbooks and papers in various stages of progress littering the desk.

She always needed ten more minutes.

Ten more minutes of lips and teeth grazing necks, gasping breaths, and grinding hips. Ten more minutes of lingering and fingers trailing beautiful cheekbones. Grey could still feel the chill air caress her breasts and shoulders. They always loved to leave the windows open when they could.

Grey adored the way her black hair contrasted against Sarah's ivory skin when it cascaded over her shoulders.

If only she could go back, finish out her degree. See Sarah. Grey could not forget their last morning together under the down comforter they had ordered from Land's End. It was slate blue, nearly the same shade as Sarah's eyes by anything other than candlelight.

"Oh, my *God*!" Sarah laughed into her shoulder. "And when she looked at you and said, 'You'd be surprised how many Democrats love Rand,' the look on your face was freaking unbelievable."

Grey had playfully smacked Sarah's smooth naked butt in response. "Yeah, you blond witch, that's when you are supposed to come *rescue* your *girlfriend* from the obnoxious and incredibly misinformed newly indoctrinated lesbian poli-sci major before she has an aneurism."

"Hell no! I wouldn't have missed that for a million dollars. All I could think was that she must have really wanted to fuck you. I mean, I just can't!"

Sarah was beyond hysterics at this point, falling dramatically to the other end of the bed and pushing a wiggling toe into Grey's face playfully. Her short blond hair was pressed into the mattress, and as usual, Grey's heart was melting at the sight of her turned-up nose and brilliant smile peeking at her from over the comforter. How could she be both sexy and adorable?

"I thought my response was brilliant," Grey teased, playing along harshly, biting the offered foot.

"Ouch!" Sarah squealed and yanked her foot out of reach. "Which response, babe? Where you said, 'Stop talking,' or where you said, 'No, seriously, please stop talking'? 'Cause that lit major is really paying off for you!"

"That's it. At least you could pretend to be a little jealous." Grey laughed, rolling over on top of her giggling lover, forcing her hands down over her head.

The playful mood had changed instantly, and Sarah locked her blue gaze on Grey intensely. There it was, the heat Grey had felt the first time she'd noticed the lanky blonde staring at her at an art show the previous semester, when she'd awkwardly walked over and offered Sarah some chardonnay, only to be told she would rather have her phone number.

"I don't have to be jealous, Grey," Sarah whispered, sucking her full bottom lip into her mouth and biting it, a signal that Grey had come to know well. "I have this. And by the way, I know someone else who really wants to fuck you."

"You do?" Grey whispered, arching her dark eyebrow. "I wonder who that could be."

"Like you don't know," Sarah murmured and ran her tongue slowly along her bottom lip. "Like you don't want it right now. Like you're not already wet, wishing you hadn't trapped my hands so I could touch you again." Sarah squirmed and arched her back, slowly grinding her hips teasingly along Grey's bare thigh.

Grey groaned and captured those sensuous lips again but did not release Sarah's hands. "No," she gasped between kisses, "my turn." The slick heat along her thigh was making her crazy, but she resisted. She did not want it to be quick and easy. She needed more time. She was going to make them miss class again, but it would be worth it.

She nibbled Sarah's ear and whispered, "You're not going anywhere anytime soon."

Before Sarah could object, Grey dipped her head lower and sucked a nipple into her mouth, goose bumps erupting all over her. She had known she had her by the sound that escaped Sarah's lips as her fingers trailed a scorching path along the dips and valleys of her soft skin.

The sensation of the damp breeze tickling her bare shoulders, the earthy smell of freshly cut grass and fallen leaves mingling with Sarah's unique scent of herbal soap and musky sex, the far-off sound of class bells ringing and idle student chatter—these things imprinted themselves on her soul in the way some memories do. For some time to come, Grey would be unable to quash an ingrained response of arousal whenever sweltering summer heat gave way to a cool fall breeze. We don't forget our first lover.

They had missed their first two classes. It was late morning before they were able to tear each other apart long enough to enjoy a quick hot shower, although they used the opportunity to share a few heated kisses, to tease a little longer. They barely managed to get dressed and get their things together so they could at least make it to their next classes.

It was Sarah who had noticed that Grey missed a call on her iPhone.

Tawny, it glowed.

"Oh, my, the stepmonster called, babe."

"Damn. Way to take away my glow." Grey laughed and sighed, reluctantly taking the cell and hitting the voice mail button.

Grey watched as Sarah slipped her laptop into her backpack and had already waved her off, when the words started to play. The door was nearly shut when the iPhone slid from her hand and clattered along the concrete of the dorm room floor, freezing Sarah's departure.

Grey jerked, and her eyes shot open again, her heart racing as though the phone had just fallen from her grasp. It had been three weeks, and the memory of that morning was still as sharp and painful as when she'd heard the words the first time. She was still on the bus. They were about three hours northwest of New Orleans now, around three in the afternoon. She looked around furtively, but no one seemed to notice her, even the woman with the purple-gray hair had nodded off over her knitting.

Grey returned her forehead to the window and let the memory consume her.

"Your father is dead, Grey."

Tawny had said it so matter-of-factly in that grating, nasally voice. Like reciting a fucking line from one of her fucking charity luncheon planning committee events. She might as well have added, "We need to order invitations, someone choose a florist, and by the way, the most important person in your life is dead. Don't forget to send a fucking handwritten thank-you note on the embossed stationery I got you for Christmas."

"Your father is dead, Grey. His plane crashed this morning on the way back from Florida. You need to come home right now. I'm sending the corporate jet for you. Get to Logan."

What her father had ever seen in that woman was beyond Grey's comprehension. Sure, the woman was attractive, if attractive meant spending the money to look like the Photoshopped models in *Maxim* magazine. She was fake from head to foot—fake hair, fake lashes, fake nails, fake tan, her face pumped full of more Botox than even Joan Rivers would have dared to try. She'd gone on vacation for six weeks one summer when Grey was in fifth grade and came back two cup sizes larger and with a new

14

nose. Grey and Bradley had laughed their heads off and had been properly admonished.

And sure, Tawny could be amusing under the right circumstances, even nearly pleasant, but it typically involved heavy expenditures at Tiffany's or similar.

Tawny had escaped the inevitable comparison by a child between mother and stepmother only because Grey's mother had died when she was still a toddler, and Grey couldn't remember anything other than a few gestures, a few snippets, a lullaby, and a brilliant smile.

Tawny wasn't completely terrible. Well, she wasn't completely sane, either. Grey could only suppose that her father's marriage to that woman was part of some trend he had picked up at the office. A big-shot was supposed to have a trophy wife a minimum of one decade younger and fitting a certain description, or something like that. His associates' wives ran in the same circle, sharing similar characteristics and the same plastic surgeon. Seeing them together was like watching *The Stepford Wives*. It was simultaneously bizarre and boring.

Bradley had coached Grey very early on not to challenge Tawny directly. He'd had enough run-ins in his early twenties to know he couldn't force their father to dispose of her or to force Tawny to be more empathetic. He expected his father to be irritated by his college antics and fraternity shenanigans. But Tawny treated his barely average rebellion as a personal insult of supreme inconvenience. She was creative and cruel with his punishments.

Tawny's voice was steady and calm in that horrible voice mail. There was no crack, no sniffling, no pause indicating a person might be struggling to deliver a terrible message. She hadn't really cried at all, from what Grey could remember of the funeral and the weeks following.

15

Grey's imagination pictured the woman applying lipstick before calling to deliver the dreadful news, vanity not allowing anything less.

The day of her father's death, September 22, the date seared into her heart forever alongside Bradley's July 30, was such a blur—clothes thrown haphazardly into a duffel bag, Sarah's tears, a reckless drive to the private airstrip within Logan. Her disbelief, her confusion. Grey couldn't even remember what Sarah said to her that last time they saw each other face-to-face. Surely, it must have been something encouraging or at least comforting. That was what her gut told her every time she tortured herself by going over what details of that day she could recall.

That half hour at the airport before she set foot on the corporate jet was one of those agonizing moments when everything shifts. Her father was gone. She would tell herself as much, and it wouldn't feel real—her brain rejected the fact, and she would have to force her mind to catch up with reality.

Her father was gone. Her support was gone. It couldn't be real. Her life with her loving family was gone. Her father was her rock, and he was gone. Perhaps there was a mistake; he had just called the night before to tell her a funny story that couldn't wait. Her father would never call her again. She dialed his number to listen to his voice mail greeting half a dozen times.

A house will not stand on a rickety foundation built on shifting sand and clay. It will collapse without the solid foundation of rock or concrete. Her foundation had been completely removed with the simplicity of a five-word sentence: "Your father is dead, Grey."

What was she going to do? Who was she going to call now when she needed a word of advice? Who was going to give her tough love and a kick in the pants when she

16

needed some strong encouragement? Who could she trust completely? He couldn't be gone. There was so much left for them to explore together.

And there was a lot of fear that day. What would happen to her with Tawny in charge and unchecked? She dreaded getting off the jet. That woman could change everything with the same cold efficiency of that voice mail.

He couldn't be gone.

Except that he was.

And for Sarah, so was Grey.

Grey felt that she would suffocate in the cramped environment of the Greyhound bus, where she couldn't scream at the universe for its insufferable blows. All these strangers, with their mingling colognes, perfumes, and body odors were making her gag. The effort to hold in the monster of grief was too much. Grey ground her teeth and squeezed her eyes shut as hard as she could, choking down the bile that rose. She barely squashed a sob, which turned into a hiccup, which led to a coughing fit that left her feeling wretched.

Chapter Three

It was finally starting to look like the Louisiana Grey imagined—endless elevated highways crossing swamplands, rivers, and lakes populated by aging houseboats, luscious pines, vines, and alligator roadkill decorating Interstate 10.

For the dozenth time, she pulled out a piece of paper from her back pocket and straightened its crumpled edges. It was an email printout, a congratulatory note for a position awarded, followed by instructions and an address. It was her new life on paper—an opportunity that would afford her both escape and a new start.

Tawny hadn't wasted any time in cutting her off, hadn't even waited until after the funeral. With figures of questionable importance parading through her father's seventieth-floor, five-thousand-square-foot penthouse in Chicago's Legacy at Millenium Park, adorned in fashionable and exorbitantly expensive Chanel suits in blacks and grays, Tawny had dressed her down within the first two hours of her arrival, in front of guests no less.

"You can stay here or you can go. But if you stay, you can't stay for long." Tawny swirled her crystal glass and took a deliberate sip of exotic wine. "Just be reasonable, darling. You had to have known that we would follow up with your performance at that school. And I have to say, we were not entirely pleased with the progress that was reported."

"Excuse me? My grades are fine. And who is 'we'? Dad is dead. There is no we. You are not royalty."

"I'm speaking of your lifestyle choices," Tawny interjected and followed up with a pregnant pause, during which her surgically enhanced lip curled with obvious disgust. "We are not going to fund that kind of perversion. You're finished. Your father may have tolerated your insolence, your 'relationship' if I'm being polite, but I will not. Consider yourself cut off until the trust he set up terminates on your twenty-fifth birthday."

Grey had felt the color drain from her face, her lips going numb. The verbal blow felt more physical.

"You can't do that!" she had blurted. "This is not what he would have wanted. I have to finish school." It was hard to breathe. Her mind was going blank with astonishment.

"It's already done. Really, Grey, your father finished school without help. He built Chesterfield Aeronautics without the benefit of a trust fund. This will be good for you—learn to value what you have. To earn respect." She took another sip of wine and smiled. "Now about the arrangements. We should use the same services we used for your brother. They dressed him up nicely."

Dismissed, practically fired, just like that, like a servant or a housemaid.

The irony of being lectured about work ethic and earning respect by a woman who had married into a three hundred million-dollar estate was not lost on Grey. Angrily, she'd pushed her way past Tawny, whose petite frame paled in comparison to Grey's own. She could have taken her five-foot-eight-inch frame and kicked Tawny's skinny ass off the balcony. Perhaps she should have.

Instead, she'd torn out of the Legacy, heart pounding, and had raced straight to the only person who could possibly help her now: her late mother's attorney and best friend. Grey hadn't seen her in the past year. They barely exchanged Christmas cards anymore, although Beth had taken an active role in her early childhood until Tawny started coming around when Grey was seven. The stepmonster didn't much care for Beth. Fairly, this was due to Beth's obvious disapproval and snarky comments to Grey's father about how he could "do so much better."

Grey knew her office was only a cab ride away, and she took the chance. She got lucky. Beth was still in her office. Her front desk clerk was none too pleased when Grey stormed past the reception area and threw open Beth's door, interrupting what had appeared to be an important phone call. It took some time before Grey could get it together and check the hysterical sobs enough to relay what had happened.

More bad news followed. Grey hadn't thought it was possible to feel any worse. But she slouched now on a plush leather couch, her heart sinking with every word.

"You can fight this, Grey, but it's not going to be cheap," Beth had said, gently cupping Grey's chin and lifting it up, forcing her to meet her eyes. "Even if I waive my attorney fees, it's still going to be costly."

Grey had shaken her head, despondent. She sighed, her throat feeling constricted and raw.

"Beth, I can't go back to school. She won't pay for it. My trust from Mom won't even cover a semester. I just...I don't know what to do. Just tell me what to do."

A few moments passed in silence, during which Grey felt she knew what was coming and still couldn't believe it was happening.

"We will file to terminate the trust. As trustee, she has authority to control distributions, but her obligation is to act in your best interest. Forcing you out of college, cutting you off," Beth's eyes sparkled with anger, "all of that clearly indicates she is not the most appropriate trustee for your portion of your father's estate."

She stood and paced the small room. "God, I always hated that plastic bitch."

"But that's good, right? I can get my inheritance and go back to school?" Go back to Sarah, she thought.

"It's not that easy. Breaking a trust takes time. Time and money. And her portion of your father's corporate shares…That's an issue, as well. I told him not to make those distributions. It's too late now." Beth had returned to her red leather desk chair and was furiously hammering away on her keyboard, scanning information popping up on the computer screen, sunset now painting the shimmering Chicago skyline visible behind Beth's well-coiffed head.

"I've pulled the trust documents and the buy/sell. We'll file the petition first thing tomorrow morning. I'm afraid I'm going to have to use most of the remainder of the small estate left by your mother to fund the trust reversion. You'll have about ten thousand left."

Grey gulped. Money had always been a pesky thing best handled by her father. It tended to slip through her own fingers like so many grains of sand in an hourglass, so she had always asked for very little, not wanting to waste it on superfluous things. Ten thousand dollars—that sounded like nothing at all. It might as well have been a hundred. Or twenty. Panic rose instantly.

"So what do I do until then? I can't even pay my semester off. What do I do until the lawsuit is finalized? How do I live?" Tears erupted as fear and grief overwhelmed her. In the span of eight hours, Grey had lost her father, and now she was practically penniless.

"Well, honey, you are going to have to do what everyone else does, I guess." Beth smiled at her kindly. "What your mom and I did when we were your age. You, Grey Chesterfield, are going to have to get a job."

Get a job. Grey had never had to get a job. The closest she ever had to a job was volunteering for her father's charity fundraising events. She didn't know the first thing about anything work-related, least of all how to start looking for a job. The idea of walking into a restaurant and having to promote herself and her own worth to obtain a position that would still not afford her the education her father had always said she deserved was beyond outrageous. She had a mind to kill that self-righteous bitch for her hypocrisy.

Grey knew the thought showed on her face. It was impossible to hide the anguish and fury. She stood abruptly, thanked Beth for her help, promised to stay in touch, shrugged off the kind hug offered, and departed as abruptly as she had arrived.

She didn't immediately return to the penthouse. Wandering the city streets aimlessly, she intended to walk off the anger before facing the "plastic bitch" again, lest she get herself thrown out before she could attend the funeral. Never had she wanted to be less alone, yet never had she needed it more than at that moment.

Her father would have been appalled, of course. She fully believed it, yet he had left her with this intolerable woman in charge of his estate. Grey thought of papers she had been working on, exams she had studied for, all for naught. Professors would surely miss her participation. Her study partners would be baffled by her absence. Even if she returned to finish out the semester, what good would it do?

She couldn't return. Tawny had already withdrawn her and cut off funding for her dorm and meal plan. Ten thousand dollars would vanish in an instant if she supplied it herself, and what would she do come January?

She should have brought her coat. Her fingers were growing numb from the chill night air, and she shoved them in her jeans pocket, shivering.

She turned toward Michigan Avenue. Maybe the cold, wet air from the lakefront would clear her mind. The wind whipped up more quickly as she rounded the corner. She saw the Chicago Art Institute looming ahead of her. Its classic architecture reminded her of college, which in turn reminded her of Sarah. This was a bad plan. She turned on her heels and headed back toward State Street.

Grey wandered up Adams and saw the red neon sign from Miller's Pub glowing to her left. Maybe a beer. She checked her pockets and was surprised to find two twenties crumpled up and shoved into the denim void. Forty bucks. She laughed out loud. Never in her life would she have believed that she would be relieved to have forty dollars. She pushed the door to Miller's open and nodded at the Greek owner standing, as he always did, greeting guests as they arrived. Grey moved to the end of the bar and waited for Kevin to see her. Kevin, like many of the servers at Miller's, had been there since Grey's father and mother, her real mother, had been dating.

"Grey, what can I do for you?" Kevin greeted her, wiping down the dark wooden bar with a white towel.

"What's the cheapest beer you have?" Grey attempted a smile.

Kevin didn't answer. Instead, he poured a large shot of Belvedere vodka into a tumbler of crushed ice and shook it until ice crystals appeared at the edge. He poured the contents into two martini glasses and set them in front of Grey.

"Just like your old man liked it, kiddo. And it's on me." Kevin gently pressed Grey's hand, then turned away, all business again.

"Just like the old man liked it," Grey echoed. She picked up the first glass and tried to drain it, the freezing vodka sliding smoothly down her throat. Searching the room, Grey realized she didn't know anyone here, which was unusual. She'd been at college too long. She put her aching head in her palm and finished the first martini.

By the time she finished the second, she was feeling much better, though the nagging loss pulled at her insides. The old man was gone. A single tear fell onto the bar in front of her, and when she realized she wasn't going to be able to stop more from following, Grey rushed back out into the city. She wandered up to State and turned right. Moments later, she found herself in the Palmer House hotel lobby staring up at the Greco moldings and taking in Tiffany fixtures. This had been her mother's favorite place.

She sat at the bar and ordered another martini.

Get a job, indeed. Boy, that lit major was going to hurt more than help her at that point. She laughed at herself and brushed away an errant tear angrily. She could have perhaps bullied her father's contacts into giving her a job if she had been studying practically anything else—finance, accounting, business, even an economics or marketing degree in progress may have helped her. They didn't need some starry-eyed kid in the office who could discuss Goethe or Hesse. Those medieval poems she'd cherished were worthless shit in her father's world, no matter how proud he had been of her accomplishments. The study of great texts only had a future in academia.

She should have paid more attention to her father's attempts at grooming her after Bradley died. But he had raised a strong-willed young woman with a deep passion for literature and wasn't going to deny his baby girl her dreams. There was an expectation that a Chesterfield would take over Chesterfield Aeronautics one day. Nobody had planned on "one day" being right then. "One day" was supposed to be on the sunset of Wilson's great career. And it was supposed to have been Bradley following in his father's footsteps.

Not that any of that mattered anymore. Plans sometimes go straight to hell. Or they burn up in a fiery plane crash.

Grey finished her drink and decided there was nothing left to do but head home. Paying her tab, she headed toward the blue glass nightmare that was the Legacy. Grey never understood why designers would take a beautiful, classic Chicago building and impale it with a skyscraper. She pressed the revolving door and entered the antiseptic lobby. Minimalist bullshit. She nodded at the security guard and turned to the elevator.

"Um, Ms. Chesterfield," the guard called after her. "I'm going to need to get your key card before you leave. Your stepmother said." He was clearly embarrassed.

"Yeah, no worries," she said. Tawny didn't waste time.

Late that night, while the penthouse was still bustling with activity related to her father's funeral arrangements, Grey slipped away into her childhood room. It was the one corner of the residence her father had forbidden Tawny from altering. Even Bradley's old room had been cannibalized to make way for a "spa." She had put in a fucking tanning bed. But Grey's room was not to be touched, as her father had said, "until she doesn't come

25

home from college anymore." That would happen soon, she thought sullenly, picking up and cuddling an old stuffed rabbit.

"Eat shit and die," she hissed, thinking of Tawny tearing down her posters of P!nk and Third Eye Blind, dismantling her bookshelves with their precious collection of every book she had absorbed since elementary school. Her Hemingway. Her Faulkner. Her Pratchett and Gaimon. Her Rice and Dupree. Her leather-bound, antique Shakespeare collection, a gift from her late grandmother. She fingered the edges of the books lovingly, sadly. What was she going to do with all this stuff? Where would she go?

The following two days, Grey again avoided the pretentious visitors Tawny entertained, refusing to fight against or object to any of the ostentatious preparations she knew were being made. Her opinions were no longer valid, after all, so there was no point in interjecting herself.

Tucked away as such, earbuds plugged firmly in place, Beyoncé helping her to drown out the world, Grey absorbed articles on her laptop for hours, studying online options and opinions on how to land a position. She explored many ideas, but in the end, with her inexperience but excellent education, few options remained available that would allow her to stay in Massachusetts or Chicago.

Sheer frustration resulted in the disastrous phone call that again shifted everything. She hadn't called Sarah for three days, her self-absorption and self-pity having prevented her from doing so. Without thinking, intending to vent, she had finally made the call.

"How are you holding up?" To Grey's relief, Sarah's voice was full of genuine concern and zero reproach. Damn, it felt good to hear that voice, better than she had anticipated. She sighed and let a few seconds tick by before responding.

"It's not so great," she finally admitted. "That bitch cut me off. He's been gone less than a week, and she just tossed me to the curb. Apparently, school doesn't matter for shit in this family. I'm supposed to figure it out on my own to 'earn respect,' when she just married into his estate and never did shit with her life except piss away his goddamned money."

"Wow." Sarah sighed. "That sucks."

Grey paused, caught off guard. That sucks? That didn't begin to describe how terrible her situation was. An irrational anger burned at the back of her throat, and tears exploded unexpectedly.

"How am I supposed to do this without him?" she demanded. "I can't even miss him without having to deal with all this crap."

Grey sobbed hysterically while Sarah remained silent.

"And there are so many people in and out of here who don't even matter!" Grey shouted. Did Sarah not understand what was happening? Of course she didn't. She wasn't there. She didn't have to live through it. Sarah could sit comfortably at school, knowing her family was perfectly safe. She could feel secure in her finances and knowing what the next semester held for her.

"It shouldn't be like this." Grey finally sighed. She could hear the defeat and childish whine in her own voice and hated it. "I just want to come back to you."

There was a long silence before Sarah said, "I'm so sorry you have to go through this. It's terrible what she's doing to you."

"Can I just come crash with you? I need to get away from this. I can't stay here. I can't do it."

Panic began to build in the even longer silence that followed. What was going on? Grey couldn't understand why Sarah didn't just jump in with a reassuring "Of course you can."

Instead, a regretful and nearly whispered, "You're not going to be in school?"

Grey froze, then slowly wiped the tears from her eyes. "No, I'm cut off. I don't have any money. I just told you that."

The silence that followed was worse than nails on a chalkboard. She imagined she could hear the crackling of static over an old-fashioned landline. It got under her skin, and she barely resisted the urge to scream at Sarah for her lack of compassion or at least obligation. The ones we love are supposed to be strong for us. But some are not. And at least Sarah was honest.

"I can't do this, Grey honey," she whispered. Grey couldn't believe what she was hearing. Perhaps she hadn't heard correctly.

"You're breaking up," she growled. "I didn't quite catch that. You can't do what?"

"This. Us." Sarah sighed in exasperation. "I care about you very much, but I can't do this. It's too much. I can't handle it. If that makes me a terrible person, then so be it. But I can't tell you what you want to hear. I can't tell you to just ditch them, come back, stay with me, crash at my place, and let me pick you up and put you back together. I can't do it. I don't even care if you think that makes me weak."

Her voice cracked, and before Grey could furiously interject, she added, "I'm sorry I'm not what you need right now. I'm so sorry, and I hate this. But I didn't sign up for this. I have to go."

"Don't go!" Grey shouted. "Just wait a minute! Let's talk about this."

"No. I can't." And the call ended abruptly. Grey stared at her phone for several long seconds until the screen went blank as her phone locked itself.

How could she? How could her lover—no, even her friend—just bow out like that when she needed her most? Was there nobody in her life she could trust and lean on?

Grey threw herself on her bed, buried her face in a pillow, and screamed.

Hours later, the stepmonster made a pathetic attempt to "comfort" her by plying her with a glass of wine and stating that, "It does not befit a woman of your father's line to be so pathetic. Get decent and come greet our guests like a proper hostess."

Grey shrieked at her to go fuck herself and bodily removed her from the room, damn the consequences. She would not play the sad but gracious hostess. She would play the genuinely pissed off and heartbroken, wretchedly distraught, and inebriated daughter. At least that was real. And from that moment on, Grey vowed to never again cave in to propriety. She prayed that karma would take that witch of a stepmother and reward her for her actions in the most appropriate and terrible way.

And as for Sarah, no matter her anger, Grey forgave her almost at once, even if it wasn't fair, even if it hurt like hell. At least Sarah was honest and hadn't dragged it out, giving her false hope. Sarah hadn't lectured her or placated her. Sarah had been just as real as she ever had.

"I can't do this" was the simplest and saddest thing, but Grey respected that. Perhaps she wasn't immune to the occasional drunken text admonishing her lack of commitment, which followed over the next couple of weeks. Or the passive-aggressive Facebook status updates and relationship status change. Or the unfollowing on Twitter and Instagram. Or the eventual deleting of all social media apps from her phone.

She forgave her, but that didn't stop her from expressing her disappointment in explicit detail to their mutual acquaintances via text message until they stopped responding. Fine. They could all go party together and leave her be.

And perhaps she would regret Sarah's inability to cope with her, to be her replacement rock. But she did eventually acknowledge that this was a pretty damned hard thing for a twenty-one-year-old to handle. Their relationship was supposed to be fun and light, and this whole event was the opposite of that. It was tragic and real. It was something that was removed from the isolated perfection of college and dorm room antics.

Grey admitted to herself reluctantly that they had only dreamed together about where life could take them but hadn't really made any concrete plans, that obligation to a fledgling six-month relationship was limited, and that, even without her father's death, it statistically had little chance of surviving college at any rate. Still, all that did not make it any less hurtful.

This was where she was now. And in those hours of desperation and sadness, surrounded in her room by pictures of her brother, her parents, and her high school friends, Grey had once again booted up her laptop in pursuit of solutions.

She gave up on the big job search sites and browsed Craigslist. She gave up on Chicago. Her gaze roved her room in search of inspiration, landing on her books and scanning the titles. She returned to the screen and selected, "U.S. Cities," then, "New Orleans." Why New Orleans? Partly because it was far, far away from the stepmonster and her bullshit, partly because it was the most opposite of Chicago that she could think of, but mostly because Grey had always romanticized about a residency in the city that set the scene for many of her favorite authors' seductive tales.

If she had to leave, if she had to start over anywhere, why not in a place she had daydreamed about a thousand times?

"Like a cat on a hot tin roof," she said out loud, tasting the salty tears on her tongue. "I'm out of here."

She started scrolling the many positions, determined to find something that worked. It was discouraging at first. They wanted résumés, job histories. She didn't have either. She felt her confidence slipping, but she pushed on. Everybody had to have a first job at some point. They got hired somehow. The trouble was, she needed something better-paying than minimum wage to survive this mess. It was tricky.

Finally, a listing that sounded promising: "Nanny wanted. Alternative lifestyle couple, New Orleans. Educated woman preferred. Click link for more information."

"Please be a fucking queen." Grey laughed, hitting the link beneath her cursor, unable to resist.

No queen. The link had been a job posting for a lesbian couple seeking a nanny for their three-year-old daughter. Although the job description was short on detail relating to her future employers, Grey was intrigued by the narrative description of home and location. It seemed almost too good to be on Craigslist.

"Lesbian couple seeking educated woman to nanny for three-year-old daughter. References a must. Room and board and $1,500 per month. Cellphone allowance included. Doesn't sound like much, does it? Picture this...

31

A colonial revival mansion in the Garden District of New Orleans—your rooms are in the west wing on the second floor (they have their own fireplace). Black-shuttered windows peering out on pink tourists meandering along uneven sidewalks. Tennessee Williams walked those lanes. Lazy mornings in the gardens behind the house chasing a redheaded imp (she will give you trouble) in the shade. The smell of magnolia and a good glass of Chablis on your nights off. We don't intend to treat our daughter's caregiver like a servant. Come down and help guide our little girl into life. Maybe even learn a little something about yourself. This town is truly transformative. The Big Easy, what will it make you? ("America has only three cities: New York, San Francisco, and New Orleans. Everywhere else is Cleveland." — Tennessee Williams) Get out of Cleveland and call us."

Well, it sounded a hell of a lot more interesting than waiting tables or working a T-shirt stand where she would still have to tutor on the side to make rent. In fact, something in the description made it feel like the ideal, wonderful escape she was looking for. Perhaps Beth could give her a reference letter. Perhaps she could find a professor to vouch for her. Maybe they would forgive the lack of experience when they discovered her love for children's literature.

Grey hopped off the bed and padded barefoot into the finally empty living room, needing to move and stretch. Tawny had roped her entourage of a dozen or more individuals into a night at Everest, a chic French restaurant. Their bill would probably pay for half a semester at Wellesley.

Grey stared at the expanse of glass framing the coast of Lake Michigan—the unobstructed, stunning view that had sold the penthouse for her father. How many nights had she watched him unwind with a martini, staring out over the water and city lights. Grey knew she'd miss this. All of it. The Windy City, the security, the ease of living.

She sighed, pressing her forehead into the cool glass.

She could do this. She could square her shoulders and walk out with her head held high. She was almost light-headed with relief and excitement about having found something that seemed suitable for her situation. Reluctantly, she tore her gaze away from the view her father had loved so much and trudged back to her room.

Grey turned the music up and typed an email.

Chapter Four

Traffic had bottlenecked in Baton Rouge. Grey managed to lean her head against the cool window pane in time to watch the seemingly endless bridges pass under the bus. She focused on one of her earliest memories, a treasure, a game she had played with her mother and Bradley.

"Hold your breath under tunnels and over bridges so the boogeyman doesn't get you!" Her mother would laugh. Then she and Bradley would watch as a chubby-cheeked Grey would puff out her face and try to hold on until the chauffeured car emerged from the other side, the three of them bursting into laughter when she could never quite make it. Bradley would always make his patented "chicken face" to kill her concentration.

"Hold your breath." Grey smiled.

She actually was holding her breath, she realized, as the bus rolled mile after mile over the bridges constructed in the early 1950s, covering the swamplands between Baton Rouge and New Orleans. When she finally spotted the profile of downtown, the sun was just beginning to illuminate the glass buildings from the west as it set on the Crescent City. From Interstate 10, New Orleans looked like any other downtown area. She was a little disappointed.

"Guess I'll have to wait to fan myself on the veranda with my mint julep."

The Greyhound bus finally pulled into its destination stop. Passengers groaned in relief and shuffled around, collecting their scattered belongings. Grey rolled her shoulders and stretched her aching knees as she waited in line to exit the bus.

The thick air felt sticky on her skin, muggy even in early October. Grey could tell that it had been sweltering earlier, before the sun had started to dip below the horizon.

Everything about that bus stop was unexpected and contradictory. It was dated but surprisingly clean. Men in polo shirts and business suits sat waiting for their bus, noses buried in their smartphones. The last station had smelled like urine or possibly vomit. This one smelled of bleach. The prior station was overflowing with unwashed bodies and loud opportunity youths, this one was quiet and professional.

Grey shouldered her messenger bag and rolled her suitcase out onto the curb. More contradictions—to the right, under the highway, she could just make out the numerous signs of homeless camps; to the left, sleek and modern office buildings, the Superdome, palm trees, and shiny hotels.

That particular city block left the impression that without the palm trees, it could have been any other city, any other downtown. The same kind of strangers meandered the sidewalks and dodged impatient drivers as they crossed Loyola Avenue. She would only have to walk five more blocks for that indistinctness to fade into New Orleans flair, but she didn't know that yet.

"Where the fuck is Canal Street?" she muttered, pulling out her phone and selecting the navigation. "Thank goodness it isn't too far." She sighed and adjusted the strap on her messenger bag, straightening her shoulders. However disappointing this first encounter was, it was still far, far away from the stepmonster, and the pictures in the email printout promised a more interesting neighborhood awaiting her. So she trudged on, trying not to make eye contact with anyone in the neighborhood.

Her new employer had offered to meet her at the station. She now slightly regretted not taking the woman up on her offer. But a newly acquired character flaw prevented her from accepting help of any kind. She had something to prove to herself and everyone she encountered.

"I will find my way," she'd texted back.

Earning that fucking respect.

The rolling case was having some difficulty with the uneven streets of New Orleans. Bobbing and weaving her way toward Canal Street, Grey had previously decided to take the St. Charles Streetcar to the Garden District and find her way to her new home. To the servants' quarters.

Twenty sweaty minutes later, there it was, the New Orleans she had only read about. Tall modern hotels leaning against eighteenth century French warehousing as seamlessly as if designed that way. Women in Christian Louboutin shoes brushing past homeless men laid out on pallets of cardboard and skirting potholes full of mud and vomit.

Grey breathed a sigh of relief when Loyola Avenue finally met Canal Street, with a streetcar station right at the center. Sweat dripped down the small of her back as she dodged taxis and tourist buses to get to the station.

She crammed the requisite two dollars into the appropriate machine, but the ticket dispenser wasn't working. Groaning in disgust—the muggy heat was already getting to her—Grey shoved her dark hair up into the Chicago Cubs baseball cap she always kept hooked to her bag and stared closer at the machine.

36

"You can just get that from the man on the car." The voice came from an elderly black man with a crutch positioned behind the ticket machine.

"Just get the ticket and take St. Charles to Washington. Tell him you want the Garden District. He'll tell you when you get off."

"How did you know where I was going?" Grey peered at the man under his purple plastic Mardi Gras hat.

"Saw the address on that piece of paper you're holding." He smiled, winking at Grey.

She really couldn't afford the dollar she gave him, but he was the first person she'd met in New Orleans, and he'd been nicer to her than her stepmother and her lover in the last week, so what the hell. He smiled broadly at her and pointed. "There's your car. Go on now."

"Thank you, sir." He just nodded.

Grey crossed to the streetcar and lugged her case up the narrow steps, bumping folks aside, though she tried her best to make herself and her case as small as possible. It was such a tight squeeze—at every stop, the driver got out and hollered at the passengers to "Move closer together now! Come on, folks, I can see there's more room in the back! Move!" He would cram more riders in, pushing the standing passengers tighter together, then resume his seat at the wheel with much muttering under his breath.

Everybody was standing entirely too close, and they were all eyeing her case with disdain and tried not to bump into it as they were jostled at each turn and stop.

A heavyset woman clung desperately to a hanging loop in front of Grey and groaned at every stop. She huffed irritably as she perspired and struggled to maintain her balance. She grumbled and huffed, then pulled a pink handkerchief with stitched yellow daisies from her front pocket and dabbed at her flushed cheeks and neck at the next stop while the driver again stepped out and crammed more passengers in the car.

"Goodness gracious," she said, fanning herself and shaking her head in disgust. She ran her hands through her wilting big hair and sighed, looking around for someone to sympathize with her. "I have back problems."

"I can tell," Grey answered, staring empathetically into the woman's eyes.

"You can?" she answered too quickly, clearly excited to finally have someone who understood how much pain she was in. "How did you know? You must be a therapist or something."

"It was the way you're bracing yourself as the car stops." Grey smiled reassuringly. "You're using your core muscles to compensate. If my brother was here, I'd make his rear end get up and give you his seat." Grey wasn't sure why she was lying to this woman about knowing she had a back problem and about Bradley being alive. She really wasn't sure why she was suddenly affecting a Southern accent, either.

The perspiring woman smiled broadly and patted Grey's hand. They were instant compatriots.

"Thank you, darling. This certainly isn't the South I grew up in." She nodded toward two twenty-something gay men maintaining their seats on the crowded streetcar. "And on top of that, Michelle Obama is here having dinner at Mothers on our dime."

Grey almost laughed at the idea that this woman considered her part of "our."

"Well, in all fairness, all the presidents eat on our dime." Grey smiled conspiratorially.

"Ain't that the truth!" The woman laughed, her paunchy belly, probably the real culprit behind her back problems, rumbling with humor.

38

The streetcar jolted to a stop, and the driver announced, "Washington."

Grey's new friend patted her hand and shoved people aside to clear a way to the door for her. So much for that frail back. Grey managed to roll her case out of the car and onto the tracks on St. Charles Avenue under a canopy of tall ancient trees, the shade of which made dusk appear thicker and deeper. She'd probably only traveled a mile or two, but downtown felt far away in this quieter neighborhood with its colonial revival architecture and lush greenery. Grey watched the streetcar pull away with a sigh of relief and decided it would be a while before she would voluntarily be its passenger again.

Grey flipped through her phone, pulling up the navigation. She glanced around to get her bearings—a boutique hotel, a neighborhood pub, a sweet little flower shop. All she wanted was to collapse on a proper mattress and give in to her exhaustion. But watching the old-fashioned street lanterns flicker on, she couldn't help but feel a second wind drive her on.

New Orleans. The Garden District. Her new home. A small smile tugged at the edge of her lips in spite of everything. Didn't Lestat roam these streets? Wasn't she but a block from the cemetery where he hid his treasures? She felt a shiver creep down her damp spine. It was supposed to be dangerous at night, yet there was something so alluring about the prospect of following in Rice's footsteps. Surely, the writer had walked these streets at night.

With great reluctance, she turned away from temptation and followed the directions on her phone. A few blocks back west, then she turned on Second Street.

Holy hell, this is some dough, Grey thought as she walked through the neighborhood. It wasn't the same as her father's slick Chicago penthouse, but money was money, and these folks sure had it.

Chicago money, at least the new Chicago money Grey was familiar with, was all shiny glass buildings and immaculately clean design. The opulent landscaping and restoration architecture of the Garden District felt a little self-indulgent, though she couldn't deny its beauty. Sprawling Southern mansions with impeccable gardens butted up to one another separated by hand-laid sidewalks of mosaic brick. Even the cracks in the walls of the older homes were interlaced with decorative ferns which, though they grew naturally, couldn't have been more perfect for the scenery than had they been planted where they grew.

Grey rolled up to the appropriate address at the corner of Prytania and Second streets, sweaty and dehydrated, at nearly eight in the evening. A black iron gate was threaded with plywood, which had been painted black to give privacy. The rest of the home was surrounded with a six-foot privacy wall made of cement that must have dated to the 1930s. Wild white lilies offset with yellow centers, and uncanopied magnolia trees decorated the walls. The beautiful fragrance was unbelievable and made up for what she had had to suffer to get from the bus station to this district.

Grey keyed the "call" button per the instruction she had received in her email.

"Yes," a low, alto voice called through the box.

"Um, hi, it's Grey Chesterfield, the new nanny." Grey spoke louder than necessary.

The gate grated as it rolled left into the wall slotted to accommodate it.

"Walk straight up the driveway, Grey, and I'll meet you at the front door."

40

Grey did as requested, glad at the chance to finally rid herself of the heavy case and bag. She was nervous, true, and a touch apprehensive, but a combination of excitement and exhaustion calmed her nerves.

The house was stunning. Although it was already fairly dark, solar-powered lights lined the front driveway, which arched from the entry gate to the front door. Grey could vaguely make out the half-round rotunda on the face of the mansion, framed on either side by colonial wings. The house was painted a light lemon yellow and trimmed in white molding. Black shutters framed the window, most of which were multipaneled and clearly French. From the roof, Grey could tell there were at least three fireplaces in the home—in other times, required for cooking and maintaining the stables, now no longer necessary.

She couldn't wait to see the inside, to find her new room, to meet her young charge. Grey squared her broad shoulders, ran her hands through her hair, and proceeded up the walk to the front door, every bit her father's daughter—curious and proud. Hours in the gym gave her a confidence in her body that might have been pure vanity prior to this point.

"Put an exclamation point on your entry into every room. Don't ever forget you're a Chesterfield," she murmured, echoing his words to her teenage self. She put on her best, most enthusiastic smile and waited for the large black mahogany door to creak open.

The woman at the door to greet her was not at all what she expected.

"Good evening, Grey," she drawled. "I'm so glad to finally meet you in person."

A slender hand extended her way, and Grey took it automatically but nearly forgot her manners, so severe was her distraction. She had tried to picture this woman to whom she had spoken on the phone, had wondered about what this family would be like. She had imagined an older, possibly heavyset or otherwise frail Southern lady. Too many short narratives of the South had clearly misled her.

This woman, her employer, she immediately reprimanded herself, was stunning—all high cheekbones, smooth skin, and molasses brown eyes, her face framed by a messy pixie cut that showed several months of neglect, making her look slightly ruffled and careless in an unintentionally alluring way. Even the dark roots at the base of her bleached blond color had the effect of making her look appropriately edgy rather than disheveled. Relaxed jeans and bare feet contributed to that effect. Her white linen shirt made her skin look almost olive, or perhaps it was the dusk light playing tricks.

Those dark brown eyes were twinkling at her in apparent amusement.

"Good evening, ma'am," Grey finally managed. "It's good to finally get here. It's so nice to see that your description of this place was more humble than its actuality."

"I'm glad to have exceeded your expectations." She chuckled, a low, comforting sound. "And don't call me ma'am, please. I'm not your grandmother. Let me help you with that." She stepped onto the porch and reached for the suitcase. "You've dragged it around long enough."

Grey stepped into the rounded entryway of the mansion. The entry gave way to a large living room—not formal, but elegant. Mahogany paneling and leather furniture dominated the room, which was filled with New Orleans antiques and well-worn rugs. Built-in bookshelves held hardback novels and various curios.

Under other circumstances, Grey would have been overwhelmed by the décor, the hardwood floors, the crown molding, the giant faux Ming dynasty vase of azaleas over the fireplace. But in the present circumstances, she simply could not take her eyes off her employer's tall, slim frame. It wasn't just the casual beauty, there was something vaguely familiar. This woman looked like someone, but Grey couldn't quite put her finger on it.

"Well, this is it. Oh, I'm Zoë Cates. But I guess you already figured that out." She smiled at Grey.

Her teeth are like angels in her mouth, Grey thought. Then she thought, What the fuck was that!

"Let's see if we can find trouble, shall we?" Zoë's eyes lit up, and Grey heard an audible giggle coming from behind a leather wing-backed chair.

Taking the bait, Grey joined in.

"I don't know, Ms. Cates, I didn't sign on for trouble. Are you sure trouble is part of my contract?" Grey said louder, edging around to flank the far side of the chair. Another smothered giggle.

"Well, Ms. Chesterfield, I think if you check the fine print of that contract, section 3, subsection 23.004 under the 'giggle puss' clause, you will see that you are specifically obligated to handle all trouble in this house." Zoë was pointing for Grey to circle behind the marble desk. Her smile was infectious.

At this point, "trouble" was full-on laughing behind the chair.

"Well, Ms. Cates, I guess if you have that 'giggle puss' clause in the fine print, I have no other choice but to grab this trouble and tickle the bejeebers out of her!"

Grey swooped in the way Bradley used to do with her as a child, grabbing the tiny redhead around the waist in a bear hug, depositing her in the middle of the Persian rug and tickling her tummy to the hysterical laughter of all three. Before she knew it, Zoë was on the floor next to her and had rolled Grey and the child over into a huge bear pile, tickling both of them until they were all begging for mercy and laughing at the same time.

It was a moment of pure joy—the first since her father's death—and she was having it with a complete stranger. Grey smiled down at the toddler in her arms. The imp was all sausagey arms and legs, freckles, and pale skin. Her baby blue eyes sparkled at Grey, and the tiny red curls that framed her face made her look all the more like a cherub. She put a chubby hand to her lips and planted a wet kiss on it. Then she deposited the same sticky hand, kiss intact, onto Grey's face.

"Well, thank you, my lady." Grey nodded in a fake bow to the little princess in the unicorn pajamas.

"Excuse me, what's going on here?"

The three on the rug separated instantly. The voice, the tone, and register alone were enough to make it happen. The toddler rolled over and pushed herself up to her feet, padding quietly behind Zoë.

"Hey, babe." Zoë jumped up and slipped her arm around the other woman's waist.

"Hey yourself. Who is this person?" The woman calling Grey "this person" was a petite, forty-something redhead. She was curvier than Zoë, but Grey could not deny that she was attractive—pale, with freckles and blue eyes mirroring the child's, only without an ounce of their joy. This had to be Zoë's wife.

"Grey, this is Bridgette, my wife," Zoë said.

"Nice to meet you, Bridgette," Grey said, extending her hand, making the eye contact her father had insisted she learn.

"Grey, we'd prefer that you refer to us by our surnames, please."

"I'm sorry, Mrs. Cates, of course," Grey deferred.

"I'm *not* Mrs. Cates. I'm Ms. Breedlove. That's Ms. Cates. That child you have there is Emily, my daughter. She has both of our last names. Emily Breedlove-Cates," Bridgette referred to her daughter with a nod. Emily was wrapped around Zoë's leg grinning at Grey.

"Technically, 'our' daughter," Zoë said calmly.

"Of course, love, you know what I mean. Why don't you take Grey to her quarters? Take Emily with you, I have a lot to do."

And with that, Bridgette left. Grey felt herself summarily dismissed.

Zoë looked at Grey, her eyes showing a combination of sympathy and humor. Emily, strangely enough, had threaded her hand into Grey's and was pulling her toward a staircase leading up to a dark hallway.

"Come with Em…"

"Looks like someone likes you already." Zoë smiled.

"Everybody loves Grey," Grey said.

They walked the carpeted hall toward the west wing. Zoë tried to lighten the mood. She pointed out the different rooms of the home, the objects of art she thought might interest Grey. Like most homes of the time, the west wing had previously been servants' quarters. The rooms, though smaller, were contemporized, and each had a small window with a view of the yard.

"Grey, you don't have to call me Ms. Cates. Call me Zoë. Bridgette is…how do I put this…?"

A raving bitch, Grey thought to herself.

"Sometimes a raving bitch," Zoë said.

Grey snorted, surprised.

"No, I'm kidding. She is very kind in many ways. She just has this 'lady of the manor' fantasy."

Emily tugged at Grey's hand to get her attention, a tiny scowl on her face. She stomped her foot and pointed at Zoë, holding out her hand, palm up.

"Oh, for the love of..." Zoë sighed and dug in her pocket. "I don't know, honey, I might not have any."

"Trouble" stomped her foot again, this time followed by a mightily exaggerated "harrumph."

"Here." She produced a quarter and slapped it into Emily's hand. She faced Grey and rolled her eyes. "I said the 'B' word. Guess who started this fun game?"

Grey giggled. She wasn't quite sure what to make of this family dynamic yet. Zoë seemed cool, and Emily was adorable. The house was beautiful. The neighborhood doubly so. She could already see herself settling in. But that Bridgette was a piece of work, she could already tell.

Zoë helped her get settled in her new room. It was lush and finely decorated—certainly nicer than her dorm room by a mile. It was more decadent than her father's penthouse. There was a large double bed with a gold threaded comforter and so many pillows that Grey was forced to remove several just to put her bag down. Venetian masks hung on the walls, a tribute to Mardi Gras. There was an over-the-top air of French Baroque decadence. Red furniture in the sitting area by the fireplace was offset by gold and purple valances. If she'd had a Louis XIV wig, she'd have put it on.

"Um, wow, this is...ornate?" Grey said.

"Yep. It's ornate." Zoë chuckled. "I told Bridge it looks like the goddamn Mardi Gras king jacked off in here. She didn't think that was particularly funny. Actually, this is one of my favorite rooms because it's not so controlled...so over-designed."

Well, Grey mused, if she had to get a job at all, at least she had wound up here and not in some dive.

Her whole body ached from being cramped in her bus seat. That second wind was dissipating fast. A deep weariness began to sink in when the door shut and she was alone. It was too quiet. She was alone. She almost abandoned her room but didn't feel comfortable roaming the house. Bridgette had popped her head in earlier to request her presence at breakfast at "seven sharp."

She sprawled across the soft king-size bed and tried not to think too hard about anything at all, least of all Sarah. She'd sent a brief email describing her new job. She'd written and rewritten it probably fifty times, more times than she had spent on her last lit paper definitely. It had to sound romantic and hopeful. Perhaps this adventure in the Deep South would allow her to write the novel they had discussed so many nights while entwined in each other's arms, all soft and wet. Maybe a little break wouldn't be so bad, she thought, trying her best to sound positive and nonjudgmental. Grey had really hoped to receive a response. Of course, she hadn't.

Despite herself, she snapped a quick photo of her room and texted it to Sarah with a simple "Not bad, right?" The text quickly showed "read," but there was no response.

Then there was another one of those moments when she would have called her father just to hear a friendly voice, maybe get some advice. But his soothing voice would never cheer her again.

She chewed her lip, trying not to cry again. It was a losing battle. Grey let the tears loose and cried herself into a dark, hard sleep.

Chapter Five

Grey woke up well before her alarm sounded, feeling surprisingly more refreshed than she had in what felt like forever.

She padded into the small but efficient en suite bathroom, intending to ease into a warm shower. She had been too exhausted the night before to rid herself of travel grime from her overnight bus trip from Chicago. It felt great to scrub herself clean. She stepped out of the shower with a contented sigh and reached for a towel. Perhaps it wasn't her favorite Egyptian cotton, such as those she had back home, but it would do. She certainly wasn't lacking for any necessities—her employers had made sure of that.

Grey toweled her long hair dry and examined herself critically in the steamy mirror, a longstanding habit. As a kid, she had always adored her brother's clean, strong features that were so distinctly Chesterfield. Now, at twenty-one, she got a daily reminder of his smile and mannerisms in her own expressions, although her lines were softer, her narrow nose long but not as long as his. Like Bradley, she, too, had given in to tweezing the family unibrow. The result was an evenness of composition— nothing particularly overwhelming, just an essential sensuality that had served her well, at least in college.

But the last few weeks had taken their toll—dark circles and a slightly splotchy complexion gave her away, had the capability of announcing her grief more loudly than any words or actions could. She looked older. She thought she discovered a new worry line on her forehead. She touched it curiously, drawing her finger along its length. She rubbed the dark circles under her eyes and sighed. It wasn't worth hiding under makeup, she decided.

Grey applied some clear gloss to her lips and pulled her hair back into a tight ponytail. She slipped on her best black yoga pants and a white oxford shirt. She opted for her white lace-up Keds sneakers and decided she had hit the mark on nanny attire for her generation. When she checked her phone, Grey realized it was just six o'clock. She still had an hour until "Bridgette Roll Call."

"Let's take a look around the plantation," she murmured.

Grey slipped out of her suite and headed down the narrow hallway. She hadn't realized how tired she was the night before. She'd never noticed the red plush carpeting under her feet or the dim lighting leading to the far end of the west wing. Four doors similar to her own marked the distance between her rooms and the back staircase down to the kitchen. Grey made the distance silently and crept down the stairs, overwhelmed by curiosity.

"Oh, my God." Grey sucked in a breath and expelled it just as quickly. "Whoa."

The kitchen was gorgeous—like something straight out of a *Southern Living* magazine shoot. Over an enormous island, every copper pot and pan hung precisely where it would catch the early morning light in just the right way. Jars of pickled vegetables and peppers lined the back butcher-block counter, the colors popping against the clean white backsplash. The appliances were modern, stainless steel—top of the line, as though chosen for a professional chef. Dark, rich hardwood floors and open

49

cabinetry stocked alternately with functional white china and antique kitchen gadgets set the whole space off beautifully.

Grey carefully pulled out a white stool from the island and sat, her mouth agape. She absently pulled a daisy from a crystal vase and twirled the flower.

It was so hard not to compare every nook and cranny of this place to the Chicago penthouse, to stack the dollar signs attached to every item to the dollar signs in her father's sleek design. Not that Grey cared so much for money—that in itself was a newfound necessity, the consideration of cost and profit curious to someone who had never had to pay for a thing in her life. The point was not to judge so much as to appreciate. Grey felt like she was in a design show. At any moment, the film crew was going to show up.

The kitchen was immaculate, not a speck of dirt or dust. Yet she had met the child who lived here. How could it be so clean?

She wished she had a cup of coffee. She scanned the kitchen and spotted an intimidating contraption, a copper espresso maker that was likely imported from Italy. Grey sighed, not daring to touch it. The thing wasn't at all like the modern automated machine she was accustomed to. She pulled out her phone and checked the time. Forty-five more minutes until roll call. Not enough time to leave and try to find a cup of coffee elsewhere. She didn't even have a key yet or access code or whatever she was going to need.

She wondered if she was going to be expected to jump right in that day or if there was going to be an orientation of sorts. Would she be given time to settle in? Not that it mattered. She had all the time in the world. It wasn't like she had to get back to school or to a life that no longer existed.

Grey sighed again, reluctantly dragging herself over to the fridge. Perhaps there was at least a bottle of water or something in there she could have to tide her over until breakfast.

"Good morning."

Grey jumped and closed the refrigerator door abruptly.

Zoë chuckled at her response. "Is there anything I can help you find?"

"I need coffee in the morning," Grey finally said, now stifling a giggle at the absurdity at having been "caught" rifling through a stranger's kitchen. "That is absolutely beautiful, by the way," she added, indicating the espresso maker, "but I have no idea whatsoever how to operate it, and I'm scared of breaking anything so pretty."

Zoë strolled over to a cabinet and removed a French press. "I hate coffeemakers. I like it old school. Here." She set the French press on the counter and removed a bag of coffee from the same cabinet. "Let's sneak a couple cups before they come down." She rolled her eyes. "Bridge is trying to get me to cut back, but I'm resisting."

Grey chuckled and settled in, watching as Zoë puttered about, getting their cups ready, her hair sleep-ruffled, clad in a simple white T-shirt and light pajama bottoms. Finally, they sat side-by-side at the island and sipped their coffee black.

"By the way," Zoë hesitated slightly but continued, "I'm sorry about your father."

Grey froze momentarily, then took another sip of coffee and shook her head, perplexed. "How do you know about that?"

Zoë cleared her throat. "Come on, Grey, we had to check you out. We're not going to invite a stranger, who we know nothing about, into our home with our baby girl."

"Hmm," Grey murmured. Just like that—precise, matter-of-fact, unapologetic—yes, we investigated you, and yes, you passed. "Nobody has said that."

"What?"

"Sorry about my father. Nobody has said that. Thank you."

Zoë stared at her for a few silent and awkward seconds. "Well, I'm sorry about that, too."

They finished their coffee in silence. Zoë took the two cups and rinsed them in the sink, dumped the coffee grinds into the trash, rinsed the French press, and began to prepare coffee again.

"I see you have coffee going. Good." That commanding voice made Grey jump, just the way it had the night before. "Perhaps the three of us can split that press. You don't drink too much coffee, Ms. Chesterfield, do you? It's not good for you."

"Not generally. I mean, I have a couple of cups in the morning," Grey lied automatically, making a mental note to pick up some VIA packets from Starbucks to hide in her room.

"Hey, hey, be nice!" Zoë deflected Bridgette's passive-aggressive criticism with an attempted kiss. Instead of lips, she received the side of Bridgette's face and hair. "If that's my biggest vice, I think I'm doing okay."

"If it was, you would be."

"Ouch! Well, that's my cue to leave. I guess I'll go to my dungeon and write." Zoë turned her back to the two women who stood facing each other across the island. The lightness she had been attempting to inflect into the conversation was totally lost. She had given up, by Grey's evaluation, on trying to end the interaction positively and was simply walking away.

Bridgette waited until Zoë was gone from the kitchen and gestured for Grey to sit back down with her.

"Emily will arrive shortly, and we will share breakfast with her. Then I will hand her to my wife for the first part of the day so that you and I can become better acquainted. We have so much to discuss, Ms. Chesterfield." Grey couldn't help but notice how sharply certain words were pronounced, likely with intended precision—wife, discuss, and most of all, Mizzz Chesterfield, the latter with simultaneous disdain and enjoyment. Grey suspected Ms. Breedlove liked the challenge of an unbroken horse, hence the enjoyment. Grey knew the morning would be spent being put in her place.

It was almost tempting to tell her off. Crazy bitch. Didn't she know what Chesterfield stood for? If they had done a background check on her or sent someone to investigate, then they would know. She wasn't just some random college kid. Chesterfield meant something. Or perhaps, she realized, it did mean something, and that was precisely why this woman was looking forward to placing herself above Grey—because then she would prove that she was better than her.

If the stepmonster hadn't cut her off... Oh, how she loathed her father's trophy wife now. All these women in her life who were so determined to put her down.

"Hmm," she murmured, more to indicate that she had heard than to contribute to the conversation. She would not make polite chitchat. That was not what Bridgette wanted anyway.

"Good. Then I shall go get the little one, and we can have breakfast." She was nearly gone when she turned around in the doorway. "I hope you don't require salt with your food. I have removed all the shakers in the house. Salt is also so bad for you."

Good lord, Grey cursed, and mentally added salt to the list of items she would have to smuggle into the house.

Twenty minutes later, Emily, Bridgette, and Grey were sitting quietly at the small dining area in the kitchen eating oatmeal with raisins and brown sugar. Emily circled her bowl with her spoon, scraping the last remnants of the sugar into each sloppy bite.

"More sugar, please." Emily eyed her mother.

"You have enough, Emily, eat your breakfast." Bridgette stood, leaving her bowl at the table. She kissed Emily on top of her head and addressed Grey.

"I've left a schedule for you. Emily must finish all her breakfast. Then you can take her upstairs to the nursery and clean her up. After that, you have play time until nine. I'd prefer you keep her inside because of her allergies. But if you must, you can go outside."

Grey nodded along to show she was listening.

"From nine until eleven, you can review the Little Einstein products, flashcards, and such in her room. At eleven, she has a two-hour nap. Depending upon when she wakes up, she can have lunch and another half hour outside. At two, generally, my wife will come take her. I'm not really sure what they do. I'd like you to keep Emily away from her until then, so Zoë can try to get some work done. Emily can be a terrible distraction. I'm usually home by six, unless I'm out of town. I'd like you to have Emily bathed and dressed for dinner. When I'm tired, it's nice to see her looking clean, you know what I mean."

"Yes, ma'am."

"Good. I think you'll enjoy it here, Grey. It's much heavy lifting. I know you aren't exactly used to heavy lifting, given your family. But it's something you're going to have to get used to from what I understand. Zoë and I have a good life. We've been very successful together, and I'm hoping with your help we can continue to be successful and enjoy this kind of life for some time to come."

Not used to heavy lifting? She'd have to get used to it from what Bridgette understood? So she was certainly aware of what it meant to be a Chesterfield—background check and all. Grey bit her tongue to trap the snarky comment threatening to escape her lips. She swallowed. Hard. Stalling. Trying to get her temper under control and find some way to push the conversation forward.

Grey looked up at Bridgette inquisitively. "Do you mind if I ask you what you do, Ms. Breedlove?" Grey said, proud of how neutral her voice sounded. "It seems like you have a passing knowledge of my situation and like I'm supposed to know something about yours, but frankly, I don't."

"Oh, dear! Did Zoë not say anything? God, that is so like her." Bridgette's face flushed pink at the perceived slight. "Nothing we did before Emily matters, goddamn her."

"Ma'am?"

"Zoë is Aimee R. Dupree, the author. I mean, that is her pen name, of course. Surely, you've read our novels."

Grey felt her stomach lurch. She spluttered and nearly slid off her chair. No wonder the woman had looked somehow familiar! Twitter. Facebook. TMZ. Articles passed by friends and friends of friends. She had just had coffee with Aimee freaking R. Dupree.

"Oh, my gosh!" Grey finally blurted and gushed. "Aimee R. Dupree, as in the *Night Shade Chronicles*... Alicia Shade, Sensual Vampire! Oh. My. God." Grey's irritation dissipated, and she was barely able to stifle a squeal of delight. She caught herself grinning from ear to ear. "Aimee R. Dupree," she repeated, shaking her head. "Holy cow! I mean, I know she lives in New Orleans, and, I mean, that's part of the reason I looked for a position here—I love her books so much! I've read them a bunch of times, they're my absolute favorite! My friends and I are huge fans, and they'll never believe I just had coffee with her...I thought she looked familiar last night. It's different in person, though, compared to online, right? But I never thought...I didn't realize...Where's my phone, I need to get a picture or..."

Grey blushed to her roots, and she cleared her throat, suddenly very aware that she was rambling like a fan-crazed teenager. She fought the grin off her face and said with as much dignity as possible, "Well, it's a very nice surprise."

Bridgette chuckled at her, amused, content to finally be recognized.

"Yes, Zoë wrote the original book when we met and the follow-up story two years into our relationship. I was her...am her literary agent and attorney."

Bridgette sat back down across from Grey. Emily had moved into Grey's lap and was playing with an orange, clearly bored with a story she had heard before. Grey, for her part, was hanging on to every word about an author she adored.

"We were at a Sisters of Sappho ball in the Quarter when we met. Zoë was no one then. Well, I mean she was from an old New Orleans family, a writer. You know the type, living in a dumpy little shack outside the Quarter, across Esplanade, for Christ's sake." Bridgette laughed at the impropriety. "Sure, she'd written a handful of short stories and a few books. Very small presses, those, moderate successes in small circles at best. I think her first book had only sold a thousand copies back then.

"Well, I saw her, and I mean goodness—she is attractive if nothing else. And there I was, this successful attorney, and it just clicked. And when I read the *Night Shade* story, I *knew* we had something. After she met me, she really started to write."

Bridgette smiled smugly. This was her favorite subject, Grey could tell. Look at how haughty she looks, Grey couldn't help thinking, and how pleased with herself for having "rescued" the now-famous Aimee R. Dupree— like she had written the book herself, or as though she saw herself as the author's muse.

She had said they knew they had had something, as though she herself had participated in the book's writing.

Probably, she thinks Zoë would still be a nobody without her influence. Grey tried not to roll her eyes. It was difficult, especially with Bridgette's gaze pinning her down, evaluating her reaction to this new bit of information. The fan in her was both fascinated and fighting the urge to defend the author and put this woman in her place. But that wouldn't exactly make the best first impression—insulting the wife. That would be terrible, right?

Grey could see how the attractive redhead could have been seen as something bordering on exotic to a penniless writer living in "a shack" on the edge of the French Quarter, how Bridgette could have swept Zoë off her feet with her cool intellect.

57

And that reference to not being used to some heavy lifting—she had momentarily forgotten in her severe distraction about Zoë, but now the irritation returned, and it caused her to bristle.

"I didn't know you two wrote together!" she gushed with fake enthusiasm. "That's got to be so amazing. How do you do it?"

For a second, she saw the façade crack the tiniest of cracks. But just as quickly, Bridgette resumed her smug smile and lifted her chin.

"Well, no, I don't write, Ms. Chesterfield. But the business end is so much more important than the actual product. I mean, without proper management, nothing and nobody ever goes anywhere, isn't that right?"

"True," Grey placated her but couldn't resist sneaking in one more jab to take the sting out of Bridgette's repeated attempts to put her in her place. "How long has it been since the last release? I always thought another book would be great. It seems like I've been waiting forever! I hope another one comes out soon. I'll have to reread the other books, just to catch up again." She laughed. "I read so many books, you forget some of the characters after a while."

Gotcha, she thought, simultaneously pleased with herself and horrified at her daring. But she had wiped the haughty look right off that face.

"That's why you're here and for no other reason. You simply must eliminate the distractions she's facing. All she ever does is dote on that child, and it's all I can do to get her to go to her studio." She sighed and again fixed her gaze on Grey. "Do your job and you'll get another book soon enough. And I think you'll find you won't have to reread a thing, darling. She's not exactly easy to forget."

Interesting. So this was the woman behind Aimee R. Dupree. Grey had always known the writer's partner had to be something else—you can read a lot between the lines of any writer's work. But this was not at all what she had imagined.

Part of Grey wanted to storm out of the room and hunt Zoë down, gush over her like some crazy teen, and demand an autographed copy of her books. Part of her wanted to continue this verbal sparring match, to twist the woman up just a little more. She settled on polite disinterest, changing the subject abruptly.

"Well, that's good to know, Ms. Breedlove. I look forward to taking Emily off her hands so she can focus." Knowing full well she hadn't yet been dismissed, she stood. "Shall we get this day started? I can't wait to see what Emily can do with those Einstein cards."

Bridgette didn't respond. She simply turned her back and walked away. So much for spending the morning together getting acquainted. That hadn't lasted long.

Grey looked down at Emily and smiled. "So, monkey pants, what shall we do this morning? Become archaeologists and dig for bones, change into mermaids and chase Neptune for his trident? Track fairies and unicorns in the gardens?"

Grey had bent down next to Emily's small face. The blue eyes stared at her wide with wonder. Her toothy grin smiling up at her in an amount of disbelief only attributable to a three-year-old.

"I say we go with unicorns and fairies in the garden," Zoë said from the doorway, smiling at the pair. "And I have just what we need."

Grey gawked at her. Zoë smiled ruefully. "Secret's out? That didn't take long. She likes to spill the beans, that one."

"Aimee R. Dupree!" was the only way Grey could respond. The grin was back.

"Momma!" Emily giggled, poking at Grey's blushing cheeks.

"Also known as Momma." Zoë grinned. "You'll have to get over it, Grey. Come on. Fairies in the garden? I have props."

She nodded mutely but enormously pleased, still blushing madly at this writer she had adored all her teenage years.

And that was how, twenty minutes later, Grey Chesterfield found herself awkwardly clad in a pink tutu, a red Dr. Seuss T-shirt that said "Thing One," a rhinestone tiara, with a wand in her hand chasing a three-year-old unicorn and a forty-year-old woman in a cape and a top hat out into the New Orleans sun.

Chapter Six

Three weeks passed pleasantly enough. Emily was a joy, smart, and entertaining. She was oblivious to the tension between her parents. Grey made sure her charge was challenged intellectually and creatively. She tried as best she could to abide by Bridgette's schedule, but she couldn't help but feel the rigidity was unnecessarily stifling for a toddler. Besides, Bridgette was gone all the time. The day after Grey's initial meeting, Bridgette had left for Los Angeles to discuss movie rights to Zoë's original novel. She hadn't returned for three days and had left almost immediately for New York. Then Chicago. Then St. Louis.

Zoë never accompanied her. There was much speculation about the aloof author online—fans alternately seemed to place her with dark secrets in the underbelly of New Orleans' shady politics or hiding a terrible and terminal illness. Grey was astounded by their creativity, knowing full well where Zoë was and what was keeping her busy: Emily. No illness, no shady political dealings. Just regular boring family stuff.

There was only one thing the fans got right—correctly assuming that it wasn't Zoë responding to and leading her social media marketing. That was Bridgette and a hired team. Grey had once unintentionally interrupted such a meeting in the kitchen one afternoon. Bridgette was dictating responses to a few young women, likely interns or college students, a stack of fan mail covering the enormous island, all four on their laptops and phones simultaneously.

"We'll be in here for quite some time, darling," Bridgette had simpered, noticing her presence. "Unless you want to stuff envelopes and lick stamps, you may want to find something else to do."

Grey went so far as to stalk Zoë online. This wasn't anything new. She'd done it a hundred times before dating back to her midteens. But she viewed the information with amusement now—the bio, the staged pictures, the speculation, the announcements. She could hear Bridgette's voice in her head while she read. Zoë really needed to get out there more, she thought, but she had to admit that part of the fans' fascination with Zoë was due to her mysterious absence.

And man, did Zoë look different in the pictures than in real life. Her daily standard of denim and linen with bare feet just didn't stack up at all against the leather-clad, goth vampire woman with black-painted nails and wine-red lipstick she saw online. No wonder she hadn't immediately recognized her.

Zoë was gorgeous either way, although she'd never have thought that denim could look better than skin-tight black leather. Grey's thoughts wandered down a familiar alley leading to nowhere PG, and she abruptly shut her laptop, shaking her head, a now-familiar "You are the nanny!" mantra soundlessly on her lips.

When Grey wasn't trying to figure out what was going on with Zoë and Bridgette, she spent her time caring for Emily and exploring New Orleans.

She quickly discovered she wasn't the only hired help.

Grey met Charlie, their landscaper, a jolly older man and New Orleans native with the loudest guffaw she had ever heard. He showed up every Tuesday at nine a.m. sharp. She could barely understand half of what he said, his Cajun accent was so thick, but he was a joy to be around, even if she could really only talk to him for a few minutes here and there.

One afternoon, she was surprised by the sound of a vacuum cleaner running in the hallway leading to her room. She discovered Maria was responsible for the impeccable condition of the house. Everything had to be kept at Bridgette's high standards. Grey shared a cup of coffee with her. The young woman seemed supremely relieved that Bridgette was in New York, although she showed Grey an extensive typed to-do list Bridgette had emailed her the night before. They had a good laugh, and because Emily was playing with Zoë and Grey had nothing better to do, she helped Maria complete her chores.

A delivery had arrived on Grey's third day at her new home. The young man had asked her to sign for a large package contained in a cooler. She opened the container to discover numerous meals in varying Tupperware sizes. When she fetched Zoë for an explanation and to sign off on the receipt, Zoë explained that a private chef hired by Bridgette prepared a few meals a week for them to "free up time for other engagements." It was good, too, all locally grown produce and grass-fed protein. Grey knew quality when she saw it.

New Orleans was growing on her. But she wasn't quite herself. Even with the distance between New Orleans and Chicago, she felt the weight of her familial litigation. Beth checked in with her once during that period. Nothing much had changed. The petition had been filed, the formalities put to paper. The stepmonster had, of course, hired the most expensive and most litigious firm in downtown Chicago. The best Grey's father's money could buy. The only message Beth had was to "be in this for the long haul."

Above all, Grey missed her handsome daddy. Never had she felt so alone. The shadow of his absence loomed over every scene of her new, surreal life. This, more than anything, was why her bond with Emily grew so strong so quickly. Emily was the only uncomplicated relationship in her life. She needed little more than attention, affection, and magical playtime. Grey gave her all she had because everyone else was emotionally or otherwise unavailable.

Sarah hadn't contacted her—not by text message or email. Not one peep. Every night, Grey checked and was disappointed. Grey reinstalled her social media apps, unable to resist the temptation to stalk online. Sarah was having a good time, checking in at bars and parties. It must be nice to move on so easily. Angry with herself for giving in to temptation, Grey decided an extended break from social media might be warranted. She posted a message to that effect on all her accounts. It would be easier to let go if she wasn't constantly able to stalk online. All she needed was a little discipline, and this, she was sure, she could learn.

Every morning after breakfast, Grey and Emily would play a fantasy game, inside or out, depending on the weather. Each game had an element of literature or art, probably way too heavy for a three-year-old, but better than forcing flashcards on the kid, was Grey's thought.

Zoë had joined them every day since Grey's arrival, contributing her own forceful creative personality to this exchange. She always insisted they wear costumes if at all possible. In fact, just two mornings before, she had leapt into the kitchen in full Musketeer regalia shouting, "All for one!" about ten minutes before Bridgette had left.

After an awkward twenty-second pause, which felt like twenty minutes, Zoë had simply said, "Sorry, wrong room," and backed out.

Grey had stifled a laugh of enormous proportions, just as Bridgette had turned an inquiring and slightly hostile eye on her.

"I have no idea." Grey had shrugged.

When Bridgette left five minutes later and they all heard the telltale sign of the gate rolling back into place, Zoë had peeked around the corner with a big shit-eating grin on her face.

"Is she gone?" Zoë asked.

"Oh, Momma!" Emily had laughed. "You are so silly."

Zoë and Grey had burst into laughter, and an epic swordfight had occurred that morning in the gardens.

These exchanges served to cut down Grey's level of awkwardness around Zoë. It was hard to see her as the writer of those alluring vampire tales when she was goofing around with her kid. Grey was able to act like Zoë was a normal person and not a celebrity—at least most of the time. It worked so long as she didn't think of vampires and leather.

For three weeks, Grey had put Emily down for her nap and crept quietly around the giant mansion, familiarizing herself with nearly every space. But there was one room she had respectfully avoided: Zoë's studio.

She could hear the music down the hall, like every other day. Jazz. Billie Holiday. The same record over and over. The door was always slightly ajar, a crack from which spilled the same soft flickering light. Grey would sneak past, tempted to knock on the door, but she hadn't yet dared.

What was she doing in there? Grey paused at the door, listening. There was no clickety-clack of fingers pounding a keyboard to hammer out a plot or a paragraph or even a sentence. Surely, Zoë didn't handwrite her work. Grey held her breath, listening hard. Nothing. She released a sigh and rolled her eyes. Here she'd been playing with this woman, wearing any number of ridiculous outfits every day to entertain a toddler, and she couldn't extend her hand and push open the door.

"Oh, to hell with it," she muttered under her breath and knocked.

There was a long pause, during which Grey furiously debated slipping back down the hallway and out of sight. Before she could act, the door swung inward.

"Sorry, wrong room," she suggested with a half-grin and got Zoë to chuckle before the woman sank back down on a lurid, ancient purple couch shoved up against the wall. Grey knew immediately this was a piece of furniture from before Bridgette or else it would never have been allowed. She found herself mildly surprised it hadn't been destroyed.

"Would you like some cognac? It's good stuff." Zoë motioned offhandedly to a small rickety table—another relic—and indicated a half-empty bottle of Rémy Martin and a glass.

"No, thank you," Grey answered quickly. "Cognac's not my thing."

"Hmm." Zoë stretched out on the couch. "Welcome to my studio, where the magic happens." A touch of sarcasm there.

It wasn't much. Grey didn't know what she had expected—maybe notes tacked to the wall, a giant expensive desk, something that might indicate that it was a writer's hangout. But there was nothing of the sort, just a small room, the bright sunlight dampened by heavy curtains, that lurid couch, a wobbly end table, a few candles, a record player on a bookshelf that held exactly two books and an interesting collection of crystal decanters and sifters, framed copies of the book jackets of her first two novels, and a few articles decorating the walls. A well-worn, midcentury American-style desk was available for work and was cluttered with notes and doodles on scraps of paper but had a look of neglect indicative of someone suffering from writer's block.

A handful of candles, flickering against the gentle breeze of the slowly rotating fan overhead cast shadows, created an intimacy that demanded privacy.

A laptop sat on the floor in the corner, closed and unused. Even by candlelight, Grey could see a thin film of dust muting its sharp red cover.

"How's the writing coming?" She knew the answer. "I really do love your work. I can't tell you how many times I read your first book. It was so beautifully put together. My friends and I are huge fans."

Nothing. No thank-you or humble acknowledgment. Grey leaned against the wall, feeling more awkward by the minute. This moody Zoë fit her idea of a vampire novelist more accurately, but it wasn't the fun and playful Zoë she had come to know. She was dealing with Aimee now. Shadows played across her angular cheekbones, darkened those molasses eyes so they appeared almost black. Her face was blank, perfectly neutral, unmoving, as still as a painting.

Grey found this shift in personality unnerving, this "Aimee Dupree effect" was making her feel like a bumbling teenage fan again.

"Where are you going to take the story?"

"I don't know." Zoë sipped her cognac. The music abruptly ended as the record played out.

"Can I ask you something?" Grey ventured, breaking the silence. Receiving no objection, she carried on. "What do you do in here every day? You play the same record, you drink cognac, but you don't know where your story is going... If you're not writing, why can't you take care of Emily? I mean, why am I even here?"

"I don't know why you're here." She stood slowly, rubbing her eyes and ruffling her hair. "Bridgette thinks that Emily is my distraction because I haven't produced anything worthwhile since we had her."

Zoë yawned and drained her glass, setting it aside. Then she fixed her gaze on Grey. "What she doesn't understand is that Emily is everything. She's not a distraction. She's my world." This last sentence came out fierce, probably more so than she had intended, Grey realized, because Zoë smiled weakly and relaxed her features with effort. She shrugged then, defeated. "So if the writing isn't happening, it's not Emily's fault. Bridgette is just trying to help, and this was her solution. And it's fine. I can already tell that you'll be good for her. Who knows? Maybe it'll work eventually." She smiled then. "But not today."

She snuffed out the candles and unplugged the old record player. "Also, don't share that you've been in here. Even Bridgette hardly ever comes in. Nobody is supposed to come in here."

Grey was taken aback but was able to stifle a response. It wasn't meant to be dismissive, it was just a fact that she had been unaware of. It was meant to be informative. She didn't really fancy having to explain to Bridgette that she had unknowingly violated a rule.

"Sure," she finally managed, trying to make the word sound light and apathetic.

They walked down the hallway in silence for several paces before Zoë stopped abruptly.

"What are you doing tonight?"

"Um…" Grey laughed and snorted. "Watching Emily, like every night."

"No. My parents are going to take her. It has been a while since they've seen her. Bridgette's gone for another few days. I feel like," she ran her hand through her hair again, making it look even more neglected and ruffled, "I don't know. This is all so quiet."

She paused for a long moment—so long Grey thought she had lost her train of thought completely.

"Here's what we need to do," she finally drawled, her eyes lighting up. "You, Ms. Chesterfield, are going to accompany me on an adventure."

"I like adventures." Grey giggled. "What kind of adventure? A quest? A treasure hunt?"

"A quest of sorts, yes." She smiled ruefully. "I want to go see my old apartment down past the French Quarter."

"What do you hope to find there?"

"My muse? Hell, I don't know. Probably mostly drunken frat boys and sailors. Maybe some worn-down queen crying because his nineteen-year-old boyfriend hasn't returned his phone call. Dirt. Mostly dirt and filth. Have you ever really seen filth, Grey Chesterfield, only surviving heir to the Chesterfield fortunes?" Her eyes were distant but teasing at the same time.

"Depends on your definition, I guess. I think my stepmother is dirty, in a sense," Grey said ruefully, staring at her shoes. She was pouting despite herself. She knew she looked childish.

"She probably feels the same way about you," Zoë said softly.

"What the hell does that mean? I have feelings, you know." Grey looked at Zoë, her voice rising more than she intended.

Zoë extended a hand, placing it on Grey's shoulder to pacify her. "It doesn't mean anything, kiddo. It just means everyone's perception of reality is just that, their own perception. And I think mine has been locked in this house and that garden full of fantasies too long. I need to get dirty."

Grey exhaled and let go of the anger that had overwhelmed her with surprising speed, suddenly realizing that she too needed to get away.

"I'm in. But don't call me 'kiddo'—no one has used that term since fire was discovered when you were five."

Zoë burst out laughing. "Touché!"

Now what the hell was Grey going to wear?

Chapter Seven

Grey had rarely felt more awkward. Emily had already taken off with her grandparents, and she was left alone in her room to get ready. What do you wear out with a forty-something on a nondate? It wasn't like she had thought to bring any twenty-something clubbing attire anyway—it hadn't seemed like the proper uniform to wear when caring for a toddler.

She sighed in exasperation and fluffed her hair dramatically. Good thing Zoë was both married and her boss, or there might be more pressure to clean up. Good thing Zoë was nearly twenty years her senior, or she might be worried about what kind of impression she needed to make. Good thing.

Yet all the nondateness of it was driving Grey to distraction as she meticulously tried on virtually every outfit she had brought from home.

"This is ridiculous," she said to her reflection in the mirror. "I am not going to pant over her like some twelve-year-old. I'm a grown woman." She giggled. "Even if she is Aimee R. Dupree."

Then she changed her shirt for the fifth time.

Finally at eight o'clock, Grey had started down the corridor to meet Zoë in the massive kitchen. She had settled on a black Pantera T-shirt, jeans, and black boots. Her hair had been brushed up into a high rockabilly ponytail. Large black hoop earrings set off her olive cheeks. She had even taken the time to apply a light amount of makeup to accentuate her natural features, finishing with a plum lip gloss that made her young lips appear full and lush—at least that was what Sarah had said when she forced Grey to buy it.

Zoë wasn't in the kitchen, so Grey, now familiar with the monstrous space, slipped into the storage room to the second fridge and grabbed a bottle of water. Bridgette had asked that she refrain from using the water in the main fridge. Apparently, that was only for the family.

"What a bitch."

When Grey stepped out, bottle in hand, Zoë was standing in the doorway. Grey gawked and dropped her bottle on the stone floor.

She didn't realize until she saw her that she had already stereotyped Zoë's "going out" attire in her mind—cotton Ralph Lauren polo, maybe some Brooks Brothers jeans. Unless she was playing the vampire author, then black leather. Nope, wrong again. This woman was an enigma.

Zoë donned on old worn pair of black men's Levis 501s, which hugged her body nicely. She was wearing a simple black V-neck T-shirt, but the V plunged dramatically to the edge of her cleavage. She had completed the outfit with a worn denim jacket with various velvet emblems stitched through it and some designer cowboy boots. Grey wasn't sure what she had done to her mop of hair, but it had more volume at the roots and fell around her face in a way that made her cheekbones and lips dominate.

In short, she was sexy as hell. But you can't just tell your employer, the famous writer, "Oh, my gawd, you are hawt!" Yet the only similarity to the woman standing in front of Grey and the pictures she'd seen by the dozens on

72

TMZ or Gawker were freshly painted black nails and wine-red lipstick. Set against the blue of her denim jacket, it read much less goth and much more indie rocker. Grey bit her tongue to quash inappropriate commentary, but she couldn't hide the appreciative grin.

Zoë, for her part, looked equally pleased.

"I love your hair up like that, Grey! It's so retro. It reminds me of when I used to try to seduce cheerleaders in high school." Zoë chuckled.

"Thanks. You look amazing." Grey decided that Zoë wouldn't have to try that hard with her, then dismissed the thought as the comical reaction from her id. Better get the old sex drive under control.

"I had Antoine bring the car around. No driving in New Orleans."

Unexpectedly, Zoë looped her arm through Grey's, snagged an Abita from the fridge, and guided her toward the driveway. Antoine was waiting in front of the nondescript black Suburban the women used for transportation in town, the tinted windows affording them, but mostly Emily, privacy.

The car rolled down St. Charles and looped around toward Canal. Grey was gaping out the windows. Three weeks in New Orleans had not lessened her fascination with the city. The myriad lights from the different districts slipped past them in long streaks of color, as though from the brush of one of the city's artists. New Orleans, it seemed to Grey, was all color. Bright pinks, lime greens, copper reds, and anything in between. Tonight, even this simple car ride was making her happy and giddy.

She turned to speak to Zoë and was caught in her direct gaze, amusement sparkling in her eyes but pain creasing the edges in a frozen expression Grey couldn't understand. She was doing that thing again, like in her writing studio earlier, her features as unmoving as a painting's. Even her breathing stilled, eyes unblinking.

"You okay?" Grey asked carefully, wary of the "Aimee Dupree effect." It wasn't exactly creepy, just unnerving.

"Sure." Her lips moved slowly around the syllable, almost hesitantly. But then she abruptly flashed a grin to take the edge off the word. "I was just wishing... regretting, maybe."

"Regretting what?" Grey nearly whispered.

Zoë slipped her hand on top of Grey's, in what Grey could tell was a nonsexual touch—a gesture to back up her assertion that she was okay.

"I just wish I could see this city like you are seeing it right now, that's all. The way you were seeing it when you were looking out the window, with your lips parted and your eyes reflecting the lights. I used to have that. For some reason, I don't see it like that anymore, and when you can't see something, you can't write about it."

Grey just stared at her. The pain on her face played through the words. How terrible to love something as much as Zoë Cates clearly loved this city and not be able to connect with it anymore. Grey imagined it would feel like losing a lover or losing one's self. No wonder the writing hadn't come easily or at all.

In the awkward silence of the dark Suburban, Grey threw out the only surefire conversation starter in her repertoire.

"So did you and Bridgette date for a while or just get married?" Dear Lord, that wasn't at all terrible.

"Ha! Do you mean was she a girl in trouble?" Zoë laughed, the wrinkles around her eyes showing her amusement.

"Well, if you're going to be rude, never mind," Grey said petulantly, realizing her own blurt was causing her to blush.

"No, not at all, I'm just teasing. You know, it was really just one of those things here in New Orleans. My folks are both doctors, pediatricians. I guess I never really got the medical bug. Biggest disappointment of their lives." She smiled at Grey.

"But you're so successful…"

"Oh, now I am. Back then, not so much. I sold some short stories and such. Wrote a few articles for *The Times-Picayune*, back when it was still in daily print, you know before fire and the wheel and such. But mostly, I begged off the parents and assured them of my pending brilliance. Needless to say, even the well-to-do parents can grow weary of that phone number on their cell."

Zoë smiled brilliantly at Grey. It seemed that Grey remembered a few conversations with her dad about "learning the importance of a dollar" and reeling in her use of the credit card he'd given her for emergencies. She felt a pang of regret.

"Anyway, I had begged a grand off Mom, who you will learn is the softy of the two. She'd been trying to get me to go to this thing when all I wanted to do was hole up and write. But there's something about getting money from the parents that makes you feel like a little shit if you can't do something in return. So I went to the ball—a Mardi Gras ball with them. Egads, terrible. Dresses…makeup…high heels." She chuckled. Grey was mesmerized.

"That night, we met and ended up back at my place. I was a little lost, in my writing and in my life, and one thing you can say about Bridge, she will get you where she wants you to go." Zoë paused. "You just have to hope you're headed in the same direction."

Their gazes met and lingered for several long seconds after that last sentence. Zoë was first to tear herself away, to run her hand through her hair and announce abruptly at a near-shout, "Here we are!" breaking the tension in the car.

Antoine dropped them on the far side of Esplanade at Chartres. The air was thick and heavy, steaming off the sidewalks even in late October, the humidity further fueled by the proximity to the river. Grey took a deep breath and felt the air settle on her skin and in her hair like a greasy film. She eyed Zoë's denim jacket, wondering how long it would last on her shoulders and not tucked under her arm.

Grey was momentarily overwhelmed by the noise and took an automatic step in the direction of the neon lights, bars, live jazz music, and general feeling of debauchery or at least mild shenanigans. But Zoë reached out and snagged her elbow, tugging her in the opposite direction. Reluctantly, Grey tore her gaze away from the block that held so much promise and followed Zoë's lead. They walked away from the Quarter to a quieter area across the street.

Two blocks, maybe three. This was definitely not the Garden District—colorful and bright but slender shotgun houses crammed together in quick succession, broken sidewalks and streets, weeds peeking out between the cracked concrete, shattered beer bottles lining the gutter, iron bars covering street-facing windows. Grey didn't necessarily feel unsafe, but she was definitely more alert. She hoped they wouldn't be wandering in this neighborhood too far.

Ahead, at the halfway mark between two streetlamps where a thick shadow fell, there was a flickering light on the sidewalk.

"What's that?" Grey asked, her voice sounding loud after the minutes of walking in silence.

"You'll see." There was a definite tone of anticipation in that statement, and their pace picked up. Zoë chuckled ruefully as they got closer.

At first, Grey couldn't understand why they were standing in front of this spot, which was clearly a memorial of some kind. The sidewalk was lined in burning candle votives depicting various saints or otherwise Christian symbols, silver crosses, bottles of red wine, roses, which looked black in the candlelight. She turned perplexed eyes on Zoë.

"Look closer."

Grey knelt on the sidewalk and peered curiously at the collection of objects. Then she saw something that slightly startled her—what looked like a pool of blood, fake, surely, and lying in it was a copy of Zoë's first novel. "What?" she stammered, trying not to laugh. "Is this a shrine?" She couldn't hold back the giggles.

"A tribute." Zoë rolled her eyes and sighed. "I forgot it was the night before Halloween and that they do this." She looked over her shoulder. "It's kind of embarrassing, actually." Her tone was deliberately nonchalant and made Grey eye her curiously. She didn't look embarrassed. That grin looked more pleased than chagrinned.

"So, um, this is a sacrifice for you?" She pointed at the book.

"Yes."

"And they leave crosses and wine and things because they symbolize things in your book?"

"Yup."

Grey burst out laughing. Was that a full-on flush creeping down Zoë's face or was it the candlelight?

"That's too awesome." Grey snorted, trying to rein in the giggles. "So where's the fan base? Shouldn't they be here to see if their sacrifice paid off? Because it has, you're here, summoned by vampire nerds."

Right on cue, the staccato of rapid footsteps echoed down the street. Zoë's eyes widened, and she grabbed Grey's elbow. "Let's go," she said urgently, trying to tug a resisting Grey away from the scene. "Come on, damn it."

"Oh, no, you don't." Grey snorted again. "No, ma'am." She seized her around the waist to prevent an escape. "You, Mizz Aimee Dupree, need this." When Zoë stopped struggling, she released her. "Besides, I have yet to see this infamous apartment of yours. Our quest is not finished."

Zoë gaped at her and indicated the sidewalk and street with a swoop of her arm. "We're here. That's it. This is the 'shack.'" Grey realized she was almost giddy.

Hardly a shack, Grey thought. Just a simple nice fourplex. Not fancy, but nothing like Bridgette had led her to expect. Clean and well kept, it was just an apartment. She turned to look at her companion but was distracted by the crowd of velvet-clad goths who were essentially running toward them.

"It's her. Oh, my God, it's her…"

"I told you it would work, just like that scene in chapter seven, where Alicia summons the elder," shouted a portly vampiress of about sixteen.

"Silence, my clan!" A tall, striking teen had emerged from the pack and was reverently approaching Grey and Zoë now, her hands extended wrist up. Grey instantly recognized the gesture as one described in the *Night Shade* stories, where a younger vampire must show submission to his or her superior by offering the artery of the wrist.

Grey would have fallen onto the ground laughing if Zoë hadn't elbowed her in the gut.

"Be nice," she hissed.

"My queen, please take such sacrifice from me as you deem necessary. Drink. Drink from all your children on this the most holy of nights before Halloween. Then we shall dance in the darkness together and swear our blood oath to your clan." The teen was kneeling now.

Zoë clasped the girl's wrist, her black nails digging into the tender white flesh just enough to leave a temporary mark, and lowered her lips toward the offered artery. For a second, Grey's eyes widened, and she believed Zoë was actually going to bite the kid.

"No, I think not." Zoë snarled, her Southern drawl now drenched with disdain. "I think before you earn this honor, the entry into this darkness and light, you will have to show me your worth by finishing school. I will find you at a later date, my children." She released the wrist and helped the girl to her feet.

Grey was actually shaking from the laughter she was unsuccessfully controlling. Did Zoë just deliver a "stay in school" message? What a mom.

She stepped back and allowed the kids to surround Zoë for photos and autographs. Several phones were thrust her way as they clamored for their idol's attention. Their vampire selfies were all poses of serious and menacing faces, of snarling and flashing plastic fangs. Then they would compare pictures and hoot with delight.

An argument ensued over a particular scene in chapter six of the second book on page seventy-eight, fourth paragraph from the top. Now that's commitment to the story, Grey thought. Her eyes hurt from the number of eye rolls she was resisting. The gushing teens carried on and on. This free entertainment was the best.

"Rochester." A teen finally cut through the rest. "We have yet to meet your young apprentice."

Grey mouthed, "Rochester?" at Zoë, who shrugged and mouthed back, "Later."

"Ah, yes, forgive me." Zoë turned to face her fully, her eyes now sparkling with glee. Grey squirmed, uncomfortable with the attention of all eyes on her. "She has only just decided to take the path and has yet a far journey to travel before she becomes one with the night. Meet Jacqueline."

"Jacqueline," the boy murmured reverently. "If only I could take your place." He sighed and took her extended hand, brushing his lips over her knuckles. Grey's abdomen hurt terribly from trapped giggles, but she raised her chin haughtily and smirked. "Perhaps one day you shall. It is not an easy path, but it will be worth the effort."

She could practically feel his pulse jump with excitement at the thought.

"Now we must go," Zoë announced in her most firm and authoritative Aimee voice. "We have yet to finish this night's quest. Leave us, young vampires. Go out into the streets and strike fear into the hearts of man."

The clan stood a little straighter, puffed out their chests with importance, and scurried away. Grey was just able to make out a whispered, "Oh, my god! That was *so* awesome!"

When they were well out of sight, Grey literally fell onto the sidewalk with laughter.

"Get your ass up off that filthy sidewalk," Zoë drawled and chuckled, unable to maintain composure.

"Ohh, but your majesty, it is the filth that you seek on this most holy of nights," Grey teased, lying flat on her back looking up at Zoë's red, laughing face. Zoë was kicking her with her boot between curses and giggles.

80

"Goddamn it, Chesterfield, get up, there's a rat right there." Zoë pointed to the street about five feet from Grey's head.

"Eee!" Grey screamed like a five-year-old and scrambled to her feet. Still squealing and laughing, the two of them ran like schoolgirls down the street, their arms intertwined.

Antoine, his eye rolls still working apparently, followed them in the Suburban.

Zoë stopped under a streetlight and caught Grey's gaze in her own, and Grey instantly had the feeling that the "adventure" that was discussed earlier in the evening was only about to begin.

"Grey, do you want to see something? Something I've never shown anyone else?" Zoë asked, her face looking ten years younger with the excitement and conspiratorial nature of the moment.

"Hell yeah," Grey said.

And just like that, Antoine was gone, and they were alone. Grey wasn't really sure how Zoë had managed to signal the car to leave, but she found herself walking shoulder to shoulder farther into the somewhat sketchy neighborhood of Zoë's creative youth. Her heart was racing, and she realized that any semblance of professionalism in this relationship was about to disappear.

There was a connection here that she couldn't quite understand. Perhaps it was simply that Zoë treated her like a human being, not an object to be controlled or a servant to be dominated. And in that moment of humanity, Grey believed that Zoë was finding something she had lost. Something that had cost her that creative spark that Grey believed she could see simmering just below the surface this very night.

The bar was nothing—a tiny narrow gin joint like so many frequented by locals in New Orleans. There were a couple of video poker games, a jukebox, and a handful of neon beer signs. That was it. Maximum seating capacity showed on the door at 45. There wasn't even a name that Grey could register as the first place she and Zoë had a drink together.

Zoë paused outside the front door and looked seriously at Grey.

"What am I doing? Hell, I don't even know if she's still here. I mean, I guess she probably is, but who knows? It has been years." It seemed as though she was talking to herself.

"Zoë, what the hell are you mumbling about?" Grey asked, clearly confused now.

"Do you want to meet her? Wait. I'm being random and weird, aren't I? Okay. Do you want to meet Alicia Shade?" Zoë asked dramatically.

"The vampire? Don't be an asshole." Grey laughed, presuming Zoë was teasing her again.

"No! I'm serious. Look, there has been so much speculation on where I got this or that character, especially in the city. I'm telling you right now. No one else knows this, not even my editor. If she's still here, the woman behind this bar is the basis for Alicia Shade. No, strike that—she is Alicia Shade."

Grey stood transfixed for several reasons. First of all, she had never seen Zoë so excited, so on the edge. This was clearly the woman who wrote the Shade novels, something she had begun to doubt watching her prance around with a three-year-old all day. This woman was wound up tightly. Secondly, Grey was literate enough to know that generations of Shade readers had debated who the Alicia Shade character was based upon. And here she was, the one person Zoë trusted to find out. And finally, as a little bit of a bitch herself, Grey was secretly pleased that Bridgette had not been the basis of the lusty scenes in the vampire novels she'd come to over and over again. Scenes that had frankly left her aching for another's body next to her own.

They stepped inside. Half the seats were empty; this clearly wasn't a popular place. Grey's attention was immediately diverted from the empty seats, however, when her sweeping gaze finally fell upon the bar.

Two empty seats, two shots of tequila, an alluring, "Well, look what the cat dragged in. Been a long time."

Zoë chuckled and put her hand on the small of Grey's back, gently pushing her in the direction of the bar, correctly interpreting her lack of progress as minor shellshock.

"Too long," Zoë said as she slid onto the barstool. "You remembered." She took the dressed tequila shot, carefully removing the lime.

"How could I forget those eyes?"

Zoë knocked the shot back and licked her lips appreciatively. "Another," she said simply and set the glass down.

Grey was transfixed. She just held her shot of tequila in her hand but didn't down it. This woman—she was sure there had been a name, a quick introduction, but it didn't matter because her mind already rejected any name but Alicia—was exactly what she had pictured when reading the *Night Shade* novels. She had fantasized about this woman doing so many naughty, dirty things to her that she was having difficulty making eye contact. Her mouth was dry. Her pulse jumped. She took the shot for something to do that would at least appear normal and so she might break her gaze.

"And who is this?" The woman sauntered over to her spot, resting her chin on interlaced fingers, her eyebrow arched. Grey gaped and said nothing, lost in the space where the woman's slender neck met a defined collarbone, exposed under the tight, low-cut tank top the woman wore. Beautiful tattoos of dripping red roses and gothic symbolism trailed from her forearm, up across the shoulder, touching the collarbone before dipping deep into that beautiful cleavage. Grey couldn't tell her heritage, but she was either half Latina or half Iranian. Or half sex goddess. What the hell ever. She was dark. Dark hair cascading around her hips in natural waves that seemed to shimmer blue in the bar lighting. Black eyes with irises so wide there seemed almost no whites peering at her. Her skin, however, was almost ivory, and the red on her lips and nails stood out with an intended shock. And when she slipped her fingers into her mouth every so often in an unconscious gesture, Grey literally thought she might pass out.

"Jacqueline," Zoë supplied helpfully, taking the empty glass from Grey's frozen fingers. "She's new to New Orleans."

"New to many things," the bartender drawled, her eyes twinkling.

The woman oozed raw sexuality. Grey couldn't tear her gaze away. She listened to the two friends' banter, subconsciously edging her seat closer to Zoë. Their shoulders were touching. Seeing Alicia was making her think of all those nights she had climaxed to the pages Zoë had written. Her breath was catching.

"I'll take another one," she blurted. The bartender arched her eyebrow, shared a significant look with Zoë, then poured the shot.

"You can have another of whatever you want, darling."

Damn. Every word out of her mouth was hawt. Grey knew if they stayed here much longer, she'd be a wet pile of quivering mess before long.

Her forearms were just defined enough to look strong. Grey liked strong hands. Damn, those tattoos were hot. She could feel the heat radiating just to her left. Look at those sensuous lips and the way they move when she speaks. They would move across her body the same way—soft and wet. Damn, her knees were weak. Damn, that woman was hot when she leaned forward and pushed her cleavage together for just the right vantage point. She was doing it on purpose. She was doing it to arouse Zoë. Damn, Zoë was hot.

Holy hell. Grey's head felt light, and it wasn't the tequila. She took a deep breath and released it.

Zoë's knee bumped up against hers under the bar, and she nearly jumped out of her skin.

"Try to blink every now and then, so your eyes don't dry up," Zoë teased. Grey saw her smiling at her under the neon "Abita" light directly above them. Alicia had slipped into the supply room to get something, which Grey had completely ignored because anything that woman said was irrelevant.

"Holy shit" was all Grey could manage.

Zoë raised one eyebrow in a "right, I know" expression and turned back just in time to see the goddess slip back into place. Grey realized she must have a deer-in-the-headlights look about her, but she frankly didn't care. She was outclassed by these two women, sexuality and experience-wise. And she was smart enough to know not to jump into the fray.

Zoë and Alicia bantered back and forth with practiced ease. At one point, Grey did pick up that Alicia must have been in the Marines because Zoë was telling the story about how the first night they had met, she heard an exchange between the bartender and a younger man in the bar.

"So I see her go up to this kid, who is clearly about to wet himself. And she says, 'Baby, have you ever been with a goddamn United States Marine?' and when he says, 'No, ma'am'—this bitch here says, 'Well, do it for your country, baby!'"

The two women burst out laughing, and Grey joined in despite herself—despite, because she wasn't sure she liked the way Alicia was running her forefinger along the curve between Zoë's thumb and palm, although she didn't know which one she was precisely jealous of at that moment.

The bar had begun to fill up, and the spell of the three of them seemed to be breaking. Grey and Zoë had had three shots of tequila and a couple of beers, and the natural warmth of the night was giving the alcohol extra potency.

"Let's get out of here," Zoë murmured when Alicia momentarily turned her back on them to get beers for a group of rowdy young men who were not shy with compliments. "I would say this quest was successful."

"Mmm," Grey murmured around a wide grin and wider eyes. "Oh, yeah. That'll tide me over for a while. Damn. How could you just come here and hang out with her without passing out all the time?"

Zoë burst out laughing then, a bright, clear, ringing laughter that interrupted the noise of the bar. Alicia shot her a dazzling smile and winked, then mouthed, "Later, ladies," before returning her attention to the clamoring men. Zoë threw a bill on the bar and gently took Grey's arm.

"Our adventure continues, my lady." Her barstool scraped along the floor as she allowed herself to be practically lifted out of her seat.

"Onward then," Grey commanded, and they exited the dingy space arm-in-arm, giggling. The second they were outside, Grey began to ramble, "Holy mother of God, that woman is a goddess! I always thought Aimee Dupree just had an amazing and sexy imagination, but no—you just had to put her down on the page." She giggled and hiccupped. "I bet you stumbled out of here and couldn't wait to get home to…write." Whoops. Her face flushed a furious shade of red. She cleared her throat. "I mean, who wouldn't want to write about her? Or paint her? Or take a picture. Damn, we should have taken a picture."

"A picture would never have been good enough," Zoë finally interrupted her, pulling her to a stop.

"Yeah." Grey sighed. "A picture wouldn't do her justice."

"And you're right. I couldn't wait to get home." She paused a beat. "You're blushing."

Zoë barely grazed Grey's face with the tips of her fingers. "So did I, when I met her. I don't think it can be helped." She grinned then, dropping her hand, turning away and releasing Grey. "Thank you."

"For what?" Grey said, her whole body still screaming from all the unanticipated attention.

"For indulging me." Zoë paused, her gaze distancing with each second. "Sometimes, I let myself forget too much, let these things slip away too far and then…then it's so hard to chase them, hard to keep a grasp on what's real and what's fiction, what I need and what I want. Who I am." She sighed. Then she looked sidelong at Grey.

"You know, she kissed me one night." Zoë's tone dropped, and her voice almost growled.

Grey gasped, then grinned. "Tell me."

"Bridge and I were fighting, I can't even remember what about. I had a couple of drinks. I guess she followed me out because she was just there suddenly. She pushed me against a wall like this."

Zoë seized Grey roughly by her shoulders and shoved her into the wall of the home next to them.

"She didn't say a word," Zoë was whispering to Grey now, her voice intense. "She just pressed me into that wall and kissed the fucking shit out of me." She was pressing Grey unconsciously into the wall, her thigh sliding neatly in place between Grey's trembling legs, her eyes remembering another night. Zoë caught herself and stepped back with visible effort.

"Then she said I looked like I needed to be kissed and left." Zoë shrugged. "But that night, I wrote a hundred pages. I didn't sleep for three days."

"I bet!" Grey laughed. They smiled at each other. To be kissed by a woman like that simply because you needed kissing, Grey mused. Wonder what cute fucking Sarah would think about that!

Grey sucked in a lungful of muggy New Orleans air, trying to clear her fuzzy head and get her trembling legs under control. She felt light-headed and giddy, woozy, and wet in her jeans. She shook her head, laughing, and didn't shrug off Zoë's hand when it clasped her own and showed her away.

One bar led to another. They slipped up to countertops between fumbling drunk couples and bachelor parties. They hammered down another few shots. They stumbled in between drag queens, dodging puddles, bursting out onto Bourbon Street in a fit of giggles under a sheet of a late evening thunderstorm, hair plastered to their faces, their clothes heavy with a proper New Orleans baptism.

Hours passed with innuendos and teasing touches. Somehow, they stumbled down Bourbon Street past hookers, human statues, and boys drumming on five-gallon buckets. They dodged beads being thrown from balconies and avoided the gutter punks as best they could. Zoë bought Grey a Lucky Dog. Eventually, they ended up on Canal Street, staring down the tracks for a streetcar to arrive, both trying and failing not to stand too close to each other.

Chapter Eight

It was late but definitely not the break of dawn Zoë had written about countless times in her novels. No lavender moon peeked through the glass skyscrapers downtown, casting any sort of luminous shadows. Nope, nothing like that. The streetcar stop was humid and stank of garbage. But they were alone, and Grey had to admit that being with Zoë, mildly intoxicated, in the dirty streets of New Orleans just seemed right.

Zoë leaned against a street pole waiting for the St. Charles line, smoking an American Spirit cigarette. A long forgotten vice from her youth—the temporary sensation long since forbidden by the authoritarian Bridgette.

"Man, I know these things aren't good for me, but every now and then..." Zoë took a drag on her cigarette, dropped it on the ground, and stubbed it out with her boot.

The St. Charles streetcar pulled up and stopped unceremoniously. The two boarded and quickly realized that, other than the driver, they were the only two passengers on the car. Grey sat in the first forward-facing bench, fully expecting Zoë to take the place next to her.

Instead, she felt a cool, soft finger trace across her hairline, gently swiping her ponytail. Zoë's voice, changed now, more sultry with its tequila-laden depth, whispered into her ear, "You sit here, I want to watch you."

Grey followed her in the driver's rearview mirror as Zoë headed straight back to the rear of the car, sat down, and squarely set her chin upon a closed fist. Grey could feel her brown eyes burning into the back of her head, her mind. The sensation was unnerving, toying with already frayed senses from a night of delicious debauchery. Those eyes on her made her hot and keenly aware of how much she wanted this woman

She tried not to squirm. She focused on looking nonchalant, casual. Grey draped an arm across the seat top aside her. The responding sexy smirk did not escape her in that rearview mirror.

It was too stuffy; she couldn't breathe. Grey opened a window to catch a breeze. Still, the eyes bore into the back of her head. Grey tried to watch the scenery slide by as the streetcar rumbled along Canal Street. Were they really just now reaching the first stop since they had boarded? Damn.

Another passenger stumbled into the car. Grey glanced briefly his way, trying to catch a glimpse and not daring to turn all the way around. Too obvious. Too interested. This ride was making her crazy.

"Stop it," she muttered under her breath, trying to shrug it off. And still, those eyes bore into her, straight to her core, like a line of heat searing a path from where those cool fingers had touched the back of her neck, down her spine. She shifted in her seat restlessly and took a deep breath. The breeze was not helping at all.

Grey found those eyes again in the mirror. That smirk had morphed into a sultry, teasing smile. Grey looked away, trying to focus on neon signs and lantern-shaped streetlamps. Cars. Pedestrians. Anything. It wasn't working.

"Damn," she hissed. It was almost a laugh. Another deep breath.

Her mind went straight to that moment when Zoë had pushed her into the wall, talking about Alicia. She imagined that kiss, how hot that must have been. Grey knew she was getting wetter by the second. Her whole body was throbbing, her shirt was too tight. Every passing minute was a struggle not to move, not to get up and walk to the rear of the streetcar, to crush her lips against that knowing smile. It was disorienting, alien. She had never had to resist so diligently.

Grey straightened her shoulders, clasped her hands in her lap. She sat up straighter, took many deep breaths of the muggy midnight air. She closed her eyes and allowed herself to imagine, just this once, she told herself, because she was drunk, she added.

Her eyes snapped open when the streetcar came to an abrupt halt and cool fingers again touched the back of her neck. Lips that were entirely too close to Grey's overheated body murmured in her ear, "We're here."

To Grey's irritation, Zoë virtually bounced off the streetcar and headed straight toward home. No hesitation, no lingering, nothing. How could anyone be that controlled?

Grey let the breeze flowing along St. Charles sober her mood and thoughts, and she found herself speeding up to match Zoë's pace. The trees facing the street, which usually provided shade from the Gulf sun, were serving up appropriate shadows to mark Grey's sudden foul mood.

But when she caught up to Zoë, Grey realized that the woman's features were not as controlled as she had originally imagined. Zoë's brow creased, her concern showing her age, yet simultaneously making her look more beautiful. Zoë's pace was quickening, her stride lengthening.

92

"Are we gonna run home?" Grey asked, her ire showing despite her attempt to seem nonchalant.

"Oh, I'm sorry," Zoë said, making a visible effort to slow down.

It struck Grey that she was trying to look relieved.

"I just didn't realize how late it was. I don't know what I was thinking. I mean, the baby is gone and Bridge is gone. Maybe we should get something to eat. Are you hungry?" Zoë was rambling. But Grey could tell she didn't mean it, and her attempt at being polite sounded more like an angry parent than a friend.

"No, I'm fine. Let's just walk." Grey was unable to control the pout.

Zoë laughed and looped her arm into Grey's. "Grey Chesterfield, you are going to have to get a better poker face if you're gonna play games. Don't be a brat. Artists get moody, haven't you heard?" Zoë playfully kicked Grey in the butt.

"Art?" Grey feigned surprise. "Is that what we're calling vampire porn these days?"

And just like that, the mood shifted. Grinning, Grey sprinted full speed, practically squealing, toward the driveway of their home. She was ashamed to admit Zoë, who was almost twice her age, was gaining ground on her.

Grey ran straight into the driveway gate and turned to face Zoë. Maybe this was it. She turned, smiling at Zoë, and laughed. But the minute she saw Zoë's face, the laughter died.

"Don't say a word," Zoë whispered urgently. "Go straight through the kitchen and up to your room. Be careful and be quiet. We were not out together, do you hear me? You were at a friend's house. Go."

"What?" Grey hesitated.

"You have to trust me," Zoë hissed, pointing at the black BMW in the driveway Grey hadn't noticed. "Bridgette's home. Please. Just go."

Her heart still hammering from the run and with heavy feet, Grey dragged her gaze and self away from Zoë and headed for the back door. She couldn't understand what had happened. Weren't they just having fun? She felt summarily dismissed and was wondering what she had done wrong. She had half a mind to turn around, march straight back over to Zoë, and ask.

Grey glanced over her shoulder, and Zoë made the universal "shoo!" gesture at her. Grey ground her teeth angrily as she slipped quietly through the door, trying as hard as she could not to let it creak. She took off her shoes and tiptoed down the hallway, through the pitch-dark kitchen, up the stairs toward her room. But when she reached her destination and tossed her shoes on the floor, curiosity got the better of her. She couldn't stand it. She had to know.

Grey could hear faint sounds from the entryway—was that a set of keys falling on the floor? Something crashed. Laughter. If Grey could hear Zoë this far away, making an entrance, she must want to be heard bumbling around. It was suspiciously loud. What the hell was going on? Grey knew Zoë wasn't completely hammered. In spite of the alarm bells going off in her head, she slipped out of her room and down the hallway, sticking to the shadows and carefully placing each clumsy step.

"Oh, it's you." Zoë giggled. Even from a distance, Grey could tell it was fake. Then she shook her head at herself—like she really knew Zoë that well. "Weren't you supposed to come home tomorrow?" Zoë's words were also much more slurred than they had been only moments before.

"Where the hell have you been? You realize it's well after midnight." There was a long pause—so long, even Grey started to shift her weight from foot to foot, anxiously waiting to see what Zoë would say.

"Aww, come on, Bridge." Again, she giggled. "It's the night before Halloween. You know what that means—fans and stuff."

"You expect me to believe that you were out mingling with your fans?" Another lengthy pause. "You haven't voluntarily done shit for your fans in ages. I have to practically drag you to signings."

"Goddamn it," Zoë slurred. "I just wanted to see if they still do that thing."

"At that old shack of yours?"

"My old rental, yes." Much less slur this time. The words were sharp, as though a full stop existed between each syllable.

"No, Zoë. You didn't go out to 'be with your fans.' You don't write. You don't care. Hell, half the time, you can't even get it together. I'm not taking your word for it. You were out with someone. I know it." Her voice had risen to a scream.

"There are going to be pictures on the site, I bet. And probably Facebook. And Twitter."

There was an enormous crash. Grey jumped and was just barely able to resist the urge to come charging down the hallway to what—help?

"Liar!" Bridgette screamed again. It was piercing, hysterical. "Fucking liar! Fucking bitch! How could you? We have a child! Who were you with?" She was sobbing.

Zoë tried to interject. Do something, Grey thought anxiously, this is ridiculous. Make it stop.

"After all we've sacrificed for this!" Another crash, glass bursting onto hardwood floors. "And this!" Another crash, this time ceramic shattering. "And this!" Wood splintering.

"Stop it!" Zoë thundered. "Shut the fuck up!"

Then there was a thud and a moan. Grey's heart leapt into her throat. She was simultaneously paralyzed with fear that Bridgette had perhaps hit Zoë and terrified of being caught in the hallway and dragged into the fight. Still, she couldn't not know. The ensuing noises sounded like a struggle that was moving from the entryway into the living room, and she was concerned enough to slowly creep forward, inching her way along the hallway until she could spy the tiniest sliver of the living room from around a corner.

Grey felt her mouth go dry. She was shaking all over, and her feet were growing numb from the cold air-conditioned floors. She crept forward and heard more movement. The sound of bodies being slammed into furniture. More moaning. Grey felt a sharp pain in her foot and looked down much too late to realize that she was walking barefoot over shattered crystal. She knelt down and quickly pulled a needle of glass from her heel. She was bleeding. Still, she leaned forward and peered into the room.

The main living area was dimly lit by the single lamp behind Bridgette's favorite wingback. There was no other light. Grey could almost imagine the scene. Zoë coming in, pretending to be drunk, only to be met with Bridgette's most disdainful look of superiority, the interrogation light directed in her face.

Grey had wanted to scream, "It's none of your damn business. You're never here." She had thought, at the very least, she could stumble into the room and pretend she had been frightened by the yelling.

But when her gaze made the corner, she couldn't say a thing.

The room was destroyed. All the lovely crystal decanters Zoë had kept in her room were lined up on the end table. Half of them were now unceremoniously decorating the floor of the living room and the hall where she now stood. The fight was over, and the two women were locked together in passion. Bridgette's Michael Kors skirt was pushed up around her waist. Her Prada shoes were still on, each ankle held tightly in the grasp of her lover. In Zoë's grasp.

Grey wanted to leave. She was both angry and embarrassed. She'd let herself be attracted to her married employer. She'd flirted and expected... Hell, she didn't know what she'd expected. But she couldn't leave. A strange mixture of excitement and repulsion had seized her. She needed to watch this. She had to know.

Bridgette was lying across the desk, her legs pulled into the air. Her blouse was ripped open, the buttons torn from the fabric. Her head was thrown back, and her red hair cascaded off the side of the desk. Zoë, still fully clothed, stood over her with her fingers working in places Grey could only imagine. She had a look of total control, total domination. Bridgette was writhing into Zoë's outstretched hand, fully controlled by the movements of the other.

"Is this what you want? Is this what will shut you up?" Zoë leaned down and brushed only her lips against Bridgette's thigh.

"Yes..." Bridgette moaned, forcing herself farther onto Zoë's fingers. "Yes, fuck me, lover. Prove you love me."

Grey could barely make out the words, but it seemed strange that Bridgette should be so submissive. So wanting.

97

The woman who didn't need anyone. The Ice Queen, as Grey had come to know her.

"Be quiet. I don't want to hear your voice," Zoë hissed and quickened the pace of her penetration, furiously working Bridgette's clit with her other hand.

Ashamed and embarrassed, angry and confused, Grey stood paralyzed in the shadows, her own clit throbbing. Jealousy and longing ate at her, rooted her to the spot, her bleeding heel leaving its mark on the floor. This wasn't Zoë. This was Aimee R. Dupree. Rochester. This was the woman she and her friends had speculated about—was she as good in real life as her writing would indicate? Was she really that good? Grey had her answer, and she didn't like it, primarily because she wasn't the recipient.

Bridgette whimpered and writhed on the desk. Zoë dipped her head lower, tearing into her thigh hard enough to make her scream, leaving angry, red bite marks. "You fucking wanted this," she growled. "You asked for it. You know better." Bridgette arched her back and thrust her hips, begging for more.

Grey sucked in a breath, still unable to leave. She knew these images would be burned into her mind. It was for the best, she told herself. She should stay and watch. Surely, that would discourage her from participating in any further drunken adventures in the French Quarter. She thought of that bartender, and her clit got harder.

"Please." Bridgette moaned. "Just do it."

Zoë pulled back and looked down on Bridgette with a smug smile playing her lips. Mission accomplished, it seemed. All she had to do was seal the deal. So she did. Grey watched, full of simultaneous agony and hot anticipation, as that shaggy blond head lowered between Bridgette's thighs, those lips Grey had been admiring in the rearview mirror of the streetcar sealing around another woman's clit, a moan rising from both women as hips bucked and arms clamped down around twitching thighs.

Grey was finally able to move. She needed to move. She was so slick and wet, she had to touch herself, and she couldn't do it in the shadows of the hallway. It would be bad enough if they saw her. It would be a thousand times worse if she were caught with her hand in her pants.

She backed up a step, then another. She discovered she could turn around. She finally crept down the hallway toward her room, being careful not to let her bleeding heel touch the floor anymore. She didn't need to leave a trail.

Slowly, she closed the door on her room and leaned her forehead against the cool wood. Her breathing sounded so loud in this quiet corner of the expansive house. The room was so empty and cold. Still leaning against the door, she unzipped her pants and slid trembling fingers beneath her panties, finding herself as slick and hot as she had imagined.

"Holy hell," she hissed and furiously worked herself until her knees nearly buckled under the release.

The room started to spin. Grey could not unsee what she had seen. How would she be able to face the women in the morning? She just couldn't think about that. She would worry about that later. She angrily shrugged out of her clothes, feeling foolish. She stumbled across the room and into her bed, half wishing she had stayed in that night, half grateful she had not.

Chapter Nine

Grey woke the next morning alone and confused. She pulled the comforter over her head and let the alarm on her cellphone buzz. What the hell was she doing? Angrily, she reached out and swatted the snooze button again, peeking at the room. The servants' quarters, she reminded herself. Images of Bridgette and Zoë flooded her mind, though she pressed her hands against her temples to keep them out.

"You are the nanny, for God's sake. You are the nanny," she mumbled, as if simply repeating the phrase would somehow rend her mind from desire. From the need to feel Zoë between her own legs, as she had seen her with Bridgette the night before.

"Well, this is going nowhere," she said aloud to the empty room, pulling the comforter back and heading into the shower. She played bad eighties music on her phone while she cleaned herself. There was nothing less sexy than bad eighties music, she mused.

After an hour of showering and getting ready, Grey headed to the kitchen to take up her duties. Her job. She pretended she hadn't spent twenty minutes selecting the right jeans and an emerald green T-shirt that set her eyes off just so.

Grey walked into the enormous kitchen to find Bridgette sitting at the table in a ridiculous satin robe with ostrich feathers around the collar. Matching ostrich slippers completed the outfit. This must be her post-coital wardrobe, Grey realized. Ludicrous.

"Oh, Grey darling!" Bridgette gushed. "Don't you look gorgeous this morning!"

Grey had to admit that Bridgette looked beautiful. Happy even.

"Listen, no Emily today, sweetie. If you don't mind, I have some errands for you to run. I'm going to make Zoë a totally delish dinner tonight. Eggplant parmigiana. It's her favorite. Oh, and I want flowers and wine. So you need to go to the grocery store and the florist. I can have the wine delivered."

"No problem." Grey smiled.

This wasn't creepy, right? This was good. These women were married, and she was going to facilitate a reconciliation dinner. That was the right thing to do.

"Wonderful! Oh, and if you don't mind, maybe you could come to the room later and help me pick from some outfits. I laid out about six. We can have a fashion show, won't that be fun? I have to look perfect tonight. Oh! And if it wouldn't be too much trouble, maybe you could just keep to your room the rest of the night. Or maybe I should get you a hotel room, what do you think?" Bridgette's eyes were glowing in an almost surreal manner.

She looks like a maniac, Grey thought. "Whatever you think is best, I guess," she actually said.

"Perfect. Oh, I'm so excited. She's in her room *writing*! Can you believe that? For hours, she has been in there. I knew I could do this." Bridgette grinned with self-satisfaction.

Right. So perhaps all the tortured artist needed was a good fuck. Perhaps dust the cobwebs off that old pussy by running around with a young thing like herself, visiting her old fuck fantasy bartender, and oh—imagine that—she was writing again. For hours. And her crazy-ass, certifiable wife was all the sudden Miss Congeniality, being friendly and almost considerate.

Grey felt so sheepish. How could she have so misinterpreted the past evening? Zoë had been toying with her. Or worse, she felt sorry for Grey and so had just been trying to make her feel better. No. Grey didn't believe that. She just tried to tell herself that it was the truth so she could get past the feeling of Zoë touching the back of her neck out of her head.

This was when she needed a close friend to call. Somebody she could just scream at and vent to, who would understand her frustration. But there wasn't really anybody close left. Instead, she was supposed to play helpful and participate in some sort of "fun" fashion show.

Grey wanted to call Beth and ask for the hundredth time when she could get her damned money so she could leave the crazy house. But it wasn't an option. She could go work in a bar or a hotel or something. No. This was probably still better. Hell, there were tons of fans out there who would just about cut off their right arm for the chance to watch Aimee R. Dupree fuck anybody, let alone her hot, albeit crazy, wife.

Shake it off, Grey, she thought.

Bridgette stood and actually leaned over to kiss her on the cheek. "I'm going to take a long bath. The list is on the table, and I left you some money. Take the car, honey, if you like. And let me know when you're back, I really need help." And with that, she sashayed out of the room like Maggie the Cat.

Grey exhaled slowly. She had a lot to do.

Grey returned to her room for her cellphone and an umbrella. It looked like rain. Somehow, rain felt right.

102

Some rain to wash away the filth and sweep away the last traces of October humidity in the city of saints and sinners.

Five hours later, Grey returned to the house with full arms. She'd taken the car to the French Market and picked up the fresh vegetables and items on Bridgette's list. She'd stopped at the bakery for bread and a good dessert. And remembering the flowers at the last moment, Grey had gone to the small specialty florist off Royal for some stargazer lilies. They had been her mother's favorite. She'd also had a dozen oysters at Acme and two Abita beers, but that was the cost of playing. At least that was what she had convinced herself.

Grey dropped the bags in the kitchen and opened the giant refrigerator for a bottle of water. When she closed the door, she was surprised to find Zoë on the other side. She was still in her clothes from the night before, and she looked exhausted. Dark black circles under her eyes showed her age.

Good, Grey thought. I hope you're miserable.

"Can I have a couple of those, please?" Zoë said, her voice softer than Grey had anticipated.

Wordlessly, Grey handed her two plastic bottles.

"You okay, Grey?"

"I'm fine. Thanks for asking."

Zoë just watched her for a moment. Grey unpacked the things she had picked up. She didn't like Zoë eyeing her, even if she looked terrible, and it was Grey's natural inclination to want to comfort. She resisted the urge this time.

"You sure?" Zoë pressed. "Do you need another bandage, some ointment maybe?"

"For what?" Grey tried to sidestep.

"You cut yourself last night." And there it was. Busted.

Grey shrugged and refused to respond.

"I told you to go to your room."

"And so I did."

"Before or after you saw what you saw?"

"Both."

There. In the open. Just like that.

"I did what I had to do."

"Of course." Grey didn't know where her cool came from. "Just like a good wife. You don't have to explain yourself to me. I get it."

"Do you?" Zoë took a step closer. Grey dodged the advance and took a step back, behind the kitchen island, and picked up the bundle of flowers.

"Do you have a vase? I need to arrange these. Your wife," she paused, carefully enunciating each word, "has special plans, I think."

Zoë sighed and shook her head, placing both hands on the island and leaning across it. "Of course you don't understand. Sometimes it just is what it is."

"People always say that, and it never makes sense. I hate that phrase."

"But that doesn't change the fact that it is what it is."

Grey shrugged and again asked for a vase. She stood there, her hand outstretched. Zoë rolled her eyes and retrieved a vase from an upper cabinet, reluctantly handing it over. Grey dutifully arranged the flowers. Then she continued to unpack the bags, no longer contributing to any kind of conversation.

Zoë took two steps, as though to leave, but changed her mind. "Look, you don't have to understand any of this. You don't know what's been going on, where we came from, or where we're at. It doesn't have to make sense. It so rarely ever does—for anybody. You'll learn that soon enough. It's not all rainbows, Grey. I know at your age, it's supposed to be, but relationships are sometimes confusing and ugly. You will learn that as you get older."

Zoë turned to leave, and Grey couldn't help herself. "I'll never be that old."

Zoë didn't even turn around. She simply walked away.

Chapter Ten

Grey was just finishing setting the table in the main dining room. Beautiful Limoges china with brightly colored pansies on a white starched tablecloth was accentuated by the stargazers she'd purchased. Silver and Waterford crystal.

Perfect, she thought peevishly.

She had to admit the dinner smelled fantastic. Garlic and chianti filled the air. Grey realized she was hungry and turned into the kitchen to forage for something edible before heading to her room to sulk. She had already accepted that she would be sulking that night and planned to binge on old New Orleans-themed movies and beer. She'd bought some popcorn and a large salt shaker just to be bitchy. Take that, Ice Queen. She'd have her salt and her third cup of coffee, too, thank you very much.

"She's not my wife, and I do what I like," Grey muttered, realizing she was reaching a new low on her maturity scale, but frankly, she didn't give a damn.

Bridgette bolted into the kitchen, startling her.

"Thank God! Come with me," she demanded, seizing Grey's hand and dragging her up the stairs to the family's section of the home. Grey realized she had never been in either woman's bedroom, but she did know from previous conversations that they generally slept separately, which was bizarre enough to deter her from sneaking into either room to check it out.

"She says I snore." Zoë had laughed in the garden one afternoon.

Grey's gut lurched a little bit at the memory of Zoë laughing with her and Emily, dancing around the garden in their ridiculous costumes. Earlier in the evening, she had even crept past the studio, thinking maybe she'd apologize or at least say hello and try to salvage their strong working relationship. But when she'd finally gotten the nerve up to approach the door, she'd been stayed by the sound of computer keys clacking. Bridgette had been right, it seemed. Zoë was writing furiously and had been ever since the night before.

The absence of jazz on vinyl was almost insufferable, even if part of her was dying to get her hands on whatever Zoë was writing. Hadn't Bridgette said it was Grey's job to eliminate distractions so that Zoë might finally write again? So didn't this mean, somehow, that she was technically doing a good job with her responsibilities? It didn't really feel that good, truth be told.

The darkness of the hallway gave way to an enormous circular bedroom master suite. The linens were yellow and white vertical stripes, and the curtains and furniture covers all matched exactly. In fact, the entire room was yellow and white, with the exception of an enormous portrait of Bridgette over the bed done in differing shades of pink. Yikes. How self-indulgent indeed. Grey resisted the urge to snort.

"You sit over here, Grey darling," Bridgette instructed, taking her hand and leading her to a plush chair situated by a floor-to-ceiling window. She drew the curtains, and Grey looked at her quizzically.

"You simply must help me choose the right outfit," she simpered, batting her eyelids playfully.

Oh, Grey thought. Right. Freak—I mean fashion—show time. Her gaze darted about the room, trying to land on anything other than Bridgette's excited and sparkling smile. But she couldn't avoid it. Finally, she met Bridgette's ice blue eyes and forcefully returned the smile. She unclenched her teeth and managed a simple, "All right then. Go ahead."

Bridgette laughed joyfully and dashed into what Grey suspected was an enormous walk-in closet full of designer clothes and shoes. She heard Bridgette rummaging around and shifted nervously in her seat. How many dresses would she have to endure?

None immediately, it turned out. No dresses. No blouses or pretty slacks. No designer shoes or expensive jewelry.

Bridgette sashayed back into the room—no, strutted—her pale, lithe body accentuated by a beautiful black and wine red silk corset, complete with matching panties, garter, and stockings. Grey gawked for a few seconds before catching herself, and even when she did get it together long enough to try to come up with an appropriate response, nothing came to mind.

"Um" was the best Grey could manage.

"I take it you approve." Bridgette's voice had dropped an octave. She took a few steps closer, running her hands up the corset, cupping her breasts. "Yes, I think this will work just fine." She laughed again—laughing so easily and quickly this day that Grey found it disorienting. The woman was like fire and ice, she thought, or hot and cold. Or manic. Or bipolar. Hot damn, she was fucking crazy.

Grey squirmed, uncomfortable.

Bridgette spun on her heel and ducked back into the closet.

Grey released a breath she didn't realize she'd been holding. She argued with herself furiously, trying to come up with a sufficient reason to have to exit the room in the quickest manner possible. Before she could come up with anything at all, Bridgette was back.

At least Bridgette wasn't half-naked. She had slipped into a cherry red dress, which was snug in all the right places and nearly, but not quite, too short to cover the tops of her garters. This time, Grey gave an immediate response.

"That dress is gorgeous."

"You think so? Not too much? It doesn't say, 'I don't want to wear this more than five minutes,' does it? Because I need to make it through dinner before she ravishes me."

"Um." So much for that lit major paying off.

"No, no. You're right. Something a little less fuck-me-now and more fuck-me-later." Bridgette practically tore the dress from her body and tossed it on the floor, giggling. Again displaying the decadent lingerie, peeking at Grey for a reaction.

Holy hell, Grey thought. This is not at all wildly inappropriate. She did her best to look out the window. Except the curtains were drawn, and there was nothing to hold her attention.

Three more dresses—emerald green, black, cream.

Same routine. Giggling. Undressing. Eyeing her audience for a reaction to skin on display.

Bridgette slipped back into the closet. More rummaging. In spite of her best efforts, images of the two women flooded Grey's mind again.

"How's this?" Bridgette demanded, startling Grey. She hadn't noticed her re-emergence.

Hands on her hips, a smirk playing along her lips, Bridgette twirled on the spot for Grey, nicely displaying a sky blue, sleeveless dress, which set off her eyes beautifully. The dress was looser, longer, more flowy and light. A perfect contrast to what lay beneath, Grey realized.

"That's the one," she said, not sure if she meant it or if she was just trying to end this. Don't take off the dress, she thought urgently. But off it came in a rush of floating fabric.

And there Bridgette stood again in all her glory. She took five very slow steps forward and casually knelt in front of Grey so their eyes were almost even. Grey's eyes widened in alarm as Bridgette extended her hand and cupped her cheek.

"Thank you, Grey darling." Her fingers lingered, tracing a line from Grey's cheekbone to her chin. Then she touched her nose and grinned. "You're the best."

That was the first time she saw the magnetism, understood what could possibly be so attractive about this woman other than superficial beauty. And it vexed her.

"Glad to be of help, Ms. Breedlove," she said with false politeness.

"Just today, you may call me Bridgette."

"Glad to be of help," Grey hesitated, "Bridgette." She swallowed hard. She needed some fresh air. She did not want to be surprised in this position. "Is there anything else that you require of me?"

"Mmm." Bridgette gave her a sultry smile. "Not tonight." Grey realized she was being toyed with. Time to end this.

"Then I think I'll head to my room. You have everything you need. It's all ready."

"Good." Bridgette released her with a shrug. She went to pick up the blue dress and slipped back into it while Grey fled the room.

Grey still felt slightly woozy and a little disoriented when she made it up the stairs and to her bedroom. A little violated even. What the hell were these women all about? She'd passed by Zoë's studio quickly and quietly to see if she could talk to her, but the sound of computer keys clicking made her change her mind.

Great, glad to help, she thought bitterly.

Grey put on some sweats and started her first movie, but salty popcorn and beer proved insufficient distraction. She paused the flick and paced in her room, feeling trapped.

Unable to stop herself, she'd crept down the stairs and into the kitchen under the guise of melting butter for her popcorn. She'd heard Billie Holiday's voice playing softly from the dining room and the sound of laughter and utensils touching very expensive china. Emily, it seemed, was to remain with her grandparents another night. At least that was what she presumed. Neither of her employers had bothered to tell her where the child was.

An empty bottle of Silver Oak cabernet sat on the kitchen table. Apparently, they were into their second bottle.

"No, I've got this," she heard Zoë say, followed by footsteps. Grey tried to make it to the back stairs, but the door to the kitchen swept open too quickly.

And there she was—blond and beautiful. Zoë's brown eyes showed instant concern, and she let the door swing closed behind her.

"Hey."

Really. Hey? After everything that had happened, all she got was a "hey." Nice.

"Hey," Grey responded in kind. "I'll take those for you." Grey took the dirty plates to the sink and rinsed them.

"You don't have to do that, Grey," Zoë said, her voice soft, almost apologetic.

"No, it's just how it is, right?" Grey managed a smile. "Go on back in. I know Bridgette spent a lot of time on this evening. You two should enjoy it."

"Okay."

Grey didn't even move. She couldn't turn around and betray how foolish she felt. Her boss standing there in a black turtleneck, black leggings, and brilliant black riding boots, looking beautiful. She kept her eyes on the remains of the eggplant as it washed down the disposal.

"I'm sorry about being a shit. You guys wouldn't mind if I went out tonight, would you? I mean, since Emily isn't here."

"Of course not. Take the whole night. In fact, I'll have Antoine drive you to the Quarter and get you a room. You should spend some time around people your own age." It wasn't Zoë's voice.

Grey turned around to find Bridgette, looking gorgeous in the blue dress she'd helped to choose, with her hand possessively around Zoë's waist.

"Actually, that would be great, Bridgette, thank you." Grey managed an appropriately grateful smile and quickly departed the kitchen.

"Ms. Breedlove, dear," she heard her call laughingly after her. They were both laughing, she was pretty sure of that much. And she didn't blame them one bit.

Chapter Eleven

The ride to the French Quarter was quiet and awkward. Traffic seemed unusually heavy, even for a Saturday night. But what did Grey know? Perhaps this was normal.

Antoine was all business and not much for conversation, it seemed. No music, either.

"So how long have you worked for them?"

"Five years."

"Do you like it?"

"Yes."

That was about all she got until they reached Canal Street, nearly forty-five minutes later.

"I'm to drop you off here. Be careful. Call me when you're ready to turn in." He stepped out of the vehicle and opened the door for her, extending a hand to help her out. She took it and smiled at him.

"Thanks for the ride, Antoine."

"Take this." He handed her an envelope. It contained a card with Antoine's cell number on the back and a scribbled note that said, "Hotel Monteleone, room 412." Two hundred-dollar bills were neatly tucked between the key and the card. "You're already checked in. I put your overnight bag in the room. The hotel is on Royal Street."

"They think of everything, don't they?" She smiled sweetly to take the bite out of the sarcasm.

Antoine peered at her curiously, then simply said, "Yes." Then he got back into his vehicle and unceremoniously took off.

It was so loud at the corner of Canal and Bourbon. Grey peered down the street at the obvious revelry—all neon lights and partygoers in the street. But the lack of personal conversation, of a companion of any kind, was nearly deafening. For a moment, Grey stood rooted to the spot, unsure what to do. She slowly folded and tucked the envelope into her front jeans pocket. Sighing, she briefly debated wandering down Canal Street in search of a quieter coffee shop where she could hide and mope. She took five steps away from Bourbon when her attention was diverted abruptly by a group of young men jogging down the street toward her.

"Holy shit." She giggled, gawking at the scantily clad hard bodies charging past her. Heavy locks and chains bounced off their bare chests. Their grinning faces were concealed by black Mardi Gras masks. Their rock-hard asses barely covered by black leather boy shorts. Their matching outfits were completed by knee-high black leather biker boots.

Suddenly, Grey noticed more bizarre outfits—Victorian vampires casually strolling along, smoking cigarettes with skeletons and pirates. Grey froze, shaking her head. "Oh, shit, it's Halloween!"

No way was she going to hide in a coffee shop. Just like that, her mood lifted, and curiosity got the better of her. Briefly, she wished she had a costume of her own, but that wasn't going to dampen her spirits now. She turned on the spot and headed back down Bourbon Street.

Now this is going to be a real adventure, she thought. Bet those boys are headed straight for the gay bars. She quickened her pace, dodging trash and beads and puddles of filth.

And sure enough, she found them. She had to maneuver her way through the tightly packed street, avoiding burning cigarettes and loose drinks, but the group was just outside of the Bourbon Pub/Parade.

The crowd was cheering and whooping as they struck poses for flashing cameras and phones. Grey giggled and got her own phone out to take a picture. But for what? To post online? To send to Sarah? Who was she going to share this with? She slipped her phone back into her pocket and sighed, wishing she had a drink in her hand, wishing she had a cigarette to go with it, even though she didn't smoke.

The boys danced, hooting and hollering, aggressively encouraging passers-by to come into the bar, where a dance party was clearly in progress. Grey took a few steps in their direction, fully intending to go inside to get a drink. Realizing there was a cover to get in, however, she turned around to head to a bar farther down Bourbon Street instead. But one of the dancing men grabbed her around the waist.

"Don't leave, honey." He spun her around and ground himself against her backside. "A hot little thing like yourself should go inside." Grey started to shrug him off, her cheeks burning with mortification, but she caught the crowd, which was cheering and clapping. Every face she saw was full of joy, eyes glassy with sensory overload and intoxication.

Fuck it, she thought in spite of her blush. "Fuck it all," she said out loud, suddenly laughing. Something was snapping inside—she could feel it. The past two months had just been too much. Too much hurt. Too much sorrow. Too much anger. Too much confusion. Too much longing. She just wanted to call her daddy and tell him everything

115

and ask for advice like she had a million times before. But she couldn't. And it pissed her off.

"That's right," the man behind her murmured and chuckled. "Fuck it all. Just relax, girlie. Dance for a minute. Look—they love it! And go find a hot woman in there."

Yes. That sounded like a brilliant idea.

Grey wasn't much of a dancer, but she could bump and grind like every other young twenty-something out there. So she did. And she didn't care who saw. When he finally released her, she wrapped her arms around him and kissed him on the cheek. He swatted her on the ass and led her to the bouncer. "No charge," he said, and the man nodded, letting Grey inside.

So many bare-chested men covered head to foot in glitter. Some of the costumes were spectacular, likely planned to the finest details for months. Techno music droned, and the massive disco ball flashed across the dance floor as Grey wedged herself between beautiful bodies until she finally reached a spot at the bar where she had the slightest chance of being noticed.

"Yeah?" A queen finally decided that she was worthy of his attention.

"Do you have Patrón Silver tequila?"

"You want it chilled and dressed, honey?"

"Definitely. Make it two. Do you sell cigarettes here?"

"Can't smoke in here, honey. They fucked that up for everybody about six months ago."

"Damn it."

He chuckled and presented her the shots. Well, good thing she didn't really smoke. That was the universe telling her not to start, she thought. Or the universe was telling her she shouldn't stay at this bar and she should continue walking.

116

She unceremoniously downed both shots in rapid succession and bit into a lime.

"So it's that kind of a night," the queen said. "You go, girl. Fuck it, am I right?"

"Hell yes."

"Another round?"

"Another."

She slammed the third and fourth shots, dug around in her pocket for the envelope, and slapped a hundred-dollar bill on the bar. The queen arched his eyebrow and grinned at her, taking the bill and disappearing for a few moments before returning with her change.

"So where's the parade?" Grey asked, still licking her lips. Those shots were already kicking in. "I'm assuming there's going to be one."

"Frenchmen Street. It'll start in about an hour." He paused. "There'll be a lot more action out that way for a while. When it's over, come back down this way. The party always moves back down here."

"Thanks." Grey took her change, dropped a ten on the counter, and exited the bar.

It took her about five minutes to find a shop that carried cigarettes. She hadn't the faintest idea what to get. She settled on a blue pack of American Spirit—the same kind Zoë had smoked the night before. Grey stood out on the street corner and lit the cigarette, coughing and hacking furiously after her first inhalation. How could anybody think that was a good idea? But she shook her head, wiped the tears from her eyes, and tried again, this time barely puffing.

Her father had always told her, "If I ever catch you with a cigarette, I'm going to make you eat it, filter and all. Smoking is a disgusting habit. No daughter of mine is going to smoke."

"Fuck it all," Grey murmured around the cigarette and marched down the street.

Frenchmen Street. That was near where she and Zoë had been the night before, wasn't it? It dawned on Grey that it was also close to that nondescript bar. She wondered if she could find it. She wondered if there would be more "sacrifices" at Zoë's old apartment.

"Fuck it all," Grey angrily muttered again, then stopped by a hurricane stand and picked up a giant drink in a plastic cup.

She stumbled down Bourbon Street until she hit Dumaine. She had to stop and ask directions multiple times and was nearly misled by drunken tourists and frat boys. But she eventually found Decatur, and eventually, Frenchmen Street.

Jazz oozed from every bar and street corner. This was what she thought New Orleans was all about. She stood at the corner of Frenchmen and Chartres for a long time with her cigarettes and her half-finished hurricane, swaying drunkenly to the music. She didn't even mind being bumped by the costumed, drunken crowd.

Slowly, deliberately, she stepped away from the safety of the wall and joined the sea of bodies moving like a river down the street until the flow came to an abrupt halt, the wave breaking against a wall of bodies jammed tightly on sidewalks.

It was impossible to move. Grey felt as though she were being swept up in a dream—colorful and frightening floats passing by periodically, the crowd roaring its approval and shouting for parade throws and candies. A moon pie hit Grey in the head, and she giggled and hiccupped, staring at the drag queens on a ghostly pirate ship float.

Three more blocks north or four? If she could wedge herself between these bodies, she could perhaps escape this trap and find that bar. But no. She couldn't move.

The air was crisper this night, a cool breeze wafting in off the river. But her throat felt constricted from the tight squeeze. She had to get out of there.

Just as she felt the edge of panic beginning to sober her mind, a raindrop splashed across her forehead. Then another. The sky popped open and delivered a downpour that sent the crowd pushing in every direction for cover. For a few minutes, Grey was tossed about as bodies scrambled to get away. The moment passed, and she could breathe a sigh of relief. The crowd had thinned, yet the parade carried on.

Grey was surrounded by a group of young women her own age. They were flashing the floats, giggling, and screaming with glee. Man, this isn't Mardi Gras, Grey thought, but she was distracted by the women nonetheless.

One girl noticed her obvious attention. She smiled slyly at Grey, her short dark hair plastered to her face, her white wet sorority T-shirt clinging to her chest. She obviously wasn't wearing a bra, and her nipples protruded prominently.

She turned her full attention to Grey and said simply, "Hi."

"Um," Grey said, dropping her cigarette and drink at the same time.

The girl laughed and shoved her friends out of the way, taking two steps closer. She wrapped her arms around Grey's neck, pressed her body into her, and locked her full lips on Grey's.

Fuck it all, Grey thought, parting her lips, allowing the enthusiastic invasion to the cheers of the girl's friends.

It wasn't at all like kissing Sarah. It wasn't sweet or sultry or sexy. It was sloppy, urgent, and raw. Her body responded, and she wrapped her arms around the girl's waist, pulling her in closer, tasting rum on her lips. It wasn't until she could feel the girl's fingers fumbling at her jeans zipper that Grey broke the kiss with a moan and stumbled away from her, down the street. She could hear the catcalls chasing her and didn't care.

The sidewalk rushed up to meet her. Embarrassed, she jumped up and dusted street debris from her jeans. At least she hadn't tripped and fallen into one of those foul puddles.

Her hands stung where she'd fallen. She stared at the raw skin for a minute and wiped them on her jeans.

"I need a beer!" she announced loudly, after bursting into the first bar she saw.

A few men guffawed, and an older gentleman said, "Don't we all."

She stumbled out, Abita in hand, back onto the street.

"Fuck it all."

Grey lit another cigarette, coughed furiously, and trudged farther along Frenchmen before abruptly turning onto Burgundy. "Was this where we turned?" She tried to remember. God, it would be so much easier if she had asked for the name of the bar. She could ask for directions. But between staring at tattoos and at luscious cleavage, there hadn't seemed time to get that information.

Yes. She could see now where she was. There was the wall Zoë had pushed her into. Damn. Her body was so overheated—even as she shivered in her wet shirt and jeans against the breeze, which suddenly felt much cooler. She licked her kiss-bruised lips and took another drag off her cigarette before tossing it away. She had found her destination.

120

Grey lingered in the doorway. She could see Alicia through the glass. The woman was even hotter from a distance.

One more shot, she thought, fully intending to go inside... To do what, exactly? Stare at her? Make a pass at her? She could have fooled around with that girl in the street if she had wanted to. She had certainly been attractive and eager enough. Why this one? Grey hesitated. Deep down, she knew the answer and didn't want to think about it. Her "fuck it all" mantra suddenly came crashing down.

No. She couldn't go that far. This was Zoë's muse. There was something sacred about that. No matter what had happened the next day, Grey couldn't bring herself to violate that trust. She decided this one was off-limits, even for a casual quick visit for a beer or a shot.

A firm hand clamped down on her shoulder and made her nearly jump out of her skin.

"Come with me, Grey."

She spun around, furious and frightened, until she came face-to-face with Antoine.

She gaped at him for several seconds before blurting, "Why should I?"

"Please."

She sighed. "Where are we going?" Then her eyes nearly popped out of her head. "Wait! How did you find me? Were you spying on me? Did she tell you to follow me? What the fuck!"

Did he see her dancing with the gay leather boys? Did he see her in the street with that girl? Did he know why she was stalking that bartender?

"Please take a deep breath, ma'am," Antoine responded calmly. "None of that matters. But I am going to help you find that hotel now."

"But I only just got here!" Grey pouted, drunk and confused.

"It's nearly two o'clock in the morning."

"No way!" Now she laughed. It couldn't be.

"Just come with me. I'm going to at least make sure you get there and find your room. If you leave again after that, well then, so be it."

"Fine." She felt like a child. Like a child with an overprotective chaperone. It wasn't like she would be able to shake him in her state anyway. How had he found her? It bugged her to no end.

She obediently took his offered arm and trudged back down the block, away from the bar with no name. Antoine tucked her away in his car and began the slow and tedious navigation through the crowded French Quarter. Grey stared out the window, her eyes drooping sleepily. She kind of wanted another drink. She kind of wished she hadn't shrugged that girl off to go chase down a forbidden dream.

They pulled up to the valet at the Monteleone. Antoine shared a few words with the attendant before opening the backseat door for Grey.

"Let's go," he said, offering to help her out.

"I suppose." She sighed and took his hand.

Grey couldn't even remember the walk through the hotel or riding an elevator or anything of the sort. She could barely remember stumbling through the front door. But she crashed in the dark room onto what felt like a large, plush bed, fully clothed, and closed her eyes.

Morning light after hurricanes and rum and cigarettes was for professionals, Grey had decided, hours later. She had crawled—literally crawled—on her hands and knees to the bathroom to vomit. But afterward, in the heat of the shower, she felt much better. She had allowed herself the privilege of drinking the seventeen-dollar bottle of Evian water the hotel had left conveniently by the toilet while sprawled on the floor of the shower.

Another two hours in the bed and a couple of Advil later, she actually felt better than ass. Ass was how she felt when she initially woke up that morning.

At five minutes until eleven o'clock, Grey packed her backpack and headed down to the famous Carousel Bar to wait for Antoine. She vaguely remembered him telling her he'd be back at noon for her when he'd poured her into her room. She gingerly took a seat on the rotating bar and ordered a Bloody Mary, her Rayban sunglasses still in place.

"Not feeling so good, huh?" The bartender smiled and winked at her.

"Understatement of the year, my man," Grey grumbled but managed a lopsided grin.

"Here's the key… You gotta rage against the hangover. You can't just whine. You gotta just say, 'Fuck this hangover, I'm gonna do it again.' So should I make it a double?"

Grey laughed in spite of herself. When she did, she saw Zoë sitting directly across from her, smiling. Of course she would show up there, where Grey looked and felt like shit. She resisted the urge to run her hands through her hair—slurping her Bloody Mary, trying to look unsurprised and nonchalant, like everything was perfectly fine.

The bar seats circled slowly, steadily. As they did, Zoë just as slowly took a seat closer to her every twenty or thirty seconds until, after a few minutes, she was sitting right next to Grey. Zoë was grinning like a Cheshire cat.

"Sister, you look like I feel." Zoë laughed.

Grey smiled. "Are you hungover, too?"

"Dude." Zoë chuckled.

And after all that drama and angst, it was okay. No more explanations and sarcastic, slightly hurt and bitchy comments. Just a smile, a nod, a grin, and a shrug. Just like that. Shake it off.

They each had another Bloody Mary and circled the bar for another hour or so. Grey told Zoë about her adventures, including the drunk sorority girl and the leather boys. They laughed like old friends. For her part, Zoë shared the end result of her romantic evening at home.

"So how was your night?" Grey asked, happy to simply have her friend back. "Did you guys enjoy the mommy-mommy time?" She winked suggestively.

Zoë shook her head in an embarrassed, resigned gesture.

"Yeah, I'm kind of in the doghouse there. It's possible that one of us *may* have had too much to drink and *may* have fallen asleep during the suggestive striptease of the other."

Grey snorted and choked on her Bloody Mary. "Oh, my God, you are such an asshole."

Zoë grinned sheepishly. "I'm sorry! I mean we had, and by we, I mean mostly me, as in I, had two bottles of wine and no sleep. It's not that I don't appreciate the effort, but I was tired and drunk. And I'm *old*, okay? I'm old, and I wanted to go to my room and sleep. And Bridgette had this whole dance number I was supposed to watch, and I don't know…" Zoë was turning red.

Grey giggled. "Stop, just stop! You are hopeless. I would have killed you."

"Grey, please." Zoë sighed and rubbed her blushing face. "You wouldn't have choreographed a dance to seduce a person, I'm guessing. Besides, I really wanted to write." Another sigh, then her face lit up. "Hey, you wanna go get Emily with me? Antoine's waiting outside."

Grey nodded eagerly and quickly polished off her drink, then grabbed her backpack. The return of Emily signaled some return to normality—nothing could have pleased her more at that moment. Running around hammered in the French Quarter was all good and fun, but it couldn't carry on forever. And neither could all the nonsense she had clearly made up in her head. Fun and games with Emily sounded like the best cure in the world.

"Yep, I'm more than ready to see that little munchkin."

Chapter Twelve

Emily babbled nonstop about her two nights with her nanny and pawpaw. She shifted between Grey and Zoë's laps, chattered about Scout, the dog, and jammed cheddar Goldfish into her mouth with filthy little hands. Zoë hung on her every word, alternatively asking questions about Scout's activities and eating the half-eaten morsels Emily offered her between bites.

"Scout likes Goldfish, Mommy. I fed Scout four Goldfish, and he ate them all!"

"Wow, Em, that's so cool," Zoë responded indulgently, eating a wet sticky Goldfish from a pudgy hand.

"Yeah, it was pretty cool."

Grey grinned at them both, and Emily crawled over and crammed a Goldfish into her mouth. She dutifully ate it. When they got to the house, Grey grabbed Emily's bags and took her by the hand.

Bridgette was just loading an overnight bag into the back of her BMW when Emily broke from Grey and bolted for her mother.

"Mommy!" she squealed happily and threw herself at the immaculately dressed woman.

"Emily, no! You are filthy! Don't touch me!" Bridgette screamed in a voice entirely too loud and hostile for a three-year-old. Emily froze, her eyes filling with tears.

Grey sprinted over and swept Emily into her arms instinctively.

"I've got her, Ms. Breedlove," Grey said coldly, unable to hide her disdain.

"See that you do," Bridgette snapped over her shoulder, sliding into the driver's seat and accelerating out of the driveway without further comment.

Zoë stepped up behind Grey and wordlessly took Emily from her. Emily was sobbing, and big round tears flowed freely down her rosy cheeks.

Grey followed them inside. Together, they gave Emily a bath, both women joking and teasing, trying their best to get the precious little princess to at least smile. It didn't take long. The girl's natural sunny disposition always overcame many things.

The three of them spent the afternoon playing games and watching *Dora the Explorer*. Emily was so tired from her adventures that she fell asleep after an early dinner.

After they put Emily to bed, Zoë invited Grey to watch an old movie with her in the theater room. They made popcorn, and Grey retrieved her salt shaker from her room and delivered it to Zoë with a smirk.

They spent the rest of the evening watching *Mildred Pierce*. But by the end of the movie, Grey, too, was yawning and trying desperately not to fall asleep in the overstuffed chair. It was so comfortable. And she had been out so late.

Zoë poked her foot playfully. "Hey, wake up."

"I'm sorry, I guess I'm still a little hungover." Grey stifled another yawn, grinning sheepishly. "I think I'll go to bed."

Zoë eyed her, a strange quizzical look on her face. Then abruptly said, "Wait here a second." She disappeared while Grey remained in her chair as instructed, feeling a little less sleepy, her curiosity piqued.

When Zoë returned a few minutes later, Grey saw that she was carrying a tube of white paper.

"Some late-night reading for you, if you don't mind," Zoë said, almost shyly. She hesitated a second or two, fidgeting, rolling the tube tighter before unrolling it and handing over the stack of pages. "I'd like to know what you think."

Grey realized immediately that it was the beginning pages of a new manuscript. Holy crap. After all this time. And it was more than just a page or two. It was more like dozens. Zoë had been busy. The words must have just poured out of her.

Then her gaze landed on the title: "*Jacqueline: An Alicia Shade Novel.*"

Her head jerked up, and she stared at Zoë, her eyes as big as saucers.

"Just tell me what you think."

Grey tried not to bolt from the room, but so eager was her desire to read what Zoë had written that she barely managed a quick, "Sure, good night. See ya," before she scampered up to her room. She shut the door and bounced onto the bed, practically giddy with delight and nervous as hell.

She snuggled down into the comforter, arranged the pillows just right, and reverently held the pages. Oh, how her college buddies would be jealous now—how few people could say they were allowed a sneak peek of an unfinished and unedited Aimee R. Dupree novel? Very few, she suspected. And how many of those could claim that they had inspired the title? Even fewer, she knew. She giggled with anticipation and set the title page aside carefully.

"Here we go, Rochester." She grinned and began to read.

Jacqueline: An Alicia Shade Novel

Chapter One

Most of my kind do not ask. Most take. If they see a human they desire, one they hunger for, they simply take her, like plucking ripe fruit from a tree. The act is ritual and delight. It is our heritage.

Human beings have been and always will be prey. We consume them. If they are fortunate enough to know of our existence, then they serve us—giving us their life's blood in exchange for the sexual fulfillment they receive when we take them. I am told there is nothing like it in their living world. The act becomes like a drug to them, and they give themselves to us over and over until they are shells. Then we no longer desire them. Then we kill them. There is no remorse.

Once in a great while, a vampire will change a human and make her an apprentice, a companion. In my long life, I have never done this. In truth, I have never wanted a human. Desiring sexual satisfaction from a subspecies has always seemed beneath me. Even attaching a human to myself for the purposes of gaining a simple servant has never seemed prudent. There were too many secrets a human could potentially expose. No, I have always walked this path alone, treasuring the freedom this has allowed me thus far.

Yet the rare companionship of others of my kind comes with a cost—tiring politics, pomp and ceremony, endless verbal and physical duels to prove faith and power. After nearly five hundred years, it is almost too shameful to admit, a seed of longing, of nostalgia, was pulling at the edges of my being with ever-increasing urgency until it could no longer be ignored. This unworthy and despicable sentiment stemmed from the last traces of humanity left within me and should have been shed centuries before.

There was a distant memory that tugged at my consciousness. A girl, a sunset, freshly cut hay, and emerald green eyes. There had been so many young women since that particular girl and that particular evening, but the memory persisted and would not release me. It was not guilt or regret that held me or questioning of how that girl met her end. Nothing should have held me to that moment, yet I was trapped. The cursed memory would not leave me be.

This past decade had been one of prolific conquests. The women of these ages were much less reluctant to follow a pretty stranger into the night. A vampire no longer had to be particularly clever or charming, or even beautiful. A vampire had only to demonstrate a certain magnetism that comes with centuries of practice to capture the eyes and the hearts of mortals.

There was not even a real need for competition among my kind. Populations had grown to such proportions that it was almost a necessity for us to thin out the herd, like chopping down so many trees in a crowded forest. Frequently, these young women were not even missed. Few investigations beyond missing persons reports ever took place. The old rivalries began to fade, and politics existed among us for politics' sake alone. It was tiring and dull.

Thus, every adventure held less and less intrigue, and the longing for that sparkle from a young girl centuries ago grew, festering deep within me, and I could not stop it. Melancholy drove me into the streets in search of a substitute.

130

For months, my old hunting grounds served me well, delivering up a variety of dark-haired young women with green eyes of every shade—grass, sea, precious stone. Nightly, I would satisfy myself and experience relief in the arms of another. Yet it was insufficient to slake my lust and still the intolerable despondency. They offered themselves too willingly, laughed too lightly, came too quickly.

My quest finally began to arouse the suspicions of the local authorities. The law enforcement of the greater area of the New Orleans province issued a televised statement, which I must admit, I viewed with a certain degree of joie de vivre, in which they declared that a serial killer was on the loose and was targeting women of a specific type.

Yes, I was.

This pathetic plea to the public to exercise caution was beyond laughable, I knew, because the authorities were not about to shut down the city to tourism, or they would soon lack the funding to function properly. Nor would humans be able to resist the temptation of a spectacle or of this city, which was a trap for those seeking to shed their inhibitions. History had shown us that much after every major event or natural disaster—authorities would plead for them to utilize what they called "common sense," and humans, in their ignorance, would prove yet again that such sense did not exist.

It was perfect, and I used it to my best advantage. I carried on for another few months, in spite of the additional security deployed to the French Quarter. They were easy to elude; girls were easy to come by. Eventually, however, my visits to the bars and streets of that area declined as the game grew old. I cursed that memory and tried to return to my old ways but could not. I was haunted.

Grey's phone chirped, indicating a text message. Grey jumped and cursed, glaring at the phone. She picked it up and stared at it for a few seconds before snorting with simultaneous laughter and irritation.

"Do you like it?"

"Hold your horses, I'm not done yet."

"Hurry up."

Grey rolled her eyes and tossed the phone across the bed. If she had been on the writing end, she may have been just as eager for feedback. But being on the reading end, she was just irritated by the interruption. She was reading an Aimee R. Dupree rough draft, for crying out loud! Her friend and employer, Zoë, could wait.

Eagerly, she consumed the pages—finally setting each one aside delicately, almost reverently. The walls of her room disappeared. The sounds of the house vanished. She slipped inside Rochester's world as easily as she had when she was a teenager. It felt like she had waited so long for another novel to carry the tale forward that she couldn't stand to linger on a sentence or a paragraph for more than mere seconds. Youth consumes with desperate intention.

I had begun to disgust myself. No, disgust myself was too strong. I hadn't even enough regard for my pursuit to feel that level of passion for the pathetic being I had become. Consuming empty vessels night after night trying to satiate some desire for, what was it—innocence? Certainly not. I found myself sitting across from yet another empty-headed darling enthralled by my natural empathy, my magnetism. I heard my own deep voice droning on with the usual seduction. It was so rote, so rehearsed. No effort expended in a hundred years. My prey excused herself to release urine, no doubt. My lighter withdrew itself to light the cigarette I didn't recall extracting from my leather jacket.

Even now, I can see the blue-red flame from her match. The black motorcycle helmet tossed nonchalantly on my table, and her emerald green gaze locked onto mine as she lit my cigarette. She was challenging me.

"You seemed bored." She laughed, staring, without an ounce of fear, into my own black eyes. "Seems a pity. If you get tired of being bored, I'll be out back for exactly five minutes. My name is Jacqueline." The arrogance of this young woman flew all over me, and the hair on the back of my neck stood up. I turned the power of my stare on her.

"I have no interest in where you will be or for how long. Leave me," I instructed.

To my surprise, she smiled, her full lips framing bright white teeth. She blew the match out and lowered her mouth suggestively toward my own, allowing her black ponytail to graze the knuckles of my hand.

"Too bad for me, I guess, not my lucky night. Enjoy the bimbo." With that, she took her helmet and turned to leave, her tall, curvy frame clad entirely in black leather walking confidently from the bar.

Then she was gone.

And for the first time in over five hundred years, I felt heat. I felt need, excitement. I felt regret. And I knew that this woman had felt nothing supernatural from me. There was no feral desire to draw from my undead pseudo-sexual stimulation, despite the inevitable end in death. She had reacted to me as though I was simply a potential sexual conquest, another woman to whom she was attracted in a bar, a woman she might undress and make love to anonymously without regret. To my newly wet and heated astonishment, this woman had reacted to me as if I was alive.

And I wanted her.

Grey snorted and tossed the pages aside—not that she wasn't interested. Giggling, she jumped out of bed and into her private bathroom. She flipped on the light and braced her arms on the counter, staring at herself in the mirror.

She touched her cheeks and rubbed her forehead nervously, batting at her jet-black bangs in a mocking manner. Her face was flushed, her breathing irregular. Her emerald green eyes sparkled back at her. She bit her lower lip through a grin, cursed roundly at herself and the whole situation, and commanded herself to take a deep breath.

No way should she allow herself to become as giddy and hopeful as the reading of each passing sentence was making her. She should shut it down. It was just a story. Zoë was having fun with her. Zoë was writing, and that was good. Grey, now considering Zoë a friend and not just an employer, should be supportive and should not allow her raging hormones and imagination to run amok.

Grey ran some cold water and splashed her face. Smirking at herself, she decided she hadn't had enough of Rochester for the night, and she could handle some more.

That night, I had run from my table, my poor conquest crying, demanding to know why I was leaving her, her own pheromones overwhelmed by my powers, leaving her needy and unsatisfied. But I had no time for explanations and no capacity for feelings. This was something I had not felt in generations. I had run to the back of the bar just in time to throw myself in front of the small Harley-Davidson Sportster.

"Hey! Whoa..." Jacqueline had shouted, clearly concerned, sliding her foot under the bike, the rear wheel rolling to the left. "Are you crazy?"

"I'm...I'm sorry. I just..."

Five hundred years, and I didn't know what to say to a woman...?

"You just what—have a death wish?" she said angrily, taking off her helmet and shutting down the bike.

I stopped and looked at her embarrassed. I didn't really know how to be embarrassed. I also didn't know how to talk without the seduction. Suddenly, I realized very intensely that I hadn't just spoken to a woman in years.

"I just wanted to talk to you. I would like to talk to you, Jacqueline," I said, knowing I must sound like her mother.

All I know even as I write this now is that the smile she gave me at that moment was as close to living, as close to breathing, as I had felt for as long as I could remember. She motioned me behind her on the bike. I straddled the seat, putting her helmet on and wrapping my arms around her slender waist. It took every ounce of restraint I had to not sink my teeth into her neck when she started the engine.

"Where shall we go?" she shouted over her shoulder.

"The sun will be up soon," I'd shouted in her ear. "Would you mind going to my place?"

Grey's phone buzzed, breaking the spell. She glanced over her shoulder at the glowing screen. "?????" was all it showed.

She dropped the pages and quickly gave word to her frustration, "If you interrupt me again, I will flush these pages, I swear to God. Go to sleep. We will talk over coffee."

With that, she powered the phone down and threw it across the room. Taking a brief respite from the manuscript, Grey washed her face with cold water, changed into her pajamas, and tucked herself under the fluffy down comforter on top of the bed. It was well past ten, and she had already convinced herself that she would not stop reading again until she finished the pages in her hands.

Taking a deep breath, she flipped the crisp white sheet over.

The Harley purred like a kitten beneath us, and I used simple hand gestures to lead Jacqueline to my warehouse near the interstate. Not quite in the chic region, lined with restaurants and newly renovated condos, but respectable nonetheless. I don't think she would have believed me had I told her that I had owned the property since it was built in the eighteen hundreds. The sensors my security company had installed read the control in my pocket, and the automatic garage opener retracted with no motion from me.

"Sweet." She'd laughed, holding the bike erect beneath us. I'd returned her laugh despite myself. I'd seen that door rise at least fifty times with other women. This was the first time I'd hoped to see it rise again with the same one.

Gently, she guided the bike into place, and we both dismounted. The garage of the warehouse left a lot to the imagination. It was rough concrete and steel. Since I spent virtually no time there, I found little use for decoration. It served its purpose. Pickup and delivery. I led her to the elevator, which provided the only access to my living quarters. As we began to descend, Jacqueline turned on me, her eyebrow raised in inquiry.

"What?" I asked.

"Why did I presume we'd be going up to a loft, not down to a basement?" She smiled. "You don't seem the goth type. You're not going to go all dark and broody on me, are you?"

In my mind, I still remember I had some ludicrous vampire answer—something about the night or darkness. It was bullshit. That's what I really remember. Because before I could say anything, she was on me.

Do you, my dear readers, have any idea the import of that sentence in my existence? She was on me. *For hundreds of years, my narrative has always begun and ended with "I was on her." The taking. And yet this is how it happened. How I found my Jacqueline.*

We were equally matched in height and figure, both of us five-seven and about one hundred forty pounds, muscular and lithe. Not slim. Hard like women who work. She had thrown her helmet against the wall of the elevator and slipped both of her hands around my waist, with her palms stretching the length of me, her thumbs plying the space from my hip bones down toward the small of my back. I realized she was measuring me. When her fingertips found the round of my ass, she cupped me roughly, feeling my shape with a wanton desire. Her face was so close to mine now, and her green eyes were burning into my own.

"Your body is really very lovely," she'd said. I felt her mouth on me, and I opened my lips to feel her tongue, angry and wet, thrust hungrily into me. Her hands pressed me into her own warmth, and she ground her pelvis against me, growling her desires noisily, like an animal. These were the noises I made when I killed. I wanted to take her then, but I couldn't let the climax end that quickly. I ripped the band holding her hair out, taking a clump with it, but the mass of dark blue-black silk released, making her even more beautiful. She tore at my shirt, our tongues intertwining between the savagery of the kisses, her lips pulling on my hard nipples, my fingers already inside her. It was ecstasy.

We were both in a frenzy. I'd seen women like this with me before—the pheromones of the kill, the seduction, overwhelming them. I'd never, however, reacted myself,

137

never found myself so raw and sexual. By now, we were both naked, and despite the power of her own personality, I could sense that she was succumbing to me, to what I was.

Jacqueline was becoming more pliant, more submissive. Her chest was heaving with each desperately sought breath. Her legs spread for me without her conscious thought. I could feel her will give in to mine, though her presence was still strong. She was still there for me—this was no fog for her, as it was with the others. She knew what she was doing. She could feel and sense the danger, as evidenced by her quivering hands, yet she made a conscious decision to give in to me. It was her choice that excited me, her strength and bravery that nearly undid me.

Her breasts were heavy with desire, and she was wet. I could smell her sex and her blood, hear it pumping through her veins. The sound reverberated through my body, vibrated along my skin and teeth. The hunger began to build, and I wanted to tear into her. The pull was too strong to resist. I slid along her body, silencing her moan of delight with my mouth, crushing my lips and cutting off her ragged breaths. My fingers crawled up along her body, grazing her ribcage none too tenderly, tearing at a nipple intently, tracing her delicate collarbone, so easily crushable. This human's instinct, I knew, was telling her to fight or to run, adrenaline was being released, and the intoxicant of fear was overloading her senses, lubricating the slippery wet folds against this beautiful woman's best defenses. She was mine, and I knew it, but because she had given herself to me in spite of the danger her body sensed, I could not sink my teeth into her. Jacqueline was at least aware that I was not what I seemed, yet she danced readily along that thin line of death and desire.

"Jacqueline," I hissed and nipped at that pulse point, just grazing the surface, barely hard enough to leave a

138

mark. Heat seared along my body where our skin met. For centuries, I had searched for this and failed. It was I who was in a fog of desire, not the human I had failed to trap.

Jacqueline drove her body against mine and raked her fingernails up my back. It was the sweetest of torture—a pain I had not ever felt, mingled with the pleasure of blood denied. I listened to a long, strange, and distant scream, then registered by the hoarseness of my voice that it was mine. It was not possible that I should have these sensations, not possible that she should be able to deny me anything or that I should need her to fulfill me.

I drove into her—greedily, my fingers slippery with her need—surprising myself with the deep desire to satisfy her, no longer worried about my own satisfaction. Jacqueline was hungry, and I had to feed her. Blood meant nothing at that moment. Every "please" she whimpered had to be met with something equally intense.

And yet. Everything that pulled me into her rejected what I was and what would eventually inevitably happen. As frenzied as my fingers worked her, the fog was beginning to lift. Even as muscles contracted around my fingers, even as I felt her orgasm building, this thing that I thought had died so many centuries ago objected: My conscience wouldn't let me drain her. She screamed her release just before I could detach myself.

"Not like this," I nearly growled, retreating abruptly to the bathroom. I returned shortly with a glass of cold water.

I threw it on her. She was not pleased.

"What the fuck!" she screamed, the spell broken.

I had a cotton towel ready and dried her face for her. She looked at me confused for a moment, then we both started laughing and rolling around like children, holding each other until we couldn't laugh anymore. It was then I really looked at her. She was so lovely.

"Jacqueline," I whispered, careful not to put too much into it. I took her hand and kissed it. Then her cheek. Then her forehead. Then finally her lips. I kissed her as though she was my lover because I knew that she was destined to be. In our short time together, I had felt more than I had over the last five hundred years—need, jealousy, desire, control, want. True, it was nothing compared to the stifling overwhelming feelings that force human behavior every day. But it was something. Something horrible and wonderful.

"Tell me your name," she said, stopping me, stroking my face with her hand, staring into the blackness of my eyes. I knew my skin must have felt cold to her now that the hypnosis of initial seduction was over. Perhaps I appeared frightening, or worse yet, unreal. Without thinking, I laid my head in her lap, holding the palm of her hand to my lips, part of me begging that she wouldn't leave me right then, even before I had an opportunity to explain to her who and what I was. She didn't leave. She simply pulled my mass of black hair around the nape of my neck, the way my mother had done when I was sick. My mother? I hadn't thought of her in centuries—I couldn't even remember her name. I was, in fact, sick, I suddenly realized. Nauseated from the overwhelming realization that I was feeling real human feelings for the first time in centuries. And my long-dead body was burning with a fever for more.

"Please, tell me your real name," she whispered.

"My name is Alicia. And I am yours." And with that simple statement, I buried my face into her lap and was reborn.

Grey's fingers were trembling as she flipped the final page over. How dearly she wanted one more page, one more paragraph—hell, she'd even take one more sentence.

Her body lamented the unfinished story. She didn't know if she was more turned on by the fact that Zoë's slender fingers had typed those sexy words or by the image of her own body intertwined with Zoë's muse. She pictured that woman with the ivory skin and the beautiful tattoos. Then Zoë's piercing eyes and full lips. Her skin was overheated, and she felt like she couldn't breathe.

The moment was akin to that drunken need she had felt after seeing Zoë and Bridgette together—dirty and raw. She knew she was wet. She resisted the urge to touch herself.

Struggling to calm her breathing, Grey slowly sat up, turned out her light, powered up her phone, and set her alarm. She considered all the possible metaphors and allusions between the story and she and Zoë.

Of course she was Jacqueline. No doubt about that. And Zoë was writing again, obviously. Wasn't that enough? Couldn't she enjoy the antics of a toddler with a new employer/friend? A simple human connection in a life so devoid of connection—Grey had no one, after all. She willed her body to be still. It was exceptionally hard.

She had finally been able to close her eyes when she heard the distinctive bicycle bell, indicating a text message. Presuming it was Zoë yet again attempting to solicit feedback, Grey was fully prepared to fire back a sarcastic "Hold your horses, Rochester," but the message fully shocked her awake instead. It was the first message from Sarah she had received in well over a month.

"Tonight I missed you. Tonight I realized what I did was wrong. There's so much to explain, so much to say. I want to come see you. Don't call. I love you."

Grey was not prepared for her reaction. She could feel the blood drain from her face so much her lips went numb. Her heart hammered in her chest. Six weeks of outreach with no response, and "Now she loves me?" she hissed to no one in the dark.

The fire from reading Zoë's writing was barely banked. Grey felt bile burn the back of her throat from frustration and fury.

Fuck this.

"There's nothing to say," her fingers pounded angrily into the phone. "You did the right thing. Don't come here."

Suck on that, bitch. Jacqueline was not in the mood.

Chapter Thirteen

Grey woke up early the next several days, thinking that at some point she and Zoë would have a quiet coffee and discuss the novel. Presuming, she guessed, that they would share knowing glances or laugh at the allusions to shared jokes in the storyline. She had so many questions. At first, she was excited. But when her first encounter with Zoë ended with a simple "Morning, Sunshine," and a view of Zoë's back, she couldn't help but feel hurt. They were supposed to talk about this new novel, weren't they?

That never happened. Instead, days turned to weeks, and before she knew it, it was Thanksgiving. Everything seemed to simply settle back into normalcy, as if no one there was aware of the fact that she was a central character in the third and final Alicia Shade novel. Or no one cared.

She decided she'd once again overinvested in her own importance. Without much self-reproach—it seemed she was becoming used to her own unimportance even as a Chesterfield—she'd thrown herself back into her regular routine for the holiday.

The household generally held a large traditional New Orleans Thanksgiving, which was completely unfamiliar to Grey. There was the requisite turkey and dressing and all the accompanying side dishes, of course. But there would also be a giant vat of gumbo to be cooked by Zoë and other seafood dishes that would be doled out throughout a day of football and family fun. Grey found herself excited at the novelty. After all, the Weather Channel was regularly reporting subfreezing temperatures in Chicago, and it was still in the eighties in New Orleans. And for the first time in ten years, she wasn't expected to attend the stepmonster's catered Thanksgiving wine fest in Christian Lacroix only to be lamented with "She's so pretty, it's such a shame she's a *lesbian*."

Grey giggled, remembering the way her dad would roll his eyes at her and flip a baby pearl pea at her with his spoon every time "lesbian" was said at the table. She'd giggled, then cried for half an hour realizing that family tradition was lost forever.

Emily and Grey had their regular morning routine down after several weeks, and Zoë was spending more and more time holed away in her studio, writing, although she regularly made time for Emily. Zoë and Grey almost never saw each other, and Grey was beginning to wonder if breaking Zoë's writer's block had cost her a friend. Did being a character come with some sort of karmic block? Who the hell knew? The more she observed the constant bickering between her two employers, the less she found she cared for Zoë's explanations or excuses. As she'd become accustomed to saying—"Fuck it all."

On Thanksgiving morning, Emily's grandparents came to get her at six o'clock to get her out of the way, so the preparations for the big party could begin. After Grey delivered the squirmy girl, fancy dress in tow, she headed back to her room to take a nap before her ordered appearance with Bridgette in the kitchen at noon. She'd managed to get a quick five-mile run in before delivering Emily, and she was exhausted.

She collapsed on top of the big comforter and was just about to doze off when she felt another body's weight next to her and an ice cold bottle placed on her forehead.

"Ahh...." she screamed, popping up and pressing her hand on her forehead to stop the ice cream headache.

Zoë had dropped down on the bed beside her, looking obnoxiously sexy in jeans and a black T-shirt with an apron sporting a giant smiling crawfish on it. She was bouncing her black Chuck T sneakers off the side. For the first time in weeks, she looked almost relaxed, her eyes less bloodshot, her hair brushed, an easy smile in place.

"Wake up, princess!" Her voice a little too friendly and too awake for Grey's liking. "It's time for the help to get up and make gumbo with the master of the plantation. Let's go, hot stuff."

She hopped off the bed and tossed an apron with the New Orleans Saints logo on it at Grey and stomped out of the room, an Abita in hand.

Grey grumpily followed Zoë down to the kitchen with much groaning and muttering, tying the apron behind her. Zoë didn't stop in the kitchen but continued out into the backyard, where a giant turkey fryer on propane was burning. Zoë grinned at Grey, then dropped stick after stick of butter into the fryer, then flour.

"Okay, kiddo, your only job is to stir this roux. Do not let it burn. Got it?"

"Really? Seven sticks of butter? Are you fucking Paula Deen? Or are you just trying to kill us all?" Grey grinned.

"Okay, home slice, how's about you don't question the master, and just do as you're told?" Zoë said, throwing a fake gang sign.

"Dear God, don't do that. I got it," Grey said. "How long?"

"An hour and forty-five minutes," Zoë said.

"You have got to be kidding me!"

"Nope, low man on the totem pole stirs the roux…sorry, it's a NOLA tradition."

Grey scowled at her, mentally striking a nap from her internal to-do list for the day. Zoë pulled up a lawn chair, put on her Raybans, and plopped down across from Grey. She chuckled at the scowl.

Charlie Parker music was blaring through the outdoor speakers in spite of the early hour.

"Don't you think the neighbors will get mad about the noise? It's still pretty early," Grey said, carefully stirring the bubbling roux, scraping the flour from the bottom of the pot. She was not about to be accused of ruining the Thanksgiving gumbo by letting it burn.

"Nope, because most of them will be here by ten." Zoë took a sip of her beer. "And this," she indicated the speaker, "is not noise."

"Aren't you going to offer me one of those?" Grey indicated the beer, resigned. She sighed, scraping flour from the bottom of the pot again, just as she would be doing for another hour and forty-three minutes.

Zoë laughed and yanked a cold Abita from a cooler next to her chair. "You won't really be stirring roux that long. We all take turns. We'll hand off to the first person brave enough to show up early."

Zoë fished out an extra pair of sunglasses from the bowl they kept outside for visitors. Her grin softened as she slowly stood. To Grey's surprise, Zoë slid up behind her, gently collecting Grey's hair off her shoulders. Her fingers trailed teasingly down along Grey's arm until she found the extra hairband Grey kept on her wrist and eased it off. She used it to make a ponytail of the long black hair, then placed the shades on Grey's head, cracked the beer open, and put it on the grill next to the pot.

"Better?" she drawled.

"Um…" Grey cleared her throat, unable to speak.

Undeterred, Zoë slipped her hand around Grey's waist and pressed her body into Grey's back. "Mmm." She sighed and barely grazed her lips along the back of Grey's neck, trailing the barest hint of a kiss, then another.

Goose bumps erupted along Grey's arms, and a flash of fire shot down her spine.

Trembling and barely able to speak, Grey whispered, "What was that?"

Zoë did not release her grasp. She tightened her hold, pressed her lips harder into Grey's skin to remove room for interpretation of her actions. "I want to thank you for Jacqueline," she whispered. "And I may never get another chance." She sighed, the warm breath tickling Grey's ear. "I'm sorry we haven't had much interaction lately. I know you've been wanting to talk about the novel." Her lips moved across Grey's skin so distractingly, it was difficult to follow the speech. "I'm just wrapped up in it—the writing. I'm in my world, and you're here."

Grey felt light-headed with the rush of unexpected physical attention. Her pulse hammered against her throat. Every inch of her body that was in contact with Zoë was on fire. She was resisting the urge to lean back into her, to throw her head back. She mechanically and poorly stirred the roux, failing to scrape flour at all.

"Thank you, Grey, my Jacqueline," Zoë murmured.

For a moment, the arm clasping Grey's waist inched higher, as though to explore, and Grey's mind jumped with the possibilities of that exploration. But the hand stilled, Zoë planted one last kiss on the back of her neck, then she released her with a chuckle and a sigh. "I've missed you."

Grey was unable to move.

Zoë cleared her throat and laughed. "Give me that," she demanded, taking over the roux duty and breaking the tension. "Do me a favor, will you? I'll handle the roux if you run into my studio and grab the cigs taped under my desk before Bridge wakes up. Maybe I can sneak one in before the holy mother descends." Zoë grinned at Grey as if she hadn't just been nuzzling her neck. "Or before my family shows up."

"Sure, drive a nail in your coffin, Rochester, it's not like you're not already dead," Grey was finally able to respond, laughing and handing off the spoon, as if she hadn't just been trembling under Zoë's lips.

"Ho ho ho…vampire joke…so amusing…"

Grey took the stairs to the kitchen two at a time.

Her heart was suddenly lighter than it had been in ages. Zoë wasn't shutting her out. She was wrapped up in her writing. There wasn't anything dark and weird happening between the two of them, aside from the attraction that had to be squelched somehow. And Grey had instinctively known to give her space. She wasn't being avoided or ignored. It was just a process. That was encouraging.

Grey dropped her Abita on the table in the kitchen and rounded the hallway toward Zoë's office. The door was closed, so without much thought, she pushed it open, threw on the lights, and turned toward the desk to retrieve the forbidden cigarettes.

Bridgette stood, her preposterous black ostrich robe hanging suggestively from her suddenly stiffened shoulders, her hands wrist deep in the upper left desk drawer.

Her blue eyes said it all.

"Why, Grey, what on earth are you doing in here?" she blurted.

Grey's mouth opened to form words, but nothing came out. Shit. She couldn't exactly give a direct answer. She saw Bridgette's eyes narrow as she slowly withdrew her hands from the drawer and shut it.

"It's just..." Grey cleared her throat, her mind racing. "My friends and I have always speculated about what would be in this particular writing studio, and well, they dared me to take a peek." Despite her best effort, her cheeks flushed. Grey had always been a terrible liar. "I just wanted to see it." She put on her best sheepish smile and added, "I'm sorry, Ms. Breedlove."

A small smile replaced the look of panic. "Of course, your friends would want to know where the magic happens." Bridgette picked up an errant feather, fallen from her robe, with red lacquered nails and toyed with it for a moment. "You realize, of course, that Zoë does not appreciate violation of this space?"

"Yes, ma'am."

A long silence stretched between them, during which neither party vacated the forbidden space. Those ice blue eyes pinned her in place, and Grey felt like she was being challenged and didn't know how to react. But before she could decide on a course of action or even back out of the room, footsteps sounded behind her.

"What are you doing in here?"

Grey had never heard Zoë's voice so calmly normal yet stern.

"Darling," Bridgette simpered. "I discovered Grey rifling through your desk."

The following silence was more deafening than the last. Grey thought she might lose a tooth or two from grinding them so hard. Talk about being caught between a rock and a hard place—she couldn't very well just say she'd come in here as told to retrieve forbidden cigarettes. Those damned women.

"I just wanted to see what your studio looked like," she said, trying her best to sound sincerely apologetic and not pissed off. "I'm sorry."

She turned to face Zoë, appealing to her with her eyes as best she could. But what could Zoë do without giving herself away?

"I'd appreciate it if you both respected my privacy," Zoë said firmly. "I don't ask for a lot of that."

Grey nodded and vacated the space as quickly as she could, sidestepping Zoë's looming figure while feeling Bridgette's scowl and glaring eyes on the back of her head.

"Don't be too hard on her, Zoë," she heard Bridgette the Barbarian coo behind her. "After all, she's just a child."

Grey made it to the kitchen just in time to shout, "Fuck you, whore," into the freezer as she extracted the bottle of Patrón and dropped a quick shot. There, that wasn't too bad. In fact, one more would make everything okay. The baby bottle was at full tilt when the freezer door closed, and Zoë stared at her with a giant shit-eating grin.

"Oh, my God! I thought you were going to poop a freaking kidney you were so pissed! Thank you for not ratting me out." She laughed, taking the bottle from her and having a shot herself.

"You can't poop a kidney, you moron," Grey said, still a little pissed at the humiliation but unable to stifle a giggle.

"Oh, come on, that was hilarious!" Zoë laughed.

Grey paused, still smiling, but catching Zoë's gaze in her own. "Yeah, it was, except it wasn't me who was rifling through your desk. I don't have your cigarettes because Bridgette was going through your desk. Sorry."

Zoë stepped back, suddenly serious but not surprised.

150

"I wondered. Things have been…off. She wants to see the new manuscript, of course. I can't let her do that for obvious reasons."

"Why not?" Grey said, eyeing her, although she knew the answer. "She's going to see it eventually."

"Come on, Grey, even though there's nothing between us…" Her voice trailed off, and she dropped her gaze. "Nothing…" she tried again and sighed. She finally met Grey's eyes again and smiled sadly. "Look, the minute Bridge reads that, she's going to make you leave. And I need you here. I haven't written a word in three years, until you got here. I can't let her make you leave. We just can't let her find that manuscript, that's all. Just get rid of it."

Grey stared at her. There was something enormously attractive about being conspiratorial with the great Aimee Dupree. But this was her job. Zoë couldn't even say there was nothing between them to her face.

"I don't want to get rid of it." She hesitated before admitting, "Because you gave it to me. It's just the one section. And I have that in my room. I doubt Bridgette would go into my room. After all, I'm the help."

Zoë took her hand unexpectedly. It was a gesture of intimacy Grey was unprepared for, and her heart responded with increasing intensity. She could feel her pulse hammering against her breast as Zoë's brown eyes searched her own imploringly.

"Grey," Zoë whispered, her face leaning in so close to Grey's earlobe she could feel the tiny hairs layering her skin stand on edge. "I need you here."

"I understand. We just won't let her find it, I promise," Grey whispered back. And with a squeeze of her hand, Zoë released her, and the spell was broken. She could still smell the other woman's scent as she watched her push the screen door open and walk into the backyard. For several seconds, she couldn't move. She had to remind herself to breathe.

Grey made to follow Zoë out into the yard but froze. She pictured the manuscript in her room, tucked neatly in her nightstand drawer, along with a few favorite books. Would Bridgette stay out of her room? She had just seen the woman rifling through a desk in a room she was technically supposed to avoid. And Zoë was right—Bridgette would and could make her leave.

She didn't want to leave.

Minutes later, she was rifling in her nightstand drawer, heart beating a little too fast.

"Thank God." She sighed, her fingers curling around the well-read and worn pages. She withdrew the unfinished manuscript and rolled it nervously into a tube, just as Zoë had done. Where could she hide it? Bridgette knew this room better, surely. Grey paced the room, searching.

What was she doing? She stopped. Those pages, so important to hide, could jeopardize her employment. She'd be back to square one—tossed out of another home, desperate, in need of assistance. And yet timidly digging into the problem, she realized it wasn't the employment she was so scared of losing. No, it was the connection, that budding unlikely friendship that blurred a little around the edges. Having found one job, she knew she could find another.

"Fuck," she whispered, searching with a little more urgency.

Grey opened the small closet door, flipped on the light, and crawled into the tiny space. There, back in the far corner, she decided. She grabbed a hunk and began to work it loose until she had pulled up a space large enough. She carefully tucked the pages beneath it, went to retrieve a stapler from her desk, and tacked the corner back down.

She placed two pairs of shoes over the area and inspected it critically. It wasn't noticeable, she decided, and closed the door with a sigh of relief.

What seemed like only seconds to her must have been more because as she emerged through the screen door, she heard Zoë's familiar voice call to her.

"Hey, everything come out all right?" to the gentle laughter of the growing crowd.

Great. Another poop joke, Grey mused, giving a smiling thumbs-up.

Zoë's mother, Anne, looped her arm through Grey's and said, "Ignore her, Grey honey. Zoë has always been a twelve-year-old boy at heart, I'm afraid. Didn't matter how many etiquette classes I sent that girl to, she always farted when she damn well felt like it."

Grey laughed and hugged the cotton-headed matriarch. "Thanks, Dr. Cates."

Grey returned to the gumbo and began to add ingredients as Zoë called them out—green peppers, onion, celery, chicken, sausage, bay leaf, filet.

Thanksgiving was an interesting gathering, to say the least. Zoë, Bridge, and Em, of course, the latter running in circles around the large magnolia tree in the backyard screaming at the top of her lungs, her white cotton dress already as filthy as her bare feet. The Drs. Cates, Zoë's parents. Several of Zoë and Bridgette's friends, several of Zoë's brother's very straight, very football-oriented male friends, all gathered around the large flat-screen television Zoë had placed on the patio, and one strange woman sitting under the shade of an umbrella with a sketchpad in her hand.

"Who is that?" Grey finally asked Zoë, pointing.

A small hesitation, just a few seconds too long. "That's Janel Coe." No further explanation.

"And?" Grey prompted.

"And she's an artist. She lives around the corner, comes around here every so often—parties and such."

"Okay," Grey drew out the word.

Zoë rolled her eyes. "She's a family friend. She does art shows. Do you want her bio?" It probably came out more snarky than intended, Grey realized. Something was up with that woman, and she intended to find out.

"No." She grinned. "I'll just go get it myself." She excused herself before Zoë could object.

She watched the woman for a few minutes before approaching her, trying to figure out if she was drawing anything in particular or just whatever came to mind. She couldn't quite see the sketchpad, a shade obscured the majority of the piece. Not that it was important, but she was genuinely curious, so she edged a little closer.

"Another few steps, and you might as well just come sit in my lap," a low voice drawled lazily, never deviating from the charcoal strokes on rough paper.

"I just—" Grey began but was interrupted.

"Just wanted to see why Zoë didn't introduce me? Or should I wonder why she didn't introduce you?" The charcoal stopped dancing across the page. The black soot-coated fingers touched the top of her oversized sunglasses, lowering them along her nose so she could peer up at Grey with pale eyes, the color of an overcast January sky, so light, Grey stared for a moment, distracted.

"Excuse me?" Grey finally said, caught off guard.

"The drawing is an excuse for you to come over," Janel stated matter-of-factly. "But that's okay, darling. Any excuse is fine with me." She set the sketchpad aside. "I'd shake your hand, Grey, but as you can see," she held up her hands, covered in charcoal, "probably not the best idea at the moment." A few seconds ticked by. "Besides, I'm not sure she wants us to become acquainted."

"Who?"

"You know who, and you know why." Janel set down the piece of charcoal, lining it up neatly with the edge of the sketchpad—methodically, Grey thought, compulsive. She felt confused. She'd come over to tease Zoë, sure, but not in the way this woman was insinuating. Right?

"And there it is." Janel chuckled, her laughter both charming and melodious, but there was something insulting about it, too. "The hesitation. It is quite attractive, I must admit." She reached up as though to trace her face but withdrew her fingers. "I was never that clueless. But that can be fun, too. I'd have fun with you."

"I just came over to say hello," Grey said weakly, not understanding why her mouth was suddenly dry and her cheeks were starting to burn.

"Sure you did. And you can say hello over at my place any time you like."

Grey opened her mouth to shoot off a furious objection when Bridgette suddenly appeared.

"Whatever could the two of you be chatting about that has Grey so flustered?" Bridgette swept her out of reach and away, much to Grey's relief and indignation.

"Just playing with your new toy," she heard Janel whisper obnoxiously loud and with deliberate intent of being overheard.

"Jay, you are so bad!" Bridgette giggled, her hands running the line between the other woman's shoulder blades. Grey had the distinct feeling this wasn't the first time she'd been a topic of conversation between the two. "Be nice to the precious thing, she's already in trouble and probably scared to death."

"Fine. But you always ruin my fun." Janel laughed, smiling up at Bridgette, who was too busy playing the vixen to notice that Grey was still standing there. Well, too busy or too uninterested, Grey had decided.

"Really? I always ruin your fun?"

And with that, the two women roared with laughter at a level that Grey found both inappropriate and a little cruel. She cut her gaze at Zoë, who was staring at the threesome with a venom Grey hadn't seen before. Just then, Emily ran up and took Grey's hand. Thank God for little girls.

"Ugh, Grey. She is filthy. Take her inside and clean her up so she doesn't embarrass me in the family photo again this year," Bridgette said, her disdain for the child obvious.

It was Anne who handled it this time.

"Well, Bridgette, that is an incredibly thoughtless and terrible thing to say to a three-year-old," Anne said without a hint of irony in her voice.

Bridgette stared at her with disbelief.

"Well, I'll just take her inside then, shall I?" Grey said, cutting the silence.

"That would be fine." Bridgette's voice was shrill with ice.

Anne had already returned to the party, but Grey was fairly sure she had heard Bridgette's parting shot.

"I have always hated that old bitch."

Grey lifted Emily over her head like an airplane and flew her up the stairs into her room. Emily was a huge Dora fan, and the room was filled with purple and pink dolls, monkeys, and backpacks in honor of her hero. Grey filled the sink with soapy water, washed Emily's feet, hands, and face, and opened the opulent closet to look for a replacement dress.

"Well, monkey pants, what shall we wear?" Grey said, pulling out five or six dresses and laying them on the tiny bed. "What do you think?"

Emily screwed up her nose and said, "No." Her tiny butt, clad in pink Dora panties scooted past Grey and to the drawer of her dresser. Ceremoniously, she pulled out a pair of shorts and a T-shirt and threw them at Grey.

"Who Dat!" she screamed in delight.

Grey examined the black and gold New Orleans Saints outfit she and Zoë had picked up at the French Market at Emily's insistence one weekend and laughed. It would serve Bridgette justly, she decided.

"Who's the sexiest man in New Orleans, Em?" Grey asked, pulling the tiny shorts on flailing legs.

"Drew Brees!" Emily giggled.

Happy freaking Thanksgiving, Bridge! Grey pulled a Nerf football from the toy chest and handed it to Emily.

"Let's go, kiddo."

Emily shrieked with delight, clutched her football under her arm, and made her best mean football player face, just like they'd taught her.

"Grr, Emily, be strong."

"Grr!" Emily growled, then giggled.

Grey was beyond caring about the upcoming reproach. She took Emily's hand and marched her happily down the stairs. Emily tore away from her when they reached the yard, storming past the schmoozing adults with their wineglasses and burst through the group of men crowding around the television screen.

"Who Dat!" she hollered with fierce pride, screwing up her face and making her best mean football player face. "Grr!"

They roared with laughter at the tiny Saints fan, cheering "Who Dat!" in response and high-fiving the happy girl. Grey watched for a moment, intensely pleased with herself, her heart melting for the little imp. She was beyond adorable. And she had stolen the show as easily and as quickly as flipping a switch. All eyes were on her.

Grey swept the crowd and spotted Bridgette and Janel. Both had identical looks of mortification. Janel was slowly shaking her head. She leaned in and whispered something in Bridgette's ear, and that piercing gaze landed on Grey. For a second, the party faded away and they locked gazes. Grey smirked, and it was Bridgette who looked away first.

"Who Dat!" Zoë burst through the group of men and swept Emily up, swinging her in the air, tossing her up and catching her to the cheers of her cousins and the giggles of Emily.

"Who's the sexiest man in New Orleans, Em?" Zoë demanded.

"Drew Brees!" Emily shouted and snorted, giggling and hiccupping. "Grr!"

The men roared again. There was no competing with that tiny redhead. A meteorite could have come down upon the house, and Zoë would never have noticed. Grey believed her when she said Emily was everything. It was undeniably true. It would destroy her if Emily were to be taken away. Grey's smile slid off her face. She dared look in Bridgette's direction again and saw the disdain and mortification. It was hard to understand the distance between these polar opposite women. And yet there was a bridge between them. Or rather, a wire. A thin line that was precarious to cross. It took a tightrope walker. It was a line that couldn't be broken, she realized too suddenly and a little painfully.

Grey turned inside and climbed the steps into the kitchen. She grabbed an open bottle of wine, breathing before lunch, and went upstairs to her room. Abruptly, she

158

didn't feel like partying or being with people. And considering the holiday, she was pretty sure there would be plenty of old movies to bury herself in, and the bottle of wine would make the perfect pairing.

In other words, time for the help to retire for the afternoon.

Chapter Fourteen

If Grey turned on the overhead fan and turned up the television volume just so, she couldn't hear the party outside. She had debated plugging in her earbuds and just listening to music in bed. But that had seemed too pathetic. At least while watching a movie, she could pretend she was relaxing or lounging and not hiding away.

It wasn't just Bridgette and Zoë's drama she was trying to escape. That was irritating enough. Her confusion didn't help. That Janel woman had infuriated her, sure. But something else had hit suddenly, in the middle of the roaring and cheering men and Emily's giggles, in the smile on Zoë's face.

Grey's father had held that same look of complete adoration.

He had tossed her in the air when she was just as small.

He was dead.

Grey was here, a bystander at another family's Thanksgiving holiday celebration. She no longer felt like celebrating. There was no one she wanted to call—certainly not Tawny. She just wanted to bury herself under a mountain of blankets, sip her wine, and be left well enough alone. There were no tears. She just felt tired and empty.

She flipped through the channels listlessly, finally settling on an old favorite, *The Day After Tomorrow*.

Nothing like a natural disaster movie that kills a ton of people to put your life's problems into perspective. She was an hour into the movie and three glasses of wine along the bottle when her door creaked open. She didn't have to look up to know who was there.

"Are you okay?" Zoë had to nearly shout over the roaring of the action flick.

Grey sighed and reluctantly hit the pause button. "Yeah. I'm fine. I just needed to get away."

"Okay, is there anything I can do?" The sincerity was real.

"Nope. I miss my daddy. Nothing you can do." Grey didn't even look up.

She hadn't noticed that Zoë had walked to the side of her bed. Zoë reached her hand out and tousled Grey's hair just slightly. Then without a word, she leaned down and kissed her on top of the head. Zoë drew in a deep, long breath and let it out with equal speed.

"Hold on," she said, walking quickly from the room. Zoë returned seconds later. "Here." She stuffed a giant Dora the Explorer doll into the bed next to Grey and placed a second bottle of wine by the bed. "Phase one works on Em when she's sad, and phase two works on me. You are officially off duty."

Grey looked up at her with grateful eyes.

"And if you are a really good little girl and don't try to help with anything else today, Auntie Zoë may even bring you something to read tonight."

Sometimes, when trying not to feel, while shutting out the world and exercising stoicism, just one gesture of sincere empathy is enough to thaw those nerves so carefully and deliberately frozen. Grey felt the back of her eyes burn and cheeks flush in a rush of feeling she wasn't prepared to experience. A tear rolled down her cheek, and she chuckled up at her friend.

"It's a deal," she whispered hoarsely.

Zoë lingered, hesitating, while Grey eyed her curiously. She eventually came closer and stroked Grey's hair. It was a gesture far more intimate than anything that had happened while working on the gumbo or traipsing along Bourbon Street. "I'm so sorry you have to go through this so young," she murmured. "I can't imagine what it must feel like not to have any parents." She leaned forward and gently kissed Grey's forehead before cupping Grey's cheeks, brushing tears away with her thumbs. "My heart hurts for you. But you are not alone." The statement drew a sad smile.

"Thank you, Zoë," Grey whispered and allowed the dam of tears to burst. Zoë comforted her as best she could, murmuring tender reassurances, scooping Grey into her arms and holding her tight. She didn't exit the room until Grey had cried herself out.

Grey couldn't quell the feeling of abandonment, particularly because it was wrapped up in guilt and frustration. For the hundredth time, she couldn't help but wonder why this was happening to her. This was not the life she was supposed to be living. This was not the family she was supposed to be with.

Her father had always told her, twisting a favorite literary quote, that she was no bird, and no net ensnared her. She was a free-thinking woman with an independent will. A Chesterfield—the family of which was now synonymous with wealth and power but had in the past been modestly and primarily associated with the black and white absolutes of loyalty and justice. Grey Chesterfield could exert her will and leave. The means existed within her if she truly wanted to exit her confusing situation.

162

And yet... The thought of losing yet another connection would have brought her to her knees if she had been standing and not tucked away in the king-size bed. She shivered and pulled the covers up around her face.

"I must leave," she forced the words into the open. A deep sigh. "But I won't." Not because she wasn't strong enough. Not because of a sense of obligation or fear or dread. She was not trapped. It wasn't the job. She would not leave because she felt the draw to another person deeply and had never experienced anything like it. It was more than longing that kept her from fleeing. It was genuine curiosity—the desire to feel more, to have more, to live more.

"Damn," she hissed, shaking her head. "I'm fucking crazy."

Grey snatched the remote and resumed the movie, angrily wiping the tears from her eyes.

Hours passed—*The Day After Tomorrow*, *The Labyrinth*, *Apollo 13*, some sci-fi movie she vaguely remembered having started and not finished when she woke up at nearly two o'clock in the morning. The television had been turned off. Grey didn't remember turning it off. Her mouth was sticky and dry. She gulped down a lump in her throat and groaned. She was so thirsty, she couldn't go back to sleep. Sighing, she pushed aside the giant doll and rolled out of bed.

The house was oddly quiet after all the noise of the afternoon. She crept through it carefully, trying to be still in her clumsy and groggy state. She wasn't quite successful, stumbling around the corner and into the kitchen without much grace. Grey fumbled for the light and flipped the switch and sucked in a deep breath at the sharp sensation popping behind her eyes. She turned the light back off, resigning herself to fumbling in the dark for a bottle of water. She convinced herself she could do it.

A beam of light appeared over her head, illuminating the refrigerator.

"What the hell?" she grumbled, still unfocused.

"Just trying to help."

"What on earth are you doing?"

"What on earth are you doing?" Zoë shot back, stifling a laugh.

"I just want a bottle of water so I can go back to bed."

Zoë snorted and easily retrieved a bottle from the fridge and handed it to Grey with a smirk. "Actually," she drawled, "I was sneaking up to your room to make a special delivery when I heard you stumbling around in the dark like a drunken sailor."

Grey groaned. "That bad, huh?" She struggled with the bottle.

Zoë snatched it from her, twisted off the cap, and handed it back. Grey smiled gratefully, though her expression was mostly lost in the near dark. "Thanks," she finally gasped after finishing nearly half the bottle in one go.

"Are you okay?"

"Yeah. Thank you for earlier."

"Take this and go back to bed." Zoë thrust another stack of papers in Grey's hand. "Thought this might cheer you up." She hesitated, lingering for a moment. "I know what you did for Emily this afternoon. You could have forced her into another dress, and you didn't. Thank you." Another pause. "She adores you, you know."

Zoë left the room before Grey could respond. Her head was so fuzzy. She stood rooted to the spot for a second, sipping her water, cherishing the additional pages. A small

164

smile curled her lips. Perhaps she could salvage a small piece of this night after all.

Grey stumbled up the stairs and closed the door to her room, her late-night hangover instantly stayed by the adrenaline pumping in her body. She brushed her teeth, an unfortunate necessity that delayed her reading, then cranked the A/C down and covered up to under her chin.

Chapter Fourteen

Chapter Fourteen? She had expected for some reason that Zoë would share each new chapter with her. It was both exciting to know that she had made so much rapid progress on the new Shade novel and disappointing to realize she hadn't been privy to so much.

"Okay, let's see what we have here."

Chapter Fourteen

For two years, we had continued together as one, my Jacqueline and I. So many things that had grown foreign to me—human things, after years of isolation and living in that void between humanity and death—had become a part of my existence again.

We traveled, not for the protection of anonymity after taking too many victims, but simply for the pleasure I took in seeing Jacqueline exploring for the first time.

We had friends, other familiar female couples with whom we could visit and speak with from time to time. The inevitable boredom or disdain I felt being surrounded by breathing, babbling humans was always overridden by the overwhelming pleasure I felt when her cheeks would flush with happiness from the companionship she felt. I knew that I could have been happy alone in a room with her

165

simply feeding off the emotions she evoked in me, the desire she gave me to please her. But I knew equally as well that she would find no pleasure in me alone and that she needed the warmth and interaction of others. And I needed her. More than I can possible express to you.

We had reached an accord on my feeding. Jacqueline was not willing to let me kill and remain with me. I was unwilling to cause her pain of any sort because in doing so I found that I could not bear the feeling of loss that accompanied my knowing that she might at some point cease to love me and that I might cease to feel. Anything.

So I took only what I needed to survive. Catch and release, we jokingly called it. And when I would return warm and pink, fresh from feeding, she would ask, "You didn't kill her, did you?" as naively as a child might ask about a pet goldfish that wasn't quite the same as the one she had left before leaving for school.

"Of course not, love," I would say. And she would giggle and jump into my arms.

Her favorite time to make love was after I fed. It was an evening like this that would end my world. I'd left as soon as the sun went down and found a young woman near the university who had been walking to the library. She would have no memory of our interlude, simply a feeling of complete sexual satiation. Not a bad reward for a few pints of what her body would naturally reproduce.

I had returned to the warehouse to find Jacqueline dressed to go out.

"You didn't kill her, did you?"

"No, my love, I didn't kill her. But she was a tasty morsel," I teased.

"You are a horrible bitch!" she yelled, launching herself at me. I caught her beautifully, my strength far superior to her own, and we tumbled onto the bed, her lips

166

finding mine. She rolled over on top of me, pressing her groin into mine, and whispered softly to me.

"Do we have time, Alicia, do you think?"

"All the time in the world, pet," I assured her, helping her pull the black leggings off over her ankles, playfully biting her with my fangs. Once she was naked, I maneuvered her beneath me and found the already moist folds of her inner thigh ready for my stroke. Her beautiful green eyes opened widely, and her firm muscular body relaxed and allowed me to touch her clit ever so gently, as I plied her with endless slow kisses. My lips, full from fresh blood, danced over her mouth and down the soft trail of flesh on her neck. When I reached her nipple, I leaned up on my elbow and looked at her, her head thrown back in pleasure, as her hips ground their way down onto me.

"Oh, Alicia." She moaned. "Please don't stop."

I put two fingers inside of her and stroked her inside out, and as I'd discovered, placed my mouth over her pulse point on her artery and let the pounding of her heart seduce me, as it had done every night for two years now. I felt my own cunt flow with wetness and pumped my hand in unison with her heart. I was at the point of abandoning myself to her orgasm when I first felt it. Tasted it even.

Bitterness. Disease. And ultimately death. A vampire can sense any weakness of the flesh; having none of our own, it stands out like a carton of spoiled milk. Without thinking, I recoiled and stood from the bed staring at her. Her eyes showed hurt but mostly curiosity.

"Alicia, what is it? Did I do something wrong? You weren't going to bite me?" she teased, reaching for me.

I pushed her hand away and looked deeply into her eyes, entrancing her in a way I had sworn never to do. Her will weakened, and she stared at me slack-jawed.

167

"Lie down, Jacqueline," I commanded. Of course, she complied. "Relax your whole body and stay very still."

"Yes," she cooed, eager to please her master. I had no time for guilt at that moment.

Slowly, methodically, I ran my tongue over her, stopping to take a small amount of blood at different places, spitting out what I could not palate. I inserted my fingers into her cunt, anus, and mouth, closing my eyes to allow her flow to find my sensitive hands.

When I was done, I commanded her to sleep, and she did.

And while she slept, I ran from the warehouse and ripped iron from walls in anger. I raged like a beast in a way I hadn't for some time. I flashed red eyes at young couples strolling hand in hand in the neighborhood and hissed at anyone daring to look my way.

It was all darkness. It was all night.

Jacqueline was dying of cancer. My life was dying, again.

After what seemed like hours, I returned to our home. I lay down next to the only thing holding me to the last vestige of my humanity and held her as though I would never hold her again. There was no question in my mind. I would not allow her to die.

Grey looked up and realized she was crying.

"Oh, my God, you bitch! You're going to kill me." She laughed. Somehow, the words Zoë had written had touched her, and biting sarcasm seemed the only way out. Grey knew on a deeper level that this chapter was given to her with a purpose.

Zoë needed her? She flipped the crisp white sheet over and read on.

168

"How long do I have?" Jacqueline asked me. She had been irritatingly calm when I explained to her that she was dying and that no doctor could save her.

"What is the point of discussing that, pet?" I gently skirted the question. "You have eternity, of course. Do you think I would let you die?" I ran my hand over her cheek as a tear flowed across my thumb. "I will change you tonight. We will spend a thousand years making love and laugh about this night when your crazy vampire lover forgot she could make you immortal. I really should apologize to the neighbors."

"Alicia, how long if you didn't, I mean?"

My eyes unintentionally narrowed as a suspicion blossomed. It was clear she wouldn't rest until I told her everything.

"I don't know, love. It feels and tastes like months. Maybe three at the most. But, Jacqueline, we can exchange blood tonight, and it won't matter." My voice had risen despite my attempt to carefully control it.

"I knew something was wrong. I was tired and achy. I didn't want to know, I guess. What a coward I am." She smiled sadly at me. I couldn't bear it. I drew her into my arms and held her. "Is it going to hurt?"

"The change? No, it's like a deep sleep, and I'll stay with you the whole time." I wiped her salty tears as they fell with more speed.

"No, the cancer. Is it going to hurt, do you think?" She pushed me away and walked to the door of the warehouse.

"No, of course not. We aren't going to let it go that long."

Each word came out more guarded than the last. Suspicion grew. Her emerald gaze locked on mine, and I did not like what I saw and nearly growled, "Jacqueline..."

"No, darling, it's no good. You realize that, of course."

"What are you talking about?" Panic began to set in—a deep dread that flooded my chest with ice.

"It's no good, Alicia. God, I wish it was. I really do. I'm no hero, lover. But you have to know you can't change me. If you do, I'll be like you. No offense. I will be dead. And this," she gestured with weak hands, "whatever this is we have will also die."

"Never!" I yelled, sweeping her into my arms. "You are everything to me. I love you."

"I know. I love you, too, too much to let you die again. Don't you see, if I become a vampire, we will simply grow bored with each other. This symbiotic—whatever it is—that we have won't be there. You know I'm right. Everything you have back, the feelings, the pleasure, the love. Every tiny bit of humanity you have that gives you a reason to not walk into the sun is because of how you react to me as a human. I won't tolerate immortality without this, not having had it already. I won't allow you to simply walk away from me after a hundred years. I won't allow you to stay because you made me. After this," she took my face in her hand and kissed me, "it wouldn't be enough. We would be bitter from the loss and learn to hate each other. I can't do that. I love you too much."

She was crying now, her head buried under my chin. I felt loss and pain, helpless like a child.

"I will make you do it," I said angrily. "You know I can. I will make you change."

She laughed. "No, you won't. Because you know I'm right. If I can give you three months of human emotion and love by being alive, I'm going to do it. That three months could keep you from walking into the sun for another hundred years. And I would live through you. This is my *life. I'm going to live and die the way I want to, in love with you."*

I couldn't have loved her more. Everything she said was true. I'd had other lovers of my kind. While the play was rougher, the connection was nonexistent. I thought if Jacqueline looked at me with disinterest, I might just kill her.

"Tell me," she said, smoothing her hair and walking to the mirror in the bathroom. "Tell me, can you give me just enough blood to keep the pain away?" She washed her makeup off and reapplied.

"Yes, I think I can."

"Good, let's try that tonight. I want to celebrate. I want energy and fun. Can we go to that bar in the Quarter where we met? I would love that. Will you wear your leathers?" She smiled at me.

It was over. I knew I would honor her request, her sacrifice.

I fell to my knees in front of her like a smitten teenager. She ran steady hands through my hair and kissed the top of my head fiercely.

"I love you, Alicia Shade. But I need you to get up and go with me. Please."

From the floor where I kneeled, I looked up at her and kissed her hands.

"Yes, my love, I will wear the leathers. Will you drive me on the bike? Can we smoke cigarettes and stare at each other across the bar?"

"Oh, yes! Let's do that. Then you can chase me out and tell me you 'just want to talk to me.' Remember?" She ran to the closet to dress.

I was still on the floor. It took all my supernatural strength to stand and change. I didn't want to live without her. I knew that the second she was gone, I would follow

*her and wait for the sun to carry me to my love. The sins of
my past were nothing. No creator would be cruel enough to
keep us apart. We would live and love every second
together. Then we would leave.*

Together.

Grey realized that her face was covered with tears.
Frantically, she wiped them away with the sleeve of her
nightgown. Damn, that Zoë could write, could move her in
so many ways. She crawled out from under the comforter
and went to the bathroom to wash her face. This day had
been a beat-down. She could not continue to be the
nanny/confidant, the muse, the babysitter, and the help.
Before reading the chapter, she had admitted to herself that
she would not leave, even though she should. Now she was
more frustrated than before—her feelings too
overwhelming. It was all too much and not enough. This
novel, this chapter too much. The contact, not enough. She
felt the undeniable urge to charge into Zoë's room and seek
reassurance or demand answers.

Worst of all, she forced herself to admit that Bridgette
was a war she was unwilling to fight. Grey would not adopt
the title of homewrecker. A new anger surfaced, spawned
by the knowledge that it would have to be Zoë who fought
for them both—not because Grey couldn't, but because
Zoë would never be able to forgive her if she lost Emily
because of something they had started that led to such a
terrible circumstance. And as such, Bridgette was their
cancer. Zoë couldn't make it go away without losing the
most meaningful and important thing in her life. She would
always be too scared to really fight for them.

Without much thought, presumably out of frustration,
Grey picked up her cellphone and fired off a quick text.

"Come see me at Christmas break," it read, intended for Sarah.

"I'm an idiot," Grey muttered to no one in particular.

Within seconds, despite the late hour and the time difference, her phone lit up.

"I can't wait."

Her heart filled with dread and anticipation. Maybe Sarah was the tonic that would break the spell—Zoë's spell—over her. Alicia's spell. She needed a reality check.

They all needed one.

Chapter Fifteen

The weeks between Thanksgiving and Christmas passed quickly, just as they always had at Grey's home in Chicago. Decorations went up, presents were wrapped, and Emily went crazy every time she saw Santa Claus on television or in a store. Her enthusiasm was overwhelming, and for some reason, Grey felt like a three-year-old herself. Giddy and excited. It was hard to remain morose and sullen when everything was so festive and beautiful.

The main hall of the house had been altered by New Orleans' finest designers to look like FAO Schwarz. A giant tree decorated with Dora ornaments and pink and purple bows took center stage. Emily spent hours going through presents and identifying her name.

"See, Grey! Emily has one, two, three, four, five presents!" She smiled at her.

"You sure do, sweetie." Grey smiled back.

"How come Grey doesn't have no presents?" Emily looked up at her inquiringly.

"'Cause you're my present, sugar butt. I don't need anything else," Grey said. But Emily did not find that answer acceptable, apparently, because she harrumphed at Grey and marched toward Zoë's studio. Grey ran to stop her but fell over the Persian rug and had to right herself before catching the little general.

Emily threw open the door. Zoë sat at the computer typing furiously, her reading glasses perched on her nose tip.

"Momma," Emily snapped, her little voice showing a modicum of disgust.

Zoë looked up, surprised to find Emily in the forbidden studio. Grey arrived behind her, hands in the air to indicate a silent apology.

"What's up, peanut?" Zoë said, opening her arms to Emily.

"Grey doesn't have even one present under the tree, and I have one, two, three, four, and five. That's not good. Grey's been good." A child's sense of justice could be hilarious.

Zoë laughed and scooped her little minion into her lap, pulled her reading glasses off, and looked at Emily seriously.

"Well now, Emily, how do you know Grey has been good? Shouldn't we leave that to Santa to decide? Maybe she's been naughty. Maybe that's why she doesn't have any presents."

Emily turned her curly head toward Grey to evaluate. She clearly hadn't considered this. Grey shot Zoë a look over Emily's head.

"Really? I'm naughty?"

"No, Momma. That's not right. Grey is good. She makes me sandwiches and plays with me. She gives me baths, even when I don't want them. And when Mommy makes me sad, she tells me it's not my fault. She's good." She turned triumphantly to Zoë and smiled.

Zoë hugged her and smiled at Grey over perfect cherry blond curls.

"And the defense rests. I give. Grey deserves a present under the tree. Run, get your coat, and we'll go to Saks Fifth Avenue and see what we can do."

Emily shot out of the room. "And Macy's," she yelled over her shoulder.

"That's Bridgette's fault, I swear." Zoë blushed. "Apparently, you get the day off!"

Grey grinned at Emily's antics. "You don't have to do this. It's no big thing. I wasn't exactly expecting anything."

An awkward pause followed. Zoë cleared her throat. "No, Emily is right. You've done a good job. I've gotten a lot of work done, and she clearly adores you or she wouldn't be advocating on your behalf. It's okay, Grey. And it should be a fun challenge."

Zoë and Emily took off in a rush of coats, mittens, and hats being struggled into and protested against. Grey watched them curiously, her mind already ticking away at what they might pick up. She decided this meant she should get the family some gifts after all. She had a few ideas and plenty of time to make it happen. She just wasn't exactly sure where to start.

The house in all its decorated splendor suddenly felt very empty. It was curiously quiet—only the whirring sound of the heater kicking in mingled with the creaking of her footsteps over original hardwood flooring as she paced.

Grey had already completed her early morning run, but she felt restless in the big house. She decided to go for a walk around the neighborhood to wear off some of the excess energy and giddiness. She could think about and solidify her plans for the holiday in the meantime.

It never once occurred to her that she should also get Sarah a gift.

The neighborhood was beautiful, as always. But the flowers, so majestic upon her arrival earlier in the fall, had faltered and taken to a winter's rest, leaving the gardens looking sparse and gray. Yet the houses were decked out in their Christmas finest. Just like Zoë and Bridgette, Grey suspected their neighbors had hired designers to elaborately decorate the façades, gates, and magnolia trees. It was stunning at night. This she knew from her daily wanderings, becoming more frequent. The cold didn't faze her at all. It wasn't the biting chill of Boston or the crisp wind and snowfall of Chicago. It was pleasant in her thick sweaters and leather jacket. With a bounce in her step, she marched out of the house and struck out along Second Street, away from the main road and deeper into the decadent neighborhood she had grown to love.

Her thoughts were a mixed bag—half excited about what the holiday would bring, anticipating Emily's antics on Christmas Day, which would surely be adorable, yet dreading the arrival of Sarah, worried about how the visit would go, how she would behave, what might happen. She muttered, not for the first time, "What was I thinking?"

Lost in thought, Grey nearly missed it. But at this point, she was so trained to keep a careful eye out for brilliant red hair against alabaster skin that it was impossible to miss altogether. There was Bridgette, traipsing down the stairs of a pink carriage house behind an impossibly large and equally pink mansion.

Grey skidded to a halt, perplexed. Bridgette never voluntarily walked anywhere. She had once witnessed Bridgette having Antoine take her two blocks to a small boutique shop on the main road. What was she doing then, on the stairs of a carriage house addition, no less, six blocks from the house when she was supposed to be on her way back from New York?

That gratingly irritating woman from the Thanksgiving party, Janel, emerged from the same doorway. Figures,

Grey thought, on edge. She nearly ducked behind a large Suburban to avoid a confrontation, but her hesitation was too long. Janel spotted her and waved. It was almost comical when Bridgette looked up to see what Janel was waving at and spotted Grey. Her mouth formed a small O of surprise before she managed to put her fake smile in place. Bridgette waved and bounced across the street, bounding off in the opposite direction. Grey kept her pace and intended to walk straight past Janel, avoiding any ugliness.

"Grey, sweet girl, don't you dare run away with your tail between your legs! Don't you want to come up here and ask me what we were up to before you report to Zoë?" Janel teased. Bitchily, Grey couldn't help but notice.

She'd had enough.

"Actually, no, Janel. First of all, I don't 'report' to Zoë. From what I've seen, she doesn't really care what Bridgette does, and frankly, I don't, either. Secondly, go fuck yourself."

Yep, that was what came out of her mouth.

To her surprise, Janel laughed loudly.

"Well, fucking good for you, kiddo! Get up here and have some champagne. I was wondering when you were going to stop acting like Prissy in *Gone with the Wind*."

Janel didn't wait for a reply. She just disappeared into the pink door and waited for Grey to follow.

Grey knew that this was one of those moments where she would make a decision that would either be extremely informative or a pain in the ass. Fuck it. Zoë wasn't giving her any information, and she liked to know what was going on around her. She was going in, drama or no drama.

Grey took the stairs two at a time, the hair standing up on the back of her neck. Janel's apartment was a freaking nightmare, paintings and paint everywhere, a small pallet piled with pillows and satin comforters in the corner.

Great, is she gonna offer to show me her etching? Grey wondered. What a fucking cliché.

Janel handed her some cheap prosecco.

"Well, since you are dying for me to ask," Grey flirted, intentionally touching Janel's hand when she took the glass, "what are you two doing up here?"

"Oh, Bridge is just having me paint a Christmas present for Zoë, that's all. Nothing untoward, I assure you. She's a real piece of work, though. Not like she doesn't try!" Janel smirked smugly.

Grey flashed her most brilliant cougar-conquering smile and began wandering, evaluating canvases.

"Nice. Very pre-Raphaelite. I like them." Janel was burning her with laser eyes. She could feel them hot on her back. "So where's Bridgette?"

"Sorry, big secret! She doesn't want anyone to see it until the party." Janel had refilled her glass again and was standing awkwardly close to her. The smell of patchouli was overpowering. "But maybe I could make an exception."

"Maybe?" Grey smiled, edging back from Janel coyly. "Sorry, I only do guarantees. It's the curse of the working girl." She giggled and pretended to trip on the blue satin comforter under her feet, falling easily onto the pallet.

Janel was on the bed next to her like a cheetah. "I bet we could negotiate…"

"Ahem…"

The interruption came loudly from the door. Bridgette stood illuminated in the doorway, her red hair blowing like fire. "You may not realize it, but Emily is home *now*. And your *job* actually is to care for her, Grey."

"Oh, I'm sorry." Grey jumped up and blurted automatically. Her apology fell on deaf ears. The unspoken dialogue between the two women was deafening. Grey glanced at the clock on the wall. She'd been gone from the house no more than half an hour. "Actually, Zoë took Emily shopping and gave me the rest of the day off." Seconds ticked by as her sentence wasn't acknowledged. "So I'll get out of here, that's fine, but I'm not neglecting any duties. The house is completely empty, and I left because it was too quiet and I was bored."

Bridgette was staring daggers at her. Clearly, the explanation had only succeeded in enraging her. Grey just couldn't help herself. She added, "It's not so boring here, as you must know."

Bridgette averted her eyes, resorting to a favorite tactic of eliminating Grey's existence from her presence. She instead locked gazes with her friend in a borderline combative way. Janel, for her part, held the gaze steadily and with a hint of sick amusement.

"Grey," Janel said, drawing the word out deliberately, almost sarcastically. Grey had never heard her name said quite like that. "You come back any time. *Any time*."

Grey hadn't even made the bottom of the steps when the raised voices pressed through the carved wooden door of the carriage house. There was something there. She wasn't sure if it was one-sided, something from the past, something ongoing, or just something, but it was there. Interesting.

She continued her walk through the Garden District, trying to plan for the evening. It was about three. Sarah would arrive at four, and Antoine was going to bring her directly to the house. Thank God, Sarah had decided to get a hotel in the Quarter so they could "figure out where they were going," whatever that meant. Grey turned for home.

180

She had about an hour and a half to shower and get ready to meet the young woman she had once believed she loved with all her heart. Strangely, she felt nothing but put out by the whole thing. If only she hadn't sent that text.

Sarah clearly wasn't her Alicia Shade.

Grey dragged her feet, returning to the familiar yellow-painted Victorian mansion she had begun to think of as home. She wanted to run away from all these women, yet she couldn't bring herself to pull the trigger. There was only one female in her life right now who appeared to be normal—Emily. She hadn't learned how to be manipulative or how to string a person along and give mixed signals. She simply was. How easy it would have been to simply be the nanny to adorable Emily. If only she didn't come attached to others. If only Grey didn't come attached to others. Not for the first time, she wondered if it was time for a do-over on the new start of her life. To be completely independent, independent from family money or emotional relationships, romantic or otherwise.

But how empty is a life without complications?

Her sneakers scraped along the sidewalk as she trudged down the blocks toward home. She wondered what advice her brother would provide at this point. But this far removed—eight years was a long time—it was hard to imagine anything beyond bemused chuckles and maybe, if she was particularly nice, a hug, a ruffling of her hair. She scrunched up her face with concentration. He would perhaps say something like, "When push comes to shove, do the pushing, not the hurting." Wasn't that what he told her when she'd had a bully in elementary school?

She didn't exactly have a bully now. No, Bridgette didn't really count. If push came to shove, as Bradley said, she'd do a lot more pushing and a lot less hurting. She only put up with the bullshit, she told herself, because of the paycheck. But at some point, money simply wasn't enough.

She finally reached the gate, punched in the code, and let herself in. No car, no Zoë, no Emily, still nobody. She knew she'd find the same weary silence inside she'd escaped an hour before. She was determined to drown it out. She pulled out her phone and started a favorite playlist. More bad eighties music.

Her room was untouched. For the first time in months, she really looked at it critically, trying to see it the way a stranger would. Zoë's description of a Mardi Gras king "jacking off in here" certainly fit the bill. Would Sarah agree? Would they have anything to talk about? Could Grey forgive her for bowing out when she had needed her to be strong? Grey just didn't know. If she dug deep, if she was honest with herself, she would have to admit that she had already let go because it had just been too much to handle on top of her father's death. Could they rekindle the spark? Did she really want that?

More importantly, could Sarah even stack up to… No, she couldn't go there. It wasn't right. But what was "right"? She had every right to think, to feel, to live, to want—yes, to desire—as anyone in this house. Her current lack of money and connections made her no less of a person than Zoë or Bridgette or Janel or Sarah. She was every bit their equal in intellect and feeling. She was more than their equal in want. And she was beginning to think that she was far superior in inspiration.

She was Jacqueline after all. Grey Chesterfield was the one true love of the greatest, most aloof erotic writer of her generation. Her head began to spin, and she felt the heat rising between her legs. It wasn't Sarah who was moving her now, and she wasn't really sure it was Zoë.

Quietly, Grey turned the lights in her room off, locked the door, and started the shower. She peeled off her Seven jeans and her black cotton turtleneck sweater. Her cowboy boots ended up in the corner of the bathroom. She stepped into the shower and let the water run over her naked body. Closing her eyes, visions of the dark warehouse came into her mind, and she whispered one word, "Alicia."

The writing with which Zoë had been teasing her flooded her mind. But the sentimentalism of it drowned under memories of older tales, those first two books that had been a favorite go-to in her teenage years. Her fingers slid along her soapy breasts and hips as she remembered earlier, far naughtier scenes, imagining Jacqueline interjecting herself in them. Alicia would have ravaged her more forcefully, more savagely than in the softer version of the newest book, in which the aloof vampire finally falls in love.

Grey growled in frustration, running her hands along her body, massaging her breasts, fingering her throbbing clit. She groaned. Part of Alicia's sensuality derived from her savagery. It was the sexual fantasy of borderline force—of absolute consumption, driven by the id and neglected by the heart. Jacqueline reminded Alicia of her humanity, but the real Jacqueline craved, at this moment, anonymity in her sexual desire. Would the real Alicia feel the same? Grey rubbed herself furiously, imagining that sex goddess of a bartender driving her up against the wall as Zoë had done and plunging her fingers deep inside as Zoë had neglected to do.

Grey gasped in the scalding water, her arms burning from the effort to alternately hold herself up and rub herself raw. Tears burned at the back of her eyes, and still she drove on. She was filling up inside, it was building, she was going to come hard, and she knew it. Too much time had passed. Too much longing. Alicia was taking her now when she needed it most. She squeezed her eyes shut and opened herself wide, filled herself up, taking herself quickly and furiously until the spasms overwhelmed her, and she couldn't stifle a cry of intense relief.

Grey took a shuddering breath and leaned against the wall under the now-cooling water. Reluctantly, she opened her eyes and returned to reality. Slowly, with trembling hands, she turned off the water and sighed. It really was too bad that she couldn't linger in her fantasy world just a little longer. It was so much better being Jacqueline than it was being Grey. Grey had to get dressed for Sarah, for reality.

She dried off with a white Egyptian cotton towel and lay down on top of the comforter. It was four twenty. Sarah would be in from the airport in twenty minutes or so, provided her plane was on time. Grey realized, a little guiltily, she hadn't even checked her cellphone. Grey grabbed her phone from the bedside table and read the first message.

"Landed!!!!!!!!!!!"

So many exclamation points.

Reluctantly, Grey peeled herself off the bed and went to her closet to pick an outfit. She'd been considering their plans for the evening during her walk. She pulled out some black leggings and an emerald green tunic that matched her eyes. She had just finished blow drying her hair when she heard a soft knock at her door.

Please don't be Bridgette, she thought.

She opened the door, revealing Zoë sheepishly holding a gold Tory Burch bag.

"Hey, I'm sorry to bother you. I just…um…I had an early present for you. I mean, since your girlfriend is coming and the party preparations start tomorrow and

184

such." This was the first time Zoë couldn't make eye contact with her.

"Oh, my God, you didn't get me *Tory Burch boots*!" Grey realized she was acting all of her twenty-one years, but she didn't care. She snatched the bag from Zoë and ran to her bed.

Zoë looked incredibly pleased and followed her into the room. "Well, you really like mine, and you have done such a great job. I just, I wanted to." She smiled at Grey, who was ripping the bag apart like a five-year-old.

Grey held the beautiful black riding boot up and stared at it as if it were a Gutenberg Bible. Even with all the Chesterfield wealth, her father had forbidden certain "frivolous" items from her grasp. She had wanted—scratch that, coveted—Tory Burch boots for five years. And despite her stepmonster's stream of Chanel suits and Prada shoes, she'd never had any.

Grey looked at Zoë wide-eyed and said, "I know I shouldn't take them. I know I should say they are too extravagant and that it would be inappropriate to take them. But I just can't." She grinned. "'Cause, and this is the worst part, 'cause I really, really, really want them." She giggled. "But I don't want you to think I need stuff like this. I *love* them, but I can do without. I'm not taking advantage."

Zoë couldn't help herself. She was laughing hysterically now, too. "Whoa! My choice, my treat. I know you'd never ask for this. That's exactly why I got it." She threw her arms around Grey and kissed her cheek. "You know, it's your honesty that makes you absolutely adorable. Merry Christmas from Emily and me, but mostly me."

Grey returned the hug, leaning in, wanting to return a kiss on the cheek, just as Zoë had done. But in the excitement of the moment, her lips missed their target and

185

landed on Zoë's lips. Or perhaps it wasn't an accident at all. She wanted what she wanted.

Those beautiful lips, which she had been admiring now for months, were as soft and luscious as Grey had imagined. Her body was still overheated from her loss of composure in the shower. There was no immediate rejection, no hands on her chest pushing her away, no head turning away aghast, no admonition of any kind. Instead, there was a barely detectable moan, more felt than heard, mumbled against her own lips in a sweet buzzing sensation that spun her head. She leaned in, her hands winding her way up Zoë's body to tangle in cropped blond hair at the nape of her neck. Instinctively, she drove her body in, crushing their lips together fiercely, not an inch separating the length of her body from her desired woman. Heat seared along her spine, curling fingers where they dug in. Grey felt Zoë teasing her along her lips, her tongue demanding entry. She allowed it, groaning into the deepening kiss.

Hands gripped her hips hard, pulling, kneading. A soft cry escaped her lips for the second time in less than an hour.

"Grey!" a shrill voice called from the bottom of the kitchen steps.

It was Bridgette.

"Your little girlfriend is here, sweetie. Come on down."

Just that quickly, the two women stood across the room staring at each other, panting with desire and confusion.

"I'm sorry," Grey said, not meaning it.

"Don't say that," Zoë replied forcefully. "Don't say that to me, please." She turned on her heels. "I'll see you downstairs."

Chapter Sixteen

Grey was alone in the room. She sat down hard on the bed, slowly pulling the boots over her leggings, dazed by what had just happened. What exactly had just happened? Kissing Zoë had flipped her nerves was what just happened. She felt raw and full of need, yet at a loss for how to move forward. Again, for the dozenth time, she was angry with herself for having invited Sarah to visit.

She sighed and took a deep breath, plucked her phone from the bed, and headed toward the stairs. Toward Sarah.

"Oh, come here, Grey darling," Bridgette simpered, no hint of their earlier meeting, like she could simply flip the off switch on her anger and all was well. "Isn't your little girlfriend just darling?" She batted her eyes, standing next to Sarah as though she could take credit for setting them up for a happily ever after.

There she was, looking just the way Grey remembered her. Nothing had changed, except her eyes—somehow they seemed colder. Or amused.

"Hey," Sarah said simply with a lopsided grin.

"Hey," Grey returned, albeit less enthusiastically.

There was a long and awkward pause, during which Grey did her best to allow Sarah to hold her attention, trying very hard not to look in Zoë's direction, trying not to wonder if Bridgette would notice the kiss-bruised lips.

"Well, now that you're all caught up," Zoë finally interjected. The sarcasm wasn't lost on Grey. "Why don't you join us for dinner, Sarah? Afterward, you and Grey can hit the streets, go explore."

"Sure." Sarah's attention now turned to Zoë. Grey had clued her in that Zoë was Aimee R. Dupree in several of the many unanswered emails. She was surprised Sarah hadn't arrived all giddy and gushing with compliments. Perhaps she was trying to play it cool.

They didn't embrace. They certainly didn't kiss. Sarah made a halfhearted attempt to take Grey's hand, but Grey dodged the gesture tactfully by moving to open the door toward the kitchen. "You want to come up and see my digs, I guess?"

"Oh, is she staying here? She can stay here, you know," Bridgette suggested helpfully.

"No," Grey and Zoë answered together.

Bridgette looked at Zoë inquisitively. "Well, goodness, why not? Emily doesn't have to know. She can use the servants' entrance like Grey."

It was Sarah who answered. "Thank you, but I have a hotel room in the French Quarter. I have some friends in grad school at Tulane, so I want to see them, as well as Grey. But thanks for the offer." She smiled her most gracious smile.

Sarah followed Grey through the giant kitchen and up the back stairs to her room. "Holy hell, Grey! Pretty nice, right?" She smiled a toothy grin, flopping on the bed.

Grey stood there and stared, frozen in the doorway.

"Oh, for goodness sake, I'm not going to rape you, come over here and lie down. Let's see if we can make this less awkward, okay?" Sarah's eyes showed sincerity, so Grey relented and lay on the bed next to her lover. Her ex-lover.

"Why did you ask me here?" Sarah asked, leaning on her elbow.

"I don't really know."

"Well, that's honest at least." She was hurt, Grey could tell, but she didn't care. "I guess maybe I should go first. I don't know, babe. You called, and everything we had planned was just gone. Just like that. Moving to New York, the little apartment we were going to get in SoHo. And you wanted me to just let you move into my dorm room and pretend like I could struggle."

Grey stared at Sarah but let her talk.

"I never lied to you in college. Maybe you have a different memory of who I was, who we were. Our plan was that you would work for your dad, and I would go to grad school, do you remember?" Sarah asked, looking into Grey's eyes. "So you call me and tell me there is nothing, no money, no apartment, no grad school, and by the way, can you crash with me in my dorm for my senior year. I just freaked. I'm not like you. I'm not strong." Tears were running down her face. Despite herself, Grey reached a hand out to wipe one away.

When she paused, Grey spoke. "I'm sorry, but I don't remember telling you any of that. I remember saying the only person other than you who I loved was dead. I remember telling you I was alone and penniless. Then I remember the phone hanging up and being alone."

She didn't have the energy to make Sarah feel better right now.

Sarah rolled over and took Grey's hand. "But look at you. Look at you here at Aimee Dupree's house. You always had that ability to fall on your feet. You're like a cat. I knew you would find a way to take care of us. And ultimately, that bitch stepmother of yours would die or the trust would expire. I just had to set you free is all. I had to make you perform." She was smiling now.

Grey wasn't smiling. Her blood was boiling. If this were a cartoon, steam would be exploding from her ears. She could feel the heat rise to her cheeks. She wanted to slap her.

"So," she forced an unnatural calm, "you cut me loose to force me to 'fall on my feet' like a cat. So I would have to figure it out. So I could 'take care' of us. Financially, I'm assuming."

"Exactly, honey." Sarah smiled, almost sickeningly sweet. "And it totally worked!"

"Right."

Sarah leaned back on the bed and grabbed a pillow, clutching it to her chest and peering out from behind it in a scene so reminiscent of their last morning together— peeking out from behind that slate blue comforter—that it was more frustrating than cute. Grey mentally rolled her eyes at this obvious attempt at pulling her heartstring with cuteness. Was she still cute? Yes. But was it an act? Absolutely.

"So are we going to be complete strangers the whole time?" Sarah teased, her blue eyes sparkling. Grey was amazed. Why hadn't she seen this chameleon-like ability in the time they had spent together in college? In a matter of seconds, Sarah had gone from serious to distraught to serious to horny. It was like seeing her for the first time, really. It was all an act.

"'Cause, if you are down for some everyday college makeup sex, I'm down. Dear God, I am so horny!" Sarah said, rolling over on top of Grey.

Grey found that her stomach had turned. Briefly, her mind flashed back to her father and her time at Wellesley. She remembered labored phone calls asking that a credit

190

card be reinstated, long lectures about the value of money and things being "handed" to her. She also remembered Sarah's insistence that, although Grey's dad could get them an apartment in SoHo, ultimately, they would need a house in the Hamptons, as well.

Was she even the same person? Grey hadn't questioned these assertions when she had been a child of privilege. But now, here in New Orleans, she was the servant to a couple of wealth. Every day, she witnessed families struggling to make ends meet. She'd seen the simple apartment where Zoë had fought to write her first novels to make her own name—to not rely on her parents' wealth. Frankly, she felt shame. She felt regret.

She sent her father a silent and heartfelt apology.

To Sarah, she simply diverted the conversation.

"Did I tell you Zoë is writing a new novel? A new Alicia Shade novel?" Grey stood from the bed, nearly dumping Sarah to the floor. Sarah looked up somewhat disturbed by the change in position but excited to know something that other people would consider privileged information about the authoress.

"No. Oh, my God! Tell me, tell me!" she gushed.

"I can't. But I can tell you it's really good. Alicia takes a lover, falls in love, really. It's hot!" Grey was freelancing at this point. She realized she was trying to readopt a collegiate language she had abandoned during her interactions with Zoë and her time in the city. She wanted Sarah to believe they were still co-conspirators if not lovers.

"No! But she is so mercenary! Can we…I mean, will she talk about it?" Sarah moved from the bed to an armchair, surrendering the idea that she was going to seduce Grey on the first night.

"I don't know. I guess I can ask her." Grey realized she had probably given Sarah too much information, but the underlying narrative between the two was too violent and painful for a three-day trip. You can't invite someone to your home over break and call them a gold-digging bitch the first night, can you? Perhaps not. Or perhaps it just required a few drinks.

"I don't want to do dinner here. I know she invited us, but let's get out of here. I'm here all the time, there are so many other things to do." Grey ran her hands through her hair in exasperation, severely irritated by the look of fascination on Sarah's face. Was she going to be repelled by every aspect of her former lover that she once found attractive? So it seemed. "I know a few cool places," she added in a rush. "Come on, let's go."

Sarah was only too happy to jump to her feet and to snag Grey's hand. It was difficult not to shake it off. She forced a calm she didn't feel, although she felt like a fraud, walking into the living room, her hand trapped in this other woman's hand. Grey spotted Zoë and watched that molasses brown gaze slide down the length of her where her hand connected with Sarah's hand. It was beyond awkward.

"Sarah's never really explored the French Quarter," Grey said, a tiny stammer in the back of her throat. "Um, we're going to head that way. Thanks for the dinner offer, but, um, we're heading out."

Zoë simply nodded, and Bridgette beamed. The Ice Queen abruptly held up her hand. "Hang on," she demanded and disappeared down the hallway toward her bedroom.

Grey counted seconds in her head. Her palm felt sweaty, like she was holding a hot, salty fish. She didn't like it. But the other hand held her in a vise grip. Sarah's

192

knuckles were probably white. It hurt. Zoë wouldn't meet her eyes and babbled about places they could visit in the French Quarter—places she'd already seen and knew about. The whole conversation was superfluous.

"You'll need this, of course," Bridgette's voice cut through the silence abruptly. She held out a wad of cash. Grey felt a moment of mortification. She had been saving her earnings. It would never have occurred to her to ask for spending money, especially after she had just received an extravagant gift from Zoë that Bridgette probably didn't yet know about. She was surprised the redhead hadn't mentioned the very expensive boots now covering her feet and calves.

"Come on, honey. You want to have a good time," Bridgette insisted.

It was Sarah who extended her hand and took the offering. "Thank you very much, ma'am," she said, grinning.

Grey felt her stomach nearly turn over. She needed some air. "Yes, thank you, Ms. Breedlove," she added, her voice almost cracking. She turned on her heel before she lost her nerve and headed for the entryway.

She was so quick to be angry with Sarah. Angry for what she had done, angry for what she was doing—in her mind, disrespecting Zoë and her money, being so callous. It was unacceptable. She had half a mind to slap her the second they stepped into the crisp winter air, but she resisted.

"You'll have to refuse anything else they offer. Do I make myself clear?"

"You're kidding, right? I mean it's just like your dad," Sarah beamed, holding up the wad of twenties. "Come on, you don't have to pretend with me. Besides, that Bridgette is quite a skeezer, isn't she! I mean she practically raped me when I came in. I think she'd do me." Sarah was already in the car before the last words were out of her mouth. Grey stared at Antoine, embarrassed that her friend was talking about her employers as if he wasn't even there. It was remarkable how quickly Sarah adjusted to having servants. For his part, Antoine simply held the door to the car open without comment.

Grey slid past him but managed an "I'm sorry" under her breath. To her relief, Antoine winked at her under his black cap before she bent to lower her head into the car.

Sarah babbled the entire fifteen minutes into the Quarter. "I don't know why you're so upset. I'm a penniless college student, and damn, Grey, you are the fucking help! So she gave us a couple of hundred? It's not like they can't afford it. They're loaded, for goodness sake." Sarah was laughing at her propriety.

"Yeah, I get it. But I know these two. You don't take money from Bridgette unless you are willing to pay for it later. And Zoë, well, she knows me better than to offer it," Grey said bitterly, hoping that Sarah would pick up on the suggestion of some intimacy between the two. She didn't.

"Look, I've been a member of the respected middle class a lot longer than you have, and I can assure you neither of those women gives a damn about your pride. That's pocket change to them, just like it used to be to you." Grey couldn't help but notice the emphasis on "used to be" in the remark.

It was amazing what a few months of separation would do to the perspective of one person over another. How could she have missed this? How hadn't she seen?

"I guess so," Grey conceded. She was tired of the fight. The truth of the matter was, she was still reeling from the kiss she and Zoë had exchanged earlier. Talk about bad timing. Zoë Cates was in her mind, had been for months.

194

Of all the days for Aimee Dupree to finally assert some fucking dominance. Grey's mind returned to the young vampire fans from their first adventure together. Perhaps she should have rolled over and shown her stomach months ago. She smiled. What the hell. Sarah was emptyheaded and vain, but entertaining. She'd focus the conversation on the "good old days" and try to have fun. And she knew just where they would go.

"Antoine, take us to that bar you scraped me off the front of on Halloween," Grey called to the front of the car.

"Yes, ma'am," Antoine responded with the usual lack of interest.

"Scraped you off?" Sarah laughed. "Now that sounds interesting."

"You have no idea."

Grey did her best to pay attention to Sarah's animated chatter. No matter the circumstances and obstacles, she told herself, there was no way Sarah was getting in her pants that night or any other. Whatever Sarah had planned, Grey vowed she would hit a brick wall. She eyed Sarah and her wide-eyed wonder, staring out the window with utter fascination and excitement. Grey couldn't help but recall the night Zoë had watched her in just the same way. The only difference was that Grey still shared the wonder, no matter how much she tried to set herself apart from Sarah.

She caught herself sharing a significant look with Antoine in the rearview mirror. Sarah was carrying on about some myth or another she'd heard about supposedly haunted locations she wanted to visit. Antoine grinned— the first time Grey had ever seen him crack a smile. She snorted and covered it as a sneeze.

Finally, Antoine had maneuvered them through the narrow streets of the Quarter until he arrived at the demanded location. "Any requests?" he asked for the first time ever. Grey realized he was being nice or watching out for her or perhaps he had orders to do so.

"Drop us here. I have your cell number. I'll call if we need anything."

"Sweet," Sarah exclaimed and hopped out before Antoine could step out and offer to open her door. "This is so awesome. So you'll come get us if we need you, buddy?"

Ugh. So condescending. Grey stifled a groan while she allowed Antoine to walk around to her side of the car and assist her out. "Thank you very much," she muttered. "Please ignore her." Antoine simply nodded in understanding and again grinned. Twice in one night. It must be some kind of record.

"What's so special about this place?" Sarah demanded, staring through a grimy window. "It looks like a dive bar."

"It is a dive bar." Grey had already eyed the bar, growing uneasy. What had she been thinking? Zoë had shown her this in confidence. Lucky for her, the bartender on duty had a handlebar mustache paired with a wife beater shirt and a mullet. "They have good tequila, and it's cheap."

"Seriously? That's just fucked, Grey," Sarah exclaimed. "Let's go somewhere else."

"Fine."

This time, Sarah ignored her hand. Grey wasn't exactly upset by the absence of crushing fingers establishing territory. She strolled alongside her, nonchalant. At the end of the street, they hit Frenchmen. Jazz trumpeted over drunken hollering and traffic horns.

"This is more like it," Sarah said happily, meandering into the first bar she saw.

Frenchmen had been a locals' haunt for years, but recently, the throngs of tourists had discovered that the real music in New Orleans had migrated from Bourbon to the less trafficked area. Sarah had already made the bar and ordered two Moscow Mules. She met Grey at their table with frosty copper cups in hand. Grey took one, thanking her, even though she inwardly groaned at the realization that her cocktail was really compliments of Bridgette the bitch.

Sarah pulled out a Gitanes cigarette, and Grey held up her hand.

"No smoking."

"What the fuck? In New Orleans? Are you kidding me? This is a bar." Sarah was clearly upset, even though Grey couldn't remember her smoking when they'd been together a few months earlier.

"Not kidding. They just passed it last year. Besides, since when did you smoke? I thought you said it was a disgusting habit. Remember that time in New York? You practically had an attack when that guy was walking in front of us up Columbus smoking."

"Well, I guess I've changed. Lilly smoked, and when we would read poetry together, she'd smoke, so you know, I started smoking. It was that easy." Sarah put the cigarette back in the pack.

So there it was. The name Grey had been waiting on for three months. Lilly. She could guess who Sarah meant. Lilly Erickson, a radical poet who'd shown interest in Sarah for over a year at varying poetry slams. What the fuck is a poetry slam anyway? She laughed to herself.

"Oh, Lilly. Well, cool, she was a nice woman. I'm happy for y'all," Grey said, smiling sincerely. She was actually relieved to have a fall guy for the petite seductress.

"Well, it wasn't like that." Sarah took her hand. "We just kind of fell together after your call. That very night actually. I cried and cried. She came over with some wine to try to help me get it together, you know. She just stayed. Then we were together. You know how it is." She looked at Grey pleadingly.

"Sure." Grey didn't care.

"Of course, then that bitch met that sophomore fucking soccer player, and that was it. I mean, what the fuck? A jock? I got ditched for a mindless jock, can you imagine? But then you texted the very next night. It was karma, it really was. I never really got over you, over this. So I told Lilly, 'See how long it took me to find someone else,' and flew down here. Fuck, I made her drive me to Logan. She cried. Ha! Isn't that funny?"

"I'd say that's pretty funny."

Grey spun around, knowing that voice instantly. Before she could catch herself, she sputtered, "What the fuck, Zoë?"

"Hey." Sarah snickered. "Don't talk to your employer that way."

"I'll talk to her however I want," Grey growled, then blushed. "I mean, hi, Zoë. What brings you here?"

"What a coincidence," Zoë deadpanned. "I would have joined you at The Over Under Bar, but you never went in. Guess Colt isn't your cup of tea."

Silence. Sarah continued to snicker, and Grey finally relented with a sheepish grin. "Nah, he wasn't. Also, I realized that there are many other places we should go—not that place. It's special." She acknowledged her transgression with sincerity.

Sarah stopped snickering and eyed them both. For once, Grey thought, she had finally cottoned on, realized there was tension there. But the moment faded as quickly as it had cropped up. "So we get to hang out with the famous Aimee R. Dupree. Can we get a selfie, or is that off-limits?"

"No," Zoë drawled without hesitation. "It's fine." She allowed the selfie with Sarah. Grey was left to sit and watch. Zoë held up her beer in salute, much to Grey's instantaneous irritation. Lilly, part II, she thought bitterly, unable to quash her cynicism. This was going to be anything but fun. Her lips still felt kiss-bruised, and her ex was clearly digging on her interest. How much more awkward could things possibly get?

"This bar is lame," Zoë announced abruptly, slamming her empty beer glass on the counter. "Come on, ladies, let's go somewhere else."

Zoë took Grey's arm, shrugging off Sarah's offer. At first, Grey was amused by the pout on Sarah's face. But Zoë hissed, "How dare you take anybody to that place—I told you nobody else knew!" forcing a flush to creep up Grey's cheeks and neck. Flushed, she gripped the offered arm tight.

"I didn't mean it," she whispered, but no acknowledgment of the apology followed. "So," Grey tried again, "Bridgette didn't want to join us?"

"No" was the only response she got. No explanation.

Sarah swept into Zoë's left, and the three walked in tandem down the corridor, stopping at Lafitte's.

"Here we go, ladies, oldest bar in America, they say, which seems appropriate given the fact that if you add both your ages together, you probably get mine." Zoë was in full Southern charm, but all Grey could do was lament her earlier mistake and hope for a moment alone when she could more fully explain. She didn't know why she went to The Over Under, but if she had to guess, it was because her heart and head both wanted to be with Zoë that evening, not with Sarah.

"You hardly look thirty." Sarah smiled, ducking into the dark bar.

A bad piano man played at the rear of the bar, and several people sat around the Steinway belting off-tune versions of Billy Joel and dropping cash into his tip jar. Zoë brought three beers to the table, and Sarah scooched in next to Grey in the booth. Grey continued to search Zoë's eyes for any sign that the tension between them had ebbed. She was relieved when she felt Zoë hook her sneakers around her right ankle under the table and pull her leg toward her. It was like an anvil off her chest.

"So what are you girls up to tonight?"

Grey looked at her with amazement. "We girls are just gonna have a few drinks and catch up." Grey stared.

"Actually, I'm really excited you came," Sarah said, raising her voice to be heard over the growing crowd. "I was just telling Grey how big a fan I am of your novels."

"Thanks, Sarah. That's very kind." Zoë looked down, feigned a blush, and looked back at Sarah out the top of her eyes. Her long dark brown lashes fluttered as though the flattery from a younger woman was making her uncomfortable.

Grey couldn't believe it. She was flirting with Sarah. This was going to be priceless. Suddenly, she was a "girl," and Zoë was a blushing middle-aged cougar.

Give me a break, she thought. Okay, if this was the way she wanted it, so be it.

"Actually, Zoë, Sarah is telling the truth. She is a huge Alicia Shade fan. She used to read me passages before we made love, do you remember that?"

Sarah laughed. "Oh, my gosh, yes. How embarrassing."

"Don't be embarrassed. What was your favorite? Come on, the one you had memorized," Grey prompted. She had been mildly humiliated by this particular performance a few cocktails in numerous times at school. Well, let the author herself enjoy it. "Do it for her."

Sarah smiled, gratified for the attention of the beautiful and famous older woman. She didn't notice the ice Zoë was sending Grey across the table.

"I'd love to hear it, truly, I would," Zoë said.

"See? Truly, she would." Grey smiled sardonically at Zoë, her long black hair whisping into her mouth as she flipped it.

Sarah stood from the table, dramatically licking her lips, and began to recite.

"And so it was I took her. Moistening my lips with the blood that flowed freely from her opened veins, as though from her womb, giving me life just as she would monthly slough her ability to do so otherwise. I sucked and sucked. I thrust my tongue into her wetness, tasting the musky earth of her life force as it left her. She moaned with desire even as I deprived her of her goddess-given right to live. It was my first kill. I taste her as though it was yesterday. Even now, my lips pulse to the rhythm of her slowing heart."

Sarah fell to the chair dramatically.

Zoë and Grey simply stared.

"Wow," Zoë said. She was speechless, but not for the reason Sarah thought.

"It is rather good, isn't it?" Sarah grinned. "I was a drama major first." She giggled. "Okay, gotta pee!" And she was off.

Zoë and Grey looked at each other and burst out laughing.

"Holy hell, did I write that crap?" Zoë demanded between snickers. "Who the hell bought that, much less memorizes it?"

"At least you aren't expected to fuck her after like I was." Grey giggled, and they burst out laughing again.

Sarah stumbled out of the restroom, stopping at the bar for three shots of Patrón, and finally made her way to the table. Grey recognized that Sarah was "acting" drunk—it was a ploy she had used at college to justify flirting with other women in Grey's presence. At the time, she'd found it endearing. Currently, she found it obnoxious.

Sarah slid into the booth next to Zoë, intentionally miscalculating her trajectory and pressing the other woman into the wall.

"Whoopsie." Sarah giggled, handing Zoë a shot.

"*Arriba, al bajo, al centro, pa dentro.*" Zoë giggled, tossing the shot down. The other women followed suit. "So, Sarah, I really enjoyed your reading or interpretation or whatever it was."

"Really? Oh. My. God. I can't believe that! Thank you!" Sarah launched into another series of selfies with Zoë, snuggling her, kissing her cheek, giving the thumbs-up. For Grey's part, she felt Zoë was enjoying it a little too much. And after the body-shaking kiss they'd shared earlier, all Grey could think was how immature the whole scene was.

"So tell me about your house. It's ginormous! Is it your only one? I bet you have several houses around the world, don't you?" Sarah was giving Zoë her most admiring gaze.

"Ha! Well, no, not really. Although we used to have an apartment in Paris. Bridge got tired of it, though, and we sold it. The market there is so ridiculous, I think we made over a million on it in less than two years."

What the hell? Grey thought. Over the last several months, she'd never heard Zoë talk about money. Ever. Sarah was drooling over the number.

"Gosh, a million? Wow. You know when I first met Grey, she had over three hundred million coming to her someday, didn't you, babe? We used to dream about

202

multiple houses and an apartment in the city. Of course, that's not likely now." She tried to make the comment seem offhanded, but it came across as critical.

"Yeah, sorry 'bout Dad dying," Grey said with a little more venom than she intended. After all, Sarah was what she was, and she used to love her. At this point, didn't that make her a worse person than her old paramour?

"That's not your fault, silly." Sarah smiled. "Besides, I never would have met Z here if you hadn't had to struggle."

Z? Dear Lord, she had given Zoë a nickname. Worse, the palm of her hand was lying gently atop Zoë's forearm, the same arm that had so furiously held Grey to her earlier that night.

Zoë was looking at Grey with concern. She'd made her point, Sarah was a gold digger. But at what cost? Her eyes burned with compassion for Grey. Grey could tell she already regretted her plan to expose Sarah. The collateral damage was too high. Grey's mind was only on her father now and her own ignorance.

"You know what, I don't feel so well," Grey said, dropping all the twenties Bridgette had given her on the table. "You guys finish without me. I'm gonna go back to the house before I get sick."

She was feeling sick. That much was true. Sick of her ex, sick of her situation, sick of the scene. She fled the bar, pushing her way through the thickening crowd of drunken patrons. She could barely hear Zoë calling behind her, "Grey, don't!"

"Too late, bitch," she hissed under her breath as hot tears spilled over and fell down her cheeks. Too late for so many things. Zoë and Sarah had both crossed lines not meant to be crossed. She felt belittled and humiliated.

And she was a Chesterfield. Nobody knocks a Chesterfield to the ground—feelings and hormones be damned. Bradley would have been appalled that she lasted through this disheartening evening as long as she did. Grey regretted not making a grander statement in her departure. It should have been more dramatic. It should have involved a hair flip at the very least.

Grey spilled out onto Bourbon Street in a huff. She was silently reciting all the things she should have said, meditating on her anger and disbelief. How could she have been so naïve? How could she have been so blind? She couldn't even decide which one of those two women back in that darkened bar was worse.

Antoine appeared out of nowhere, as per usual.

"How the fuck do you do that?" she growled. "Leave me alone."

Stoic as ever, he shrugged but did not leave. Grey immediately regretted her outburst. None of her current plight was his fault. "I'm sorry," she muttered, chagrinned. "Can you take me back? I need to get out of here. If you want to wait for Zoë, that's fine. I can take the streetcar, and I'll understand."

He pinned her with his dark gaze, the slightest narrowing of lips apparent. Then, wordlessly, he offered his arm, and she took it. The Suburban was only two blocks away. He tucked her away neatly and pulled away from the curb.

"Thank you," she said with as much sincerity as she could muster.

"Of course, ma'am." There was hesitation in his tone, as though he meant to say something more. But he didn't. Grey probably imagined it.

Her stomach was tied up in so many knots she couldn't imagine it ever being untied again. She rolled the window

204

down and gulped lungfuls of chilly air. She felt like she couldn't breathe.

Grey had regretted inviting Sarah, but no more. It was good, really. Zoë had exposed them both. Hopefully, this whole episode would cure her of her ridiculous infatuation with the famous and aloof author. She continued to imagine all the angry things she would say to Zoë later. And as for Sarah, she was cut off. Forever. Period. Damned gold digger.

Antoine finally pulled up to the house. As always, he opened the door like a gentleman. Again, he looked as though he wanted to express an opinion, but she could see the effort on his face in keeping it tucked behind those tight lips.

Grey watched the taillights fade down the street as he took off, probably headed back to the Quarter, she thought, and her anger built.

She stomped up the driveway and entered through the back door, not taking any care whatsoever in being quiet. She tromped down the hallway, practically seething with irritation. But she came to an abrupt halt when she burst into the kitchen.

Bridgette sat poised on a stool at the kitchen island, looking immaculate and livid.

"Where is Zoë?" she demanded without preamble. "I know she tore out of here to go meet up with you and your little girlfriend, although she refused to provide that information."

"Whoa!" Grey threw up her hands, equally livid by the whole situation. "I didn't invite her to join us, and I don't know where she is. I ditched them at Lafitte's because Sarah was irritating the crap out of me, and I don't feel like I should have to deal with her fucking shit anymore."

"Language, darling." Bridgette snarled.

"Fuck this," Grey growled. "I don't know what's going on. I don't know where she is now. And I don't care. I just want to go up to my room. Do I need permission for that, or are you going to deny me my sulking?"

Bridgette stood slowly. Her face was dangerous. Too calm. Too clean. Her hair too perfect and makeup too fresh. This was going to be like the night Grey and Zoë were nearly caught after their last French Quarter adventure. She just had a gut feeling about it.

"We are both upset, it seems. I would appreciate it, however, if you could not speak to me in this manner." Bridgette was too close. She touched Grey's face. "As for your sulking in your room—no, I think you will wait with me here in the kitchen." She laughed then. It was a maniacal sound. "I shall make you some tea. Sit down, Grey darling."

"No, I don't think I will wait with you here in the kitchen. Bridgette, I'm tired and pissed. I don't know how you deal with her, she's impossible. Arrogant and self-involved."

Bridgette measured her silently as she put the teapot on the stove. She still didn't agree to Grey's release; instead, her body language had become more menacing. She placed herself between Grey and the back staircase.

"She is impossible, isn't she? Poor Grey. Did she suck you in? Well, don't feel foolish, darling, you're not the first, nor will you be the last. I imagine she is face-down in your friend's lap right now at whatever dumpy hotel she's taken her to. But don't cry, dear. She always comes home to me." Bridgette was methodically dipping the tea bag into the cup, over and over. She never looked up. Grey was glad for this at the very least.

"She's quite adept at being dishonest and manipulative. Did she tell you I was crazy? Bipolar or some such

206

nonsense? That I needed medication, and that's why she needed another outlet? A beautiful young lover to fuck and fuck and fuck." Bridgette was stabbing a knife into the muffin she'd taken from the pantry.

Grey stared at her. Fear shot up her spine—the woman's imbalance fully exposed, dangerous.

"No, she never said anything like that. And we are not lovers. I wouldn't do that with my employer. Ma'am." Grey had added the "ma'am" after a slight pause. She hoped the formality would bring Bridgette back to reality. Bridgette pointed the knife at her, a wicked smile filling her face.

"Grey, go upstairs!" The commanding voice broke the spell, and Grey realized Zoë was standing behind her in the doorway to the kitchen. She spun around to find cold, controlled eyes—all seriousness. This wasn't a game.

"No!" Bridgette screamed. "No, don't fucking send her upstairs. You can fuck both of us, you worthless whore. You can fuck us both. Fuck you!" Bridgette launched herself at Zoë, who caught her in an embrace.

"For god's sake, Bridge, look at her." Zoë turned her face toward Grey. "Do you really think I would fuck that over you? That is laughable. Her friend was charming, but you know that's all bullshit for me. What is wrong with you?" Zoë forced out a laugh.

Bridgette turned her gaze on Grey, then looked up at Zoë, who was cradling her in her arms. A sudden realization seemed to overtake her, and Grey saw her body relax. Her eyes blinked off time, as though she wasn't fully aware of where she was. Then she simply smiled.

"Oh, my god! I am crazy." Bridgette laughed. And just then, Zoë leaned down and kissed her in much the same measure she had kissed Grey earlier. It was too much.

"I'm leaving," Grey said, walking past the couple still engaged and heading out the back gate. She made it to the backdoor before she heard footsteps. She ignored them.

She made it to the gate. Then, "Don't leave. Seriously. Please don't leave."

"No, Zoë. Fuck you. It's laughable, right? I'm so outta here. I can't with this shit anymore. Bridgette, as crazy as she is, kind of makes sense. Don't fucking follow me and don't send Antoine to tail me. I'll come back when I'm good and ready."

"But…"

"No!" she thundered. "Go back inside and deal with your crazy. I'll go deal with mine."

Without another word, Grey stormed down the street.

Chapter Seventeen

The streetcar rumbled down St. Charles. What a night—it was well past midnight. Yet the city had a feel as though just starting to awaken, and there was Grey, too many bad things for one evening already behind her.

She had dug her phone out and had her face buried in it. She'd had half a mind to text Sarah to find out where she was, to try to salvage whatever piece of this night she could—with what? A reconciliation? Ludicrous. Perhaps some amenable agreement at best. But she remembered all the selfies, all those cutesy pictures she'd taken with Zoë, and for the first time in months, Grey reinstalled Facebook and Instagram on her phone. She skipped the gazillion notifications—acquaintances surely wondering what happened to her—and went straight to Sarah's page. She didn't like what she saw there.

Picture after picture of her cute ex with her sexy employer. They looked ridiculous. Drunk or stupid or both. She tortured herself by looking at each picture, resisting the urge to post snarky comments. She couldn't even understand why she was doing this to herself.

Sarah had just checked in to another bar in the French Quarter. It would be easy to chase her down. The girl couldn't stay off her phone. But she had tagged several people Grey wasn't familiar with. These must be the Tulane friends.

Then there was a new picture. Sarah doing shots while making goofy duck lips and snuggled up to some redhead.

Grey deleted the Facebook app from her phone again.

She rushed out of the car at the next stop, preferring to walk off her anger. It was closer to Esplanade anyway. She didn't want to run into Sarah on Bourbon Street. A terrible idea already took shape in her head. She talked herself out of it, even as her feet took her in a beeline for her pinnacle of personal betrayal. She eventually denied, out loud, that she was that much of a bitch, the words echoing as she stood under the lone streetlight.

She was standing outside The Over Under Bar.

Grey tucked her hands in her pocket, her face red with unfulfilled desire, confusion, and anger. She had just worked up enough courage to go in when the small neon sign, the only identification for the club, clicked off. The bar was closed.

Grey dropped her head and laughed softly. What the hell was she thinking? She wasn't woman enough to fuck Alicia and betray Zoë. She hiccupped as she wiped a lone tear from her face, inhaling deeply and pulling her leather jacket closer around her. She was staring at her new boots trying to think of what to do next when she heard the voice. Her voice.

"So you coming in, young blood, or are you just gonna stand there and cry like a little girl?"

Alicia stood in the door, her black wife beater pulled tightly over her ample chest, combat boots encircling her black skinny jeans. Her blue-black hair was piled up in an Amy Winehouse beehive, and she wore two black leather wristbands. A Camel Light hung from her lips.

"I was just walking. I'm sorry. I didn't have a lot of money, so I came here." Grey looked at the other woman

210

for the first time straight in her beautiful eyes. She was wearing her pain openly, she knew it.

"Oh, little girl." Alicia's eyes softened and read Grey up and down. "Fuck me, come in. I've always had a soft spot for puppies." She stepped aside and let Grey slide through the screen door. Grey sat on a barstool, surprised when Alicia slid the bolt and pulled the blinds behind her. She was hoping for a beer, but Alicia passed her flipping the lights off behind the bar.

"Follow me," she said, winding up the stairs hidden behind a small door in the storage room.

Grey swallowed hard. It felt like a point of no return. Yet she couldn't deny the anger that still simmered beneath the surface making her arms feel like they were crawling with ants. A shiver ran down her spine, and she jumped off the barstool. Determined. Hurt. Needing.

She slipped behind the bar and into the tiny backroom. The space stank of stale beer and cigarettes. She pushed that out of her mind deliberately, consciously stepping through the tiny opening to a set of very old and very narrow stairs. She thought she knew damned well what she was doing.

The steep and claustrophobic staircase opened up into a tiny studio. A soft lamp in the corner revealed walls draped in various fabrics. A queen mattress on a worn brass frame with wine red sheets—the color of rust by the single light. Two floor-to-ceiling windows revealed the dark night, only a hint of neon from blocks away highlighting a rooftop or two. Alicia stood in the center of the small space, her dark eyes appearing black.

"Come here," she beckoned, her hand extended in an inviting gesture. Grey froze, struggling with the last of her inhibitions.

Tinkling laughter filled her buzzing ears. Her feet and heart felt so heavy. The anger was evaporating quickly. She was already regretting her choices. But it was too late.

"Come," Alicia said again, this time with a tone of command that was not to be denied. With a pang, Grey remembered Zoë's description of how this woman had kissed her, shoved her against a wall, practically body-pressed her into the side of a building. Her knees felt weak.

She took a few shaky steps forward and took the offered hand.

"See? That wasn't so hard," Alicia murmured, bringing Grey's knuckles up to her lips, trailing light kisses and pressing her face against the now-upturned palm. The contact was electric. In the semi-darkness of the room, unable to tell the woman's dilated pupils from her dark irises, it was easy to imagine that this was indeed the vampire she'd read about—had fantasized about. She sucked in a shuddering breath through clenched teeth.

Suddenly, her world shifted and spun. She found herself pressed face-first into the windowpane opposite where she had just been standing. Being slammed into the window stung her cheek, and her shoulder hurt where Alicia was gripping her hard, grinding her body into the back of her. "Fuck," she hissed in response.

"That's the idea," Alicia said, those strong hands winding their way down, cupping her breasts, kneading her hard, pulling her closer, crushing their bodies together, her lips locking over the pulse point of her main artery, teeth playing along its length. Grey couldn't hold back the groan that escaped her lips. She'd been holding back too long. Her skin screamed from the needed contact.

All the confusion, the anger, the jealousy melted under the feeling of those teeth on her neck, those hands winding under her shirt and bra, those fingers finding and teasing

212

her erect nipples. Grey cried out, pushing against the glass, trying to escape the position into which she was pinned. She wanted to dip her hands into the gothic beauty's tight pants. She wanted to smell sex on her lips. But she was trapped in the woman's firm grip against the open window. She could feel her shirt being torn up closer to her chest, exposing her breasts, just as her gaze landed on a couple of drunken sailors wandering the street below. But she looked away just as quickly.

This vampire goddess had sexually satisfied her so many times before, she just didn't know it. And Grey had been insatiable in her teens, needing her to ravish her again and again. It had been too long. It was almost familiar. This was nothing like fooling around with Sarah. Nothing like flirting with girls at the bar. Nothing like kissing Zoë.

Shamelessly, she begged without words, grinding her ass into Alicia's hips, moaning against her touch. This was like her best masturbation sessions in her dorm room alone, when Sarah was stuck in her lab class, after reading Aimee R. Dupree's sex scenes for the hundredth time, then driving fingers into her slick desire as hard and as fast as her hands could handle. She cried, it was so intensely familiar and yet alien.

"Fuck," she hissed again and again. She wedged her hands down the edge of the glass until she could reach her waist and unzipped her jeans in a gesture of complete surrender. Alicia was quick to take advantage, ripping the loose pants down to her knees.

Strong fingers slid beneath her panties and circled her swollen clit. Grey ground her teeth and groaned long and hard, begging shamelessly, "Please, please, please." She was rewarded for her eagerness. Alicia cupped her groin, pulling her even closer, biting her neck, before she drove two fingers deep into her center, penetrating her hard and fast.

Grey slammed her hand against the window and screamed. She was almost surprised it didn't shatter. Fingers were thrusting into her while another hand rolled a nipple between forefinger and thumb. She was close, so close.

Alicia released her too soon. Grey growled her disappointment and made to move, but strong arms clamped around her hips as Alicia dropped to her knees. Understanding dawned on Grey, and she arched her back and widened her stance in anticipation. She wasn't disappointed. The tongue running the length of her from clit to anus was the sweetest experience she had ever had.

Now she was truly light-headed, gasping for breath she couldn't hold. She wouldn't be able to stand it much longer. She leaned into the glass for support, unable to fully comprehend that a sexual fantasy so long entertained was becoming a reality. She was quivering from impending release, a thin sheen of sweat breaking out along her spine. When Alicia's lips wrapped around her clit, she couldn't hold back the flood any longer. Her muscles spasmed and knees shook from relief.

One earth-shattering minute of bliss followed—heart pounding in her ears, fingers still teasing her, a tongue tickling her anus. Too fast. Way too fast. She quivered and tried to catch her breath, her knees weak and mouth watering. It wasn't enough.

Grey struggled against the window, determined to become unpinned. She thrust herself backward, knocking Alicia away.

"What the fuck?" Alicia hissed, tumbling onto her back.

214

"Shut up," Grey growled, dropping to the floor, crawling on top and burying her face in those luscious breasts.

They struggled for control, Alicia's bemused laughter bubbling up between groans of surprise and delight. Grey, undeterred, advanced until she was straddling her hips. She dipped down and captured those dark lips, moaning into the crushing kiss while her hands tore at those skinny jeans. She bit down on that lower lip and tasted copper.

Her world spun, and she was on her back, a hand clamped down on her throat. Teeth grazed her earlobe and a whispered, "How dare you?" made her wetter than she already was.

"Just tear me up," she moaned, "because I dared."

"No." The pressure on her throat eased, but lips grazed her cheek, licked a lone tear that had suddenly leaked from Grey's eye. "Not until you say her name."

The angry ants marching along her overheated arms disappeared abruptly. A sick feeling built in Grey's gut and spread like ice into her chest and hands.

"What?" she tried, knowing it wouldn't work.

"Say her name right now."

"No."

"Say it."

"Fuck you."

Mocking laughter. "That's not her name, darling." Those soft, full lips wrapped around Grey's earlobe and suckled gently. "I know why you're here. Just say it. You'll feel better. Just let it out."

Another tear leaked out, and that feeling of ice intensified. Guilt. She knew it was the feeling of intense, devastating guilt.

"Zoë," she whispered.

"That's right," Alicia encouraged, her voice darker and more throaty, nearly breathless. "Again but louder."

"Zoë," Grey repeated obediently, tearfully, desperately.

"Fuck, you're in love with her." Alicia sighed.

"No…" Grey started, her eyes wide open in the dark. "No, it's not true!"

"Shh." A finger on her lips. "Only say her name. Nothing else." The finger dipped between Grey's lips, and she sucked it deeper into her mouth automatically.

The sound of a zipper shattered the sound of their heavy breathing. Grey watched—fascinated, terrified, guilt-ridden, and hot all over in spite of the icy shame—while those skinny jeans came off. Her gaze trailed those fingers removing a lacy black thong. Her vision was finally obscured when Alicia pressed herself into Grey's face.

She could barely breathe. That slick sex ground into her kiss-bruised lips. It was spicy and sweet and too much. She tried to keep up and couldn't catch a breath. She could barely hear Alicia's groans and tried to dip her tongue into that opening, tried to capture her clit between her lips, tried to wrap her arm around strong thighs pinning her down to still the riding and grinding hips. Her head felt light. Just when she thought she would pass out, Alicia stood.

"Fucking say her name again," she demanded, rifling in a drawer nearby.

"Zoë," Grey whispered, gasping.

"That's right." She held something up to the light. Grey saw the leather straps, and her eyes widened. "You can take it," Alicia assured her, running her hand teasingly along the length of a very thick, long and very real-looking yet silicone cock.

Grey scrambled to her feet, her heart hammering in her chest. What the hell was she doing? How could she even be in this particular place with this particular woman? She had to get out. Now.

"So no." It didn't sound like a question. Alicia had stated it flatly, like she knew the answer and didn't appreciate it.

Grey quivered and tried to catch her breath. Her whole body was still on fire. And she was scared. And felt guilty. And was so tired—tired of feeling confused, tired of drama, tired of finding herself in every impossible and unfortunate situation. The urge to escape overwhelmed her. It spilled out through her eyes, and she couldn't stop it.

Alicia stood and stared at her, composed even in this heat.

"I'm guessing those aren't for me." She reached down and wiped a tear from Grey's face. It was the only gesture of compassion she would receive. Alicia walked to the small fridge and took out two cold Abitas, the humidity forcing steam to rise from each.

She thrust one at Grey, who was busy pulling her clothing around her and trying to formulate an excuse or explanation for Zoë.

"Oh, for god's sake, Jacqueline, I'm not gonna tell her," Alicia said without a note of patience.

"I'm sorry?" Grey asked through tears of confusion and doubt.

"I'm not going to tell Zoë, sweetie. I mean, I wish you were game for this." She touched the equipment, running her fingers lovingly along its length, stroking it. "But what the hell. You can't fuck someone when you're in love with someone else. Drink your beer and leave." Alicia was pulling on camo pajamas and brushing out her hair. "Maybe you can get the fuck out now that I've shown you what's out there. 'Cause, babe, that shit is crazy, and you don't have a chance, know what I mean?" She stepped into her bed, flipping the light off.

"I'm not in love with Zoë, not at all," Grey protested, the cold beer sweating over her grasp.

"Whatever, doll. Don't let the door hit you on the way out." And with that, she flipped off the light, leaving Grey to find her way down the stairs and out the back door. She emerged in the alley, her skin still on fire, tears still spilling over, and a semi-warm beer grasped in her hands. Suddenly, she realized that her pants were still unzipped, and her bra, though on, was clasped under her breasts. She felt like an idiot.

Slowly, she admitted to herself what the seductive bartender had figured out in one short covert seduction.

She was in love with Zoë.

Thirty minutes later, she was back on the streetcar toward the mansion. Even though the evening was chilly, Grey was still sweating and hot. As the historic streets of the Garden District passed her vision, she felt her heart rate rise, and doubt shadowed her brain. What was she going to say? She had violated Zoë's trust, and whether Zoë was willing to admit it or not, Grey felt as though she had cheated on her lover. She let out a primal scream that caused the driver to turn and smile at her.

"It can't be that bad, honey." She smiled into the mirror.

"Oh, it can. It can be *that* bad." Grey laughed while crying.

The walk from the stop to the mansion calmed her mind. She hadn't done anything wrong, really. She'd had sex with a free single woman, and she was a free single woman. Did it really matter that she was in love with Zoë? It wasn't like anything was going to happen. Zoë herself had declared it ridiculous. She continued this dialogue even as she mounted the stairs to her room. And by the time she flipped the light on by the door, she was satisfied that no harm had been done.

Then she looked down and realized she was standing on several sheets of white paper covered with typing. It was a chapter, and it had been shoved under her door sometime in the hours she had been gone, sometime in the hour she had spent fucking Zoë's muse.

Grey reached down and picked up the scattered paper, arranging it in order. Even before she began to read, the tears started again.

"Oh, Zoë," she cried to herself. "This is impossible. It's just impossible."

For several long minutes, she just stood there, letting the tears fall. She felt like she didn't deserve those pages. She didn't deserve to be allowed to read the new novel before anyone else did. She didn't deserve to be the basis for a main character. She wasn't Jacqueline. Who had she ever been kidding? The pages shook in her sweaty palms.

But what would she say to Zoë in the morning if she didn't read them? Would it really matter? Usually, Zoë ignored her after any new pages surfaced. This probably would be no different. She debated hiding the pages—unread—with the rest in her closet. Yet somehow, she couldn't.

She kicked off her new boots and placed the pages reverently on the bed. She had to get out of those clothes. She had to wash off Alicia. A hot shower would do wonders, this she was sure of, and she trusted her instincts.

After she had scrubbed herself clean—the smallest of after-shivers cascading the length of her spine when she washed where Alicia's tongue traced her length—she emerged pink and steaming, wrapped in a towel, ready to hit the sheets.

Rifling through the pile of clothes, she fished out her phone and was about to plug it in to charge overnight when she noticed a message indicator.

"I can't believe you ditched us. That was about the most insecure, immature, and ridiculous thing I think I've ever seen you do. Don't bother contacting me again."

"No problem," Grey muttered, deleting Sarah's message. At least that solved one problem.

She pulled the paper to her and sighed.

Chapter Twenty

Every day, every hour, every second of the time we had together was precious. I watched as Jacqueline had to take more and more of my blood just to get through each day without pain. It didn't matter. No matter how many times I approached her about the change, no matter how many ways I assured her things wouldn't change between us, she would simply smile and nod at me and move the topic to some human joy we would share together the next day. The next memory we would create.

In the early morning as we would fall asleep, I would sit next to her growingly frail body and watch as she labored to breathe. Every second with her was worth more than each of the thousands of lives I had sacrificed in the years before I knew her. After several weeks, I noticed that Jacqueline had been waking up before the sun set each evening. She'd begun to leave the warehouse two or three hours before I awoke from my slumber, returning in time to guarantee that we never missed a waking second together.

One morning when I awoke, I found her pink and happy from a strong sun, sitting at the side of the bed holding my hand.

"Good morning, my sweet love," I whispered, pulling her to me. She buried her head in my chest and sighed.

"I'm afraid I need more blood, Alicia," she apologized. "It just hurts a little today."

I sat straight up and pulled her to me, simultaneously slashing my own wrist and pressing it to her lips. When she finished, she wiped her mouth and smiled at me.

"I made a new friend," she beamed. "I want us to go meet her tonight."

"You did?" I said, trying to hide my ire. She didn't need friends. There wasn't enough time.

"Don't be like that." She laughed, kissing me. "I won't see anyone but you when you're awake, but I've been getting up a little early. There are things I want to see…the sun, daytime things." She looked at me hoping for my understanding.

"Of course," I said. She was still human, I had to remind myself. She was human and facing her own mortality with more bravery than most soldiers I had known, and killed, in my long life.

"Her name is Chloe. She is adorable. I met her in a cancer support group." She hopped off the bed and headed to the closet, the vampire blood had already taken hold. "You are going to love her so much. We meet in the afternoon about four and talk and share stories about dying. Of course, it's not like being with you. But she is someone who understands, you know?"

"Of course, my pet." I didn't understand at all, but I would try.

"I want you to meet her tonight, Alicia. She needs treatment. I mean, her treatment could save her, but she *can't afford it. I thought maybe we could, well, you could help." She looked at me with anticipation. "You are going to love her."*

Thirty minutes later, I was seated at a table with three human friends of ours and Chloe. Perhaps it was my own ire that made me instantly dislike the woman. She wore her bravery and desire to "beat" the cancer within her like a badge. Or perhaps it was the adoring look my sweet Jacqueline was giving her across the table. Who can tell? When you haven't felt anything for so many centuries, I suppose you feel things, even jealously, more intensely.

"I wish I had the money for the treatment," Chloe was saying bravely. "But since they can't guarantee me a cure, my family deserves to not have to pay for a guess. Besides, I have lived more in the last thirty-three years than most people do in a lifetime! You know what I mean, Alicia?" She reached her hand out to touch me. "I'm so grateful for Jacqueline's time and love, she means so much to me." She smiled a dazzling white smile at me.

All I saw was red. That one touch had revealed all to me and in doing so had released a fury I thought had long gone dormant. It took all the strength I had not to take her right there at the table. Instead, I saw the look of admiration in my love's green eyes. Frankly, it only stoked the fire within me, but I held it.

"So, Chloe," I said, layering my tone with all the powers of persuasion natural to one of my kind. "Tell me all about yourself and your family."

The dissertation she gave painted the picture of a loving and supportive family losing a daughter too early. The daughter bravely facing a long and painful death to keep her aged parents from having to suffer the consequences of her death. She regaled me with stories of

222

trips to the Mayo Clinic, afternoons spent jumping from airplanes or riding horses up Pike's Peak. Fulfilling her bucket list before dying. She explained that all of these had been paid for by her loving friends who had donated money to her once they understood she was terminal.

I took this in as long as I could bear it. Then I told my love that I needed food and rest. Of course, she understood this in a way no one else at the table could. I gave her a hundred-dollar bill and asked her to pay the tab when I was gone, telling her I'd meet her at home.

"But I want to go with you." She looked at me questioningly.

"No, sweet, you stay, and I'll see you back at the warehouse." I gave her all the assurance I could muster considering my dark intent.

Before I left, I leaned in and whispered to Chloe, "Meet me by Lafitte's at three tonight. Come alone."

I knew even before the words left my lips that she would comply. I hadn't asked this human, I had commanded her. Just as I had commanded thousands like her to their deaths in the centuries before I met Jacqueline. She nodded thoughtlessly, unaware that my entire being, my smell, my gaze, my thrall if you will, was mandating her obedience.

All I saw was red.

At three, I stood beside "the oldest bar in America" (laughable arrogance of humans), when Chloe appeared as commanded. She was breathless, her own erotic inner nature having taken control already.

I gazed into her eyes, my strong vampire hand holding her left wrist.

"Tell me all about yourself. Tell me why you lie about dying and about your cancer. Do it quickly and now."

223

She had no chance to resist. Conmen and tricksters for generations had been my food. Taking the wicked always seemed less vulgar, though before my love, I was far removed from such genteel concerns. Chloe freely told me of her game, faking cancer and taking advantage of people in dire circumstances, living on the good intentions of others. Even under my spell, she couldn't hide her disdain for the sick and elderly she abused without remorse. She laughed and told me how my own Jacqueline had given her money and how she'd spent it on clothing and food for her boyfriend, a heroin addict named Brad.

"That's all." She smiled and pressed herself into me. I could smell her desire for me. It only angered me more. This creature had taken valuable time from my love, had robbed her of money, and was perfectly willing to continue to do so. "Take me," she begged, tilting her head up, exposing her neck as human victims instinctively did.

"I will take you, whore," I spat. And in a second, my fangs ripped a four-inch gash across her throat. She tried to scream, but her vocal chords had been severed in my initial attack. Blood flowed in an arch from her carotid artery and bathed me in a river of death. I wouldn't deign to drink from her neck, but instead caught droplets of blood on my tongue.

Chloe's eyes showed nothing but horror as she watched her own blood drain onto the uneven sidewalk. But I was not done.

With both hands, I grasped her wrists and pulled, severing both arms from her body, drenching her blond hair in gore. After that, though I knew she was dead, the violence of my nature took over. I tore this human to pieces, inch by inch.

The whole attack took seconds, but even in my mind's eye, I play it in slow motion, reveling in her shock and

224

pain. She had no value, other than her life's blood, which I would feed by proxy to my love. I took a life in the most violent and bloody way I could, and frankly, it freed me and brought me to the point of climax, just as it had for centuries before I regained some of my "humanity." And I would do it again.

Walking toward Jackson Square, I realized I was drenched in the blood and flesh of this carrion. Although I don't remember how I got there, my next waking memory was baptizing myself in the waters of the fountain in the square. Washing the blood from my kill so I could return to my beloved cleansed. I lay in the waters, running my hands through my hair and over my body. And even as the water closed around my face, I closed my eyes and whispered, "Jacqueline, it's not fair."

Life is not fair, it seems. Even when you're dead.

Right. Life isn't fair. The whole situation wasn't fair. It wasn't fair that Grey had basically been ejected from her comfortable life. It wasn't fair that she had had to abandon her education—temporarily or not. It wasn't fair that her girlfriend turned out to be a gold-digging whore. It wasn't fair that she had lost her father. It wasn't fair. It just wasn't.

Jacqueline and Alicia would never be able to grow old together. Or grow eternally.

And it wasn't fair that Grey was in love with her teenage idol, who was married and had a child. Life wasn't fucking fair. Dead or not.

"Fuck you, Zoë," Grey whispered in the semi-darkness of the room. "Fuck you, Alicia. Fuck you, Bridgette. Fuck you, Sarah. And fuck you, Rochester."

She was beyond tears. She felt so lost and empty. She rolled over and sighed, hugging the pages to her chest.

Before Sarah had arrived, before that disastrous outing in the Quarter and her consequent encounter with Zoë's muse, before she'd betrayed herself, the excerpt she'd just read might have given her hope in spite of its implications. Was it not proof that Zoë definitely had strong feelings for her and felt just as trapped and helpless as she did? Yet at that moment, it served to fuel her own sense of helplessness and hurt. Everything seemed painted in shades of regret and remorse. Her senses were poisoned with it, and she felt cold.

She saw what Aimee R. Dupree was doing in this novel. It was an explanation and a plea for understanding. It was anger and disappointment. Opportunities lost and hurting hearts. Grey saw it and despised it. Instead of sadness, she felt anger.

"You coward," she growled, tossing the pages onto the floor. "Have some fucking courage. Fight for what you want."

Did it matter that Bridgette was holding her hostage through Emily? Of course. And yet she couldn't forgive or lend understanding. The hurt took her beyond that.

She wanted out. The violence of that scene left her reeling. It reflected her own internal rage stemming from too many losses too closely. She wasn't ready for anything this real. She needed time and space to grieve and grow. This place offered no reprieve.

Another deep sigh. Grey pulled the cover over her head and closed her eyes. Let sleep come if it could.

Chapter Eighteen

Seven days. Seven days of silence since the core of Grey's world was exposed as both essential and unimportant on white pages of eight-and-a-half-by-eleven paper. Grey and Zoë had passed in the kitchen numerous times during the preparations for Aimee R. Dupree's annual Christmas party. And yet Emily seemed the only true bond between them, innocent to the pain and anger exchanged in each glance between the two people who had become the most important to her in the world.

Bridgette had come and gone three times to Los Angeles during this period. She was negotiating film rights to the first Shade novels and seemed on cloud nine since Zoë had begun to write in earnest again. She never questioned the motivation beyond the creative outpouring. Bridgette only appreciated the financial ramifications.

"There she is!" she'd practically shouted the morning of the Christmas party when Grey had entered the grand ballroom with Emily in her arms. Bridgette rushed her, planting a moist, lippy kiss on her cheek. "There's my little enabler. My little goldmine. Darling, without you? Who knows if she'd have put Emily down long enough to write again!"

Grey wanted to slap her despite the child cradled in her arms.

"Emily doesn't feel well," she said without emotion. "I don't think she or I will make the party." Grey's relief when she realized Emily was running a fever had been palpable. Putting on the strapless black leather dress Bridgette had purchased especially for her seemed too painful to bear. "I'll stay with her in the nursery tonight."

Emily had her pink face tucked into Grey's neck.

"Nonsense. I'll call Clara, and she can come sit." Bridgette unceremoniously plucked the sleeping child from Grey's arms. "Grey, I need you at this party in that dress looking every bit the sexy vampire bait, sweetie. We are selling tonight...*selling*! LA and New York will both be here. I need you here, no arguments." Bridgette was already heading up the stairs, where Grey had no doubt she would deposit Emily in front of an Elmo video with little or no concern.

"Yes, ma'am," Grey responded flatly.

What did it matter?

Around seven, Grey found herself in the awkwardly familiar situation of having a hairdresser and a makeup artist knock on her door. It was so reminiscent of countless holidays with Tawny and her attempts to "de-gay" her that she couldn't help but feel nostalgic.

"Come on in, guys." She laughed, opening the door to her quarters.

Thirty minutes later, Grey found herself sucked into a three thousand-dollar couture Donna Karan strapless leather cocktail dress, a full size too small, complete with built-in bustier and ostrich feather skirt. Her hair had been piled on top of her head in a traditional eighteenth century pomp, and her makeup screamed goth hooker. Staring in the mirror, the ridiculous spectacle made her laugh for the first time in weeks.

"Dear God." She smiled. "I look like Elvira meets David Bowie meets Tri Delts!"

Her stylist Manuel managed to look hurt and exit with a disgusted flip of his Chariots of Fire hair. "Well…ungrateful much."

Grey braced herself and walked down the stairs and through the back kitchen to the party. The Aimee R. Dupree Christmas party was both for the literary elite and the literary subversive, she'd been informed. Her "job" was to look like a vampire slut and not speak. No worries there.

When she entered the grand ballroom, it took Grey a minute to take in the flamboyant decorations that had consumed the classically beautiful room. The crown molded ceilings were draped with red and emerald velvet. The tables were set with grandiose flair. It was truly Bacchanalian. Grey walked, as best she could in her restrictive wardrobe, to the bar and ordered vodka. Straight.

Through the influx of New Orleans elite, Grey saw a tousled blond head tilted back with laughter across the room.

"Don't look," she whispered to herself, polishing off the iced drink in her hand.

It was too late. Zoë spotted her instantly, her eyes flashing with opportunity. The crowd, Grey realized, provided them with anonymity, the ability to speak without notice. There was no way she would avoid her flame tonight.

Zoë maneuvered between the guests, her gaze locked on Grey, a toothy, semi-drunk grin on her face. Surprisingly, she passed Grey and headed straight to the bar behind her.

"Two shots of Belvedere, Maurice. Iced." The bartender handed her the drinks, and just as quickly, Zoë handed one to Grey.

229

"Let me guess," Zoë smiled at her, staring at Grey out the tops of her eyes, "wardrobe by Bridgette?" Zoë glanced Grey up and down and chuckled.

Grey fixed her with a sardonic stare, though she felt her heart melting.

"No, I just felt like wearing a Glad garbage bag and a feather duster tonight. I really feel fashion is headed toward cleaning fucking utensils. Cheers." She shot her most sarcastic glare at Zoë.

Zoë threw her head back and laughed, slipping her arm around Grey's waist.

That seemed a dangerously familiar act, but Grey didn't care. She loved this woman.

"Grey, I want to talk to you. About Sarah," Zoë said, looking just a touch sheepish.

"I think we have better things to talk about than my gold-digging ex."

Their gazes met. Understanding was instant. They were in love. *In love.* It was terrible. And exciting. And awful.

Grey smiled slyly, unable to maintain composure. She was leaning into the arm around her waist. Zoë was babbling about something. Surely, it was clever and funny. She caught herself laughing easily, as though the last week hadn't happened. Love was insanity.

She touched her neck subconsciously, trailing fingers along her collarbone as though demonstrating where Zoë should lay her lips. New York and LA were in the room. It didn't matter. Aimee R. Dupree stood in front of her, yet it was just Zoë—the woman she'd pranced around in the yard with, entertaining a toddler. Just the two of them, no spotlight, no drama.

Grey went to place her empty glass on the bar. In doing so, she happened to glance over Zoë's shoulder.

230

Bridgette stood frozen, framed in the grandiose stairway. For all the world, she could have appeared to simply be caught between two thoughts, like a pause, but for Grey, who had learned to distinguish the mask of propriety from the mask of barely contained crazy, it was a moment of impending disaster.

Their gazes met. It was only a second, perhaps two. In that timespan, Grey knew that Bridgette knew.

"You look like you just swallowed a bug," Zoë said, chuckling, grazing Grey's cheek with her fingertips. "What is it?"

"Nothing," Grey whispered and tried to take a step back.

Zoë turned and looked over her shoulder, her whole body stiffening. When she turned back to face Grey, her smile was still in place, but it was forced. She tossed back her drink and said, "*Fantastic*. Let's get this party started, shall we?"

Zoë walked forcefully to the center of the ballroom and signaled the band to stop the music. A single hand gesture, already recognized by the other partygoers, and silence engulfed them all.

"Ladies and gentlemen, if I could have your attention," she articulated through the white noise of the party. "At this time every year, as many of you already know, Bridgette and I present our Christmas presents to each other. So, Bridge, if you wouldn't mind…" Zoë stretched her hand out to the visage frozen on the staircase. It was an effort at concealing something that would not be concealed, Grey realized. She turned on her five-inch stilettos to walk to the kitchen.

"Don't go anywhere, Grey." Bridgette's voice sounded the edge of madness across the room. Even the revelers had begun to glance at one another questioningly. Grey stopped and turned on her heel. Tonight she would not be cowed by Bridgette's aggression. She placed a smooth palm on her twenty-seven-inch waist and turned confidently.

If you could have worn this dress, you would have, bitch, she thought.

Zoë continued. "As many of you know, a few years ago, Bridge gave me the ultimate gift—Emily. So I decided that Emily and I would give Bridge a little magic this year. I have arranged for the three of us and Emily's nanny to go to the Magic Kingdom and stay in Cinderella's Castle."

The crowd broke out in the customary oohs and ahhs. But Bridgette remained silent, alternating her visual accusation between Grey and Zoë. Saying, without ever opening her mouth, "I know." Grey stood frozen until she heard Emily squeal from the stairs. The little redhead, who was supposed to be tucked away in her room, rushed full force into her—all pink glitter and unicorn pajamas, red hair flying in a fit of excited giggles.

"Cinderella! Cinderella!" she squealed to the amusement of all. Grey felt a knot form in her stomach. Yet she maintained her stance.

"I know, pumpkin. It's going to be awesome." She tried to inject the appropriate amount of enthusiasm and not just for the child. All eyes were on Emily.

Grey's response seemed to jog Bridgette. "Yes," she simpered madly. "That's absolutely marvelous, darling!"

Awkward applause followed.

"And now, my beloved wife," the words "beloved" and "wife" were enunciated particularly sharply, "may I present my gift to you?"

"Of course," Zoë said without enthusiasm. Her smile was in place, but it looked more like a grimace than an expression of joyous anticipation.

232

"Wonderful. Janel?" Bridgette beckoned her friend forward.

Janel glided confidently over to a rather large velvet-draped object. It was obviously going to be a painting, Grey realized a split second before Janel grabbed the red velvet with both hands and yanked it off the piece in one swift and rather aggressive movement.

Grey nearly choked. Utter silence filled the room as no one initially was able to react.

The portrait was graphic. That was the only appropriate descriptive word that came to mind. It was hard for the eye to travel to anything past the giant vagina painted directly into the center of the six-by-ten-foot canvas. It seemed like it was at least half a square foot in size, glistening in luxurious linseed oil and cadmium red with obsidian black and a variety of shades in between. It was difficult to discover that there was more to the painting, that it was a rather revealing pose of Bridgette herself, fully nude, the haughtiest of looks on her smug face. It was so wildly inappropriate that it took several long seconds before the first gasp from the crowd erupted.

"Mommy?" Emily broke the silence.

Zoë jumped as though struck. She snatched for the velvet, tearing it from Janel's hands, and threw it over the painting, her face white with mortification.

"What, darling? Don't you like it? You've always liked it in the past." Bridgette sneered at Zoë in disgust. "I apologize for dropping the G rating folks, but my God, this party is not a romper room!" Bridgette signaled the band to resume the music, and the guests tried their best to laugh in agreement. Grey for her part had enough. She grabbed Emily up off the ground, kicked her high heels into the corner by the band, and padded barefoot up the stairs to the nursery.

233

Emily asked her several awkward questions, which Grey managed to end by bathing her and dressing her for bed. By the second chapter of *Green Eggs and Ham*, Emily was out. Grey took the back stairs to her room, peeled off the dress, and lay down naked and exhausted on her bed. She decided she would unpile her hair in the morning.

In a matter of seconds, she felt her eyelids growing heavy and thick. The last thing she saw that registered was the clock showing ten thirty.

Grey started in the dark, fully awake. She looked around, alarmed, not understanding what had woken her. Perhaps it had been a dream. She tried to relax back into the soft bed, but she couldn't seem to.

There. A noise—muffled voices, a crash. That must have woken her. She sat up in bed. If she could hear them from her room, they must be yelling, fighting. Grey tried to settle back in. She remembered all too well the last time she had followed the sound of their fighting. The last thing she wanted to experience was a repeat.

She picked up her phone and glanced at the time. Three o'clock in the morning.

The voices continued. Another crash.

"Shit," she hissed, arguing furiously with herself. She didn't really want to sneak downstairs and expose herself to another one of their crazy fight-then-fuck episodes. And yet, with each muffled scream, she became more anxious. Surely, they would wake Emily. Shouldn't she perhaps ensure Emily's safety and well-being at the very least?

She groaned and struggled to her feet. "This is bullshit."

She didn't bother trying to be quiet. Neither of them would be listening for creaking floorboards or muffled footsteps. As soon as she opened her door, the yelling intensified. As she crept down the stairs, she could tell it was coming from beyond the entryway and down the hallway. They were in Zoë's studio. The muffled yells became distinguishable as Grey traversed the kitchen into the entryway.

"Don't stand there and tell me this is inappropriate!" Bridgette was screaming.

"You're telling me it's *'just a painting'* when we both know what it is!"

"Go ahead and say it!"

"You fucked her! She painted your goddamned cunt in such loving detail that you didn't even notice how fucked up your face is!"

"It's supposed to be an expression of my love for you! And what do you care if I fucked her? You're in love with the fucking nanny! How cliché is that? Jesus, Zoë!"

"An expression of love?" Zoë laughed, sounding maniacal. "It's the most self-indulgent nonsense I've ever seen, worse than the one you already have in your room! And the fact that you thought it was appropriate to reveal to a house full of guests, especially the guests we had tonight, proves that you're an egotistical freaking maniac! This isn't a gift, it's a threat and a punishment."

"And yet you didn't deny that *you're in love with the fucking nanny!"*

"Fuck you, Bridge. I'm so over you and your bullshit. You. Are. Fucking. Crazy!"

Another crash. "Jesus, not the laptop!"

Grey stood frozen in the entryway, not daring to move in the sudden silence.

"That's it," Zoë growled. "I'm done. Fucking *done!* I want a divorce. Immediately. I want you to *get the fuck out of my house!"*

It was Bridgette's turn to laugh. "So you can shack up with that *penniless teenage whore?* Good Lord, Zoë. I wasn't born yesterday. You're not going anywhere, and I'm certainly not leaving this house. You're not getting divorced."

"Oh, forgive me for possibly being too subtle. *I don't love you.* I haven't loved you since you went bipolar fucking apeshit crazy the last time and nearly killed us on the highway when you threatened to drive off the overpass. Fuck you, Bridge. I want out. *Out!* And she's not a teenager. And she's not a *whore,* unlike you and Janel. "

Bridgette screamed. "You'll never see that fucking child again! I have friends—the best attorneys in town. I will erase your beloved Emily from your life! I'm not going to let you ruin us for some little *whore.* You're sick. You could be her mother. It's not right. It should be illegal. I will not allow this *perversion* around my child!"

Crash. "Go ahead and break another one!" Zoë shouted. "I don't give a fuck! Go ahead, break it!" Crash. "Hey, look, there's another one you missed! Why don't you smash it over the busted fucking laptop?" Crash. "There ya go! Perfect. And while we are fucking in this, who the fuck is her father, goddamn it? Who the fuck is Emily's father, Bridgette? It was supposed to be my fucking brother, remember?"

"Don't you fucking dare! Don't you dare! What the hell do you care anyway? You have no fucking claim to her. *None.* You will never see her again, do you hear me?" Bridgette was growling her words, feral at this point.

"Fuck off. Fuck the hell off. Fuck Janel for all I care. We? There is no 'we.' And we will see who gets Emily, you fucking unmedicated nightmare. You freaking call me a cliché, but you are banging the fucking neighborhood artist. You say I'm sick? *Look at you!* Go to hell."

236

The sound that escaped Bridgette's lips was startling in its intensity. So primal and raw, it made the hair stand up on Grey's neck.

"You really think you can threaten me with that?" Silence. "Go ahead, Bridge. Attack me with it. You think you'll get to keep me away from Emily if you've attacked me with *a fucking hatchet?*" She laughed. "You are so goddamned crazy!"

Crash. The sound of wood splintering. Grey was torn between rushing into the room to protect Zoë and running to her room to barricade the door. She thought of Emily. Her gut wrenched at the thought of the tiny imp walking into this mess. She decided Zoë could handle herself.

Grey sprinted to Emily's room and threw open the door. Emily sat in her bed, a teddy bear hugged fiercely to her chest. She was trembling. Grey swooped her up into her arms and made for her own room as quickly as she could. She placed Emily on her bed and struggled with the desk, gradually maneuvering it in front of the door.

Sweating and nervous with fear, she held her phone. Should she call the police? How damaging would that be? She could see the story on TMZ. Zoë would not be pleased. This was clearly not the first time this sort of thing had happened. She trusted Zoë to handle her crazy wife and went with her gut, tucking herself and Emily into bed. She selected some music on her phone and played it for Emily, trying to cover the muffled noises from down below.

Trembling like the child she held, Grey was determined to stay vigilant, her eyes wide in the dark as she recited a story to soothe Emily. But emotional exhaustion eventually overwhelmed her.

Chapter Nineteen

Grey woke, the warm body next to her being unceremoniously plucked from her arms. She sat bolt upright. Eyes still fuzzy, she watched as Zoë deposited Emily in the arms of Clara, who quickly exited the room. Grey hadn't even realized Clara stayed the night. She was suddenly wide awake and very aware of being alone in her room with the woman she loved.

Zoë's expression told her everything.

"Zoë, no. Please don't." Grey moved toward the exhausted blonde.

"No. Grey, you have to go," Zoë said, refusing to meet Grey's eyes. "I need you to pack up your belongings and leave now." She hesitated just a beat and added, "Please."

"You don't mean that. You can't." Grey slid off the bed, taking a step closer. Zoë backed up a step.

It felt like a rock dropped into her stomach, like she couldn't catch a breath. Grey swallowed hard, willing her voice not to tremble. She knew Zoë had been through a lot, but this was ridiculous. They couldn't be apart. It all seemed so severe. "Please don't," she whispered. "Please. Let's just talk."

Grey reached out, a gesture of understanding. Her hand was met with a cold swat from her would-be lover. Zoë wouldn't even touch her. Her gaze never left the oriental rug that covered the floor of Grey's bedroom. Zoë wasn't even trying. What happened to "I want out!" and "I want a divorce!" in the few short hours she'd fitfully slumbered with Emily?

"Don't touch me." Zoë sighed and rubbed her eyes wearily. "I've been up all night. I just can't. This isn't negotiable. Pack your things. I've already made a reservation back to Chicago and called your family."

"Goddamn it, Zoë, you *are* my family! You and Emily. You are such a fucking coward. I swear to *God*." Grey lunged forward and caught her around the waist, grabbing that beautiful face with both hands and crushing their lips together.

The kiss began fierce but softened—a sad and gentle exploration, salty with tears, confirming what they both already knew. Zoë wrapped her fingers into Grey's hair, deepening the kiss, drawing out the inevitable.

Zoë broke their contact, ending the kiss. But before she pulled away, before Grey reluctantly allowed her to disentangle herself, Zoë whispered, almost as a surrender, "I love you, goddamn it. I love you. I love you. *I love you.*"

Then they stood apart.

"I don't understand." Grey sobbed.

"I know." Zoë sighed and finally met her eyes. Grey stared at her imploringly. Zoë took her hand. "Let me show you."

Grey allowed herself to be led out of the room and down the stairs, through the kitchen, and into the entryway. Zoë flipped on a light, and Grey gasped.

The wreckage was unreal. It looked like a ransacking. Or a terrible break-in by very destructive vandals. Bits and pieces of holiday decorations littered the floor and furniture. The Christmas tree, so lovingly decorated, lay on its side in sad disarray. The leather wingback chairs were slit, vases smashed, artwork slashed, frames busted throughout the room. Broken glass was everywhere. Furniture overturned. Books strewn about. Even a window had been knocked out.

The hatchet was lodged in the wall above the fireplace.

"Do you see?"

"Oh. My. God."

"And you want me to leave Emily with this? With *this?*" Zoë threw her arms out in exasperation. "I won't. So you have to leave."

Grey's shoulders slumped. "Zoë." The name came out like a sigh or a dream. "Fight for us."

"I have no ground to stand on." They stared at each other. "Bridgette was supposed to use my brother to get pregnant. She didn't. If we divorce—and hell, the laws are still so new for us—I have little faith I'll be able to take Emily. If she had used my brother like she was supposed to, maybe we could have had some claim on her. Even with the adoption papers, I'll never get full custody. Bridge will never relinquish her rights. I can't stand the thought of my poor baby girl alone with that crazy bitch during one of her episodes."

"I should have called the cops last night," Grey lamented. "Then there would be a police report to back up your assertions that she's certifiable."

Zoë laughed, the sound clipped and sharp. "We were both drunk as hell. Wouldn't have done any good. Can you imagine? My word against hers, two crazy drunk lesbian bitches and their drama. I see what you're trying to do there, but don't beat yourself up. You did exactly what I would have wanted you to do by protecting Emily."

"But they would have…"

Zoë held up a hand. "Don't you see? I fucked up. A long time ago. You can call it lunacy. You can say fate wronged me. I'm surprised you haven't straight up asked me what I ever saw in her or why I fell for her or why I didn't keep my head and not let myself get wrapped up in this situation." She groaned in frustration. "I have no right to get upset about anybody else's drama. I'm forced to admit that I'm no better. God, I wish I had dealt with it earlier. Dread this remorse shit—whenever you are tempted to fuck up big-time, Grey, because remorse is the poison of life."

"And yet there is a cure for that poison: repent."

"It's not enough."

"But…"

"No, Grey."

She had never heard a "no" that sounded so final. Grey opened her mouth to continue her objections, then shut it just as quickly. Anger simmered in her gut.

She was crushed under that "no," the word uttered through lips so kissable. That ruffled hair, even now, was so appealing. Grey's heart was so broken. She loved Emily, too, and it was of the utmost importance to keep her safe. Still, Grey couldn't comprehend that this woman would not stand up for herself. Or for the two of them.

"Antoine will help you pack," Zoë continued, her tone one of complete defeat, sad eyes again averted. "You have no idea, Grey, no idea at all what I'm giving up. But you have to understand. Please. No matter what the cost, I can't lose Emily. I just can't. And especially not to this."

"I have a pretty good idea exactly what you're giving up. It's the same thing you're forcing me to give up."

Zoë dropped Grey's hand, strode over to the fireplace, tore the hatchet from the wall in one vicious movement, and tossed it in the corner. Then, without a backward glance, she strode out of the room and was gone.

Grey trudged back up to her room. Antoine was there, all understanding and utter silence. Slowly, Grey went to

241

her closet to pull out the same rolling bag that had brought her to New Orleans. When she removed it, she noticed the carpet was loose. She dropped to her knees and felt around for her hidden bits of manuscript. The pages were gone. Bridgette had torn her room apart, and she hadn't even known.

"Fuck," she whispered, comprehension dawning. "After Sarah was here."

Bridgette watching them at the party. Her frozen look wasn't just for seeing them close. She'd read the pages. She knew about Jacqueline.

It was her fault. The whole fight started because of her. Grey felt sick and light-headed.

But then the simmering anger in her gut exploded. It wasn't her fault. None of this was her fault. Zoë was trapped in a loveless marriage with a certifiable crazy person. Sure, she herself could have left or kept her feelings in check a little more. But she never forced anybody to hatchet the shit out of everything in the house with a toddler present.

She stood slowly, took a deep breath, and stiffly turned to pack her things while Antoine tried to assist. She didn't take her time. She didn't double-check to make sure she had everything. She just grabbed whatever she saw through a blur of tears and crammed it unceremoniously into her bag.

"Your phone, ma'am," Antoine offered, handing her the device. "Your purse."

"Thank you," she answered automatically.

The rest of the next few hours slid by in a stream of unreality. Grey vaguely remembered Antoine packing her into the car with her belongings. He had her wait there for what seemed like forever, returning with a few additional items. He had combed the room thoroughly for her.

There was a ride to Louis Armstrong Airport at six o'clock in the morning. It was still dark.

"Your plane doesn't leave until ten. Just lay back and try to sleep, Grey," he had told her, his tone a lot softer than she remembered it ever being. He had called her by her first name.

It hadn't taken long to get through security. She had two or five cocktails at the bar before boarding the plane. First class. Of course, how else would you send your whore home to stepmama? She had no idea what she was going to do. The dread of getting off that plane wasn't quite as bad as it had been when she'd flown home after her father died, but it was close.

Most of all, her heart just hurt. She thought she had cried for Sarah, but now she realized that even then she had been mourning something that truly meant nothing. Now she was feeling real loss. A lover. A child. Her life. She was losing the life that she had earned, not the one her father handed her. Aching, she leaned her head against the window and whispered to her dead brother, "Please help me," and fitfully dozed.

Two and a half hours later, Grey disembarked the plane more than a little hungover and made her way through O'Hare security to the pickup and drop-off area. It suddenly occurred to her that Zoë had called her family and that she might round that corner and not see a familiar face.

She turned the corner anyway. She could call a cab. The day could not possibly get any worse than it already was, so it didn't matter anyway. Yet to her surprise, and through cloudy eyes, she identified not one but two familiar faces. Beth she could understand. But Jonathan had joined her.

After all that time, estranged, rarely keeping in touch, there he stood. As beautiful as ever. A tentative smile curling his lips. Bradley's fiancé. He'd kidded around that she should have been his sister all along, always following that up with "brat" or "trouble."

It didn't matter that he had avoided her because he couldn't bear to be around her without his lost love. She had needed him. And although he showed up well past due, he had finally shown up.

Grey dropped her bag and ran straight for him, throwing herself into his arms tearfully.

"Greyby, what's up, kiddo? What's wrong?" The now-bearded man stroked her back, just as Bradley used to. "We've got the company limo waiting, honey, we can get out of here. It's okay." He grinned. "I'll make it okay."

Grey smiled. Bradley used to swear to make things okay when she was a child with a skinned knee. She put her head on Jonathan's shoulder. He pulled her in tighter. "I'm sorry," he whispered. "I should have been there. I should have come down there to steal you back."

Grey cried around her smile. "I know you would have. Just don't go away now."

Beth joined them, wrapping her arms around their shoulders, squeezing tight. "Come on," she said. "Let's get out of here."

They slipped into the limo, and Beth took her hand.

Grey was home. At least, she was as home as she was likely to get in Chicago.

Jonathan and Beth shared a furtive glance. After a few silent seconds, he cleared his throat and said, "Grey honey, I didn't think you would take it this hard. I mean, you didn't really like her."

Beth stroked her hand. "Honey, I know this is hard, but ultimately, this will end the trust. This is what we want."

244

It finally dawned on Grey that the sympathy she was getting was completely unrelated to her lost love. These two had no idea what she was mourning. Something else was going on here.

"Wait. I thought you said it would take years to break the trust. What are you talking about? What's going on here?" Grey was almost afraid to ask.

"Grey, didn't you get my email?" Beth demanded. "My certified letter? Somebody signed for it. We thought…"

"Ever heard of a phone call?" Grey snapped, more out of fear than anger or impatience.

"You blocked my phone."

"And mine," Jonathan chimed in helpfully. "And Tawny's."

"No," she started, but trailed off. "Fuck it all," she whispered. "Damn it. When I was…" wasted, she thought, but said, "I didn't mean to. I deleted a lot of shit on my phone that day. I was mad and upset and had a few too many drinks."

"Well, you never check your voice mails, so the inbox is full." Beth sighed. "Look, you've always been terrible about checking messages or answering numbers you don't know. At any rate," she held up her hand to forestall any rebuttals, "we tried. I was about to go hunt you down when that woman called your stepmother."

"It doesn't matter. This is about Tawny, honey. She is ill, gravely ill. Grey," she took a deep breath, "she won't be around much longer."

Grey flinched. Tawny ill? She couldn't picture her father's young buxom trophy bride as sick. It seemed impossible.

"I don't understand," she said, sitting up straighter. "What could be wrong with Tawny? She's more than half plastic." It was funny how quickly she could slip back into sarcasm.

"Grey, this is serious. She had a new breast augmentation done, and it went septic. She's been on IV antibiotics for months. It's just a matter of time, then this will be your company. No trust. No controls. Over three hundred million dollars, all yours."

"Wait." She had to see for herself. "Reggie, take me to the condo, please."

Just like that, Grey realized that as imperfect and self-absorbed as her stepmother was, she didn't want her to die. She was, after all, the last connection to Grey's father. She was all the family Grey had left.

The long black limo turned on State and headed toward her home.

The elevator to the condo seemed to take forever. Grey stood silently, her rolling bag crammed with belongings packed too quickly and without much care. Reggie stood silently next to her, his uniform and chauffer's hat as spotless as she always remembered. When the doors slid open, nothing seemed amiss. The large professional flower arrangement that Tawny had brought in every two days stood, as usual, on the Grecian column in the entryway, a gift from her father, she remembered. She walked the few steps to her bedroom and dropped her bags.

"She's in her room," Reggie said, urging her along but making it clear that he would not be joining them.

With more than a little trepidation, Gray knocked softly on the door to her parents' room.

"Come in," a small, weak voice called from within.

Grey pushed the door aside and stopped. This wasn't the luxurious palace Tawny had so carefully choreographed when Grey was a pre-teen. It was a hospital room. The

246

large mahogany bed had been replaced by a hospital bed, complete with IV and heart monitor. And though the handmade silk curtains still adorned the windows, they seemed awkward and out of place amid the beeping medical equipment surrounding her stepmother.

Beyond the massive changes to her parents' room, it was Tawny who shocked Grey with devastating change. The stepmonster she had conjured so many years ago was no longer the strong, robust blond beauty who would stare her down when Grey issued a well-timed insult she presumed the woman wouldn't understand. She looked, well, *old*. Old and tired.

"Grey, is that you? Come over here where I can see you."

Grey approached the bed and took a seat in the chair opposite her. Instinctively, she intertwined her fingers into Tawny's own.

Tawny was at least thirty pounds lighter than when Grey had left for New Orleans. She couldn't help but think that it had only been a few months.

Had it really? So much had happened in such a short time. She'd lost her father and her heart. And now she'd lose a woman she'd despised for so many years and didn't know how to feel. She stared into those eyes—that overworked face, now sunken and nearly ruined—and didn't know what to say or do.

"You've been crying," Tawny said. "Goodness, your face is blotchy and puffy. I'll have the nurse bring you a cold cloth. You can't very well be seen like this."

Grey snorted, then a slow chuckle built around all the hurt. Even in this state, Tawny was still Tawny.

"I'm sure it's not for me," she said flatly, "though I'd be flattered if it was. Come now, what has happened that has you all worked up?"

"Nothing you'd understand or that I want to talk about." Grey paused awkwardly. "What happened to you? I had no idea. I would have called. I would have come back sooner."

"We sent word."

Silence.

"But you're here now." Tawny struggled to sit up. "Help me. I don't like looking at you from down below."

Grey fumbled with the controls until she figured out how to change the bed. She tucked and fluffed pillows around Tawny until she was satisfied.

"Where the hell is that nurse?" she said abruptly. "Reggie!" she hollered, though it was much weaker than Grey was accustomed to.

Reggie appeared in the doorway instantly. "Ma'am?"

"Find the goddamned nurse. I need my meds, I need my lunch, Grey needs her lunch, I want a cocktail, Grey needs a cocktail, I need my wheelchair, and I'm not staying in this fucking room all day long when my daughter is here."

"Yes, ma'am."

Grey started. Her daughter? Since when had the stepmonster ever claimed her as a daughter and not a nuisance?

"Tawny?"

Tawny leveled her gaze on her. "Oh, don't look so shocked. I'm dying, and I can be a sentimental fool lately." She smiled. "You know, things might have been so much better for both of us if you hadn't been such an entitled brat. It didn't help that your brother poisoned you against me from the start. He thought he was such a rebel. Didn't take to discipline at all. Your father spoiled you both rotten. So there's that."

Grey opened her mouth to furiously interject, but Tawny held up her hand.

"No, let me finish…" Reggie entered with cocktails in hand—two cosmopolitans. "Thank you, Reggie. At least you know how to do your job."

"Angela will be here shortly. She went out to retrieve some necessities for you."

"Fine, thank you." Tawny took the pink martini and sipped it gingerly. "Angela tells me not to have this," she winked at Grey conspiratorially, "but what is it going to do—kill me?" She cackled and took another sip.

Grey grinned sadly but took her cocktail and sipped it obediently. "It didn't help that you forced me to quit school and threw me out, penniless," she said flatly.

"That was your father's call, Grey. I would have just handed you the trust and said, 'To hell with it, let her throw it all away.' But your father was adamant in his discussions with me and in his will. You needed to learn the value of a dollar. Period."

Grey was stunned. "Dad did this?"

"Yes."

"But…"

"He was right to do it."

Grey shut her mouth. She remembered her musings with Sarah in New Orleans and guiltily recalled maxed-out "emergency" credit cards, trips to the Hamptons to house shop, thousands of dollars spent at American Outfitters for the needy blonde. How had she ever been so blind to her own problems?

"I don't know what to say, except you're right." Grey squeezed Tawny's hand.

"Dear God, I'm right and you're my daughter. We better get someone to roll me into the living room before lightning strikes us." Tawny laughed at her own joke, which led to a coughing fit so severe that Grey jumped up to find the nurse.

"Oh, stop it. I just have some fluid on my lungs, give me a second. I'll be fine."

Grey looked at her with concern, perhaps for the first time in their relationship.

"Now, my dear, let's chat. I understand that you'll be taking over a rather large aviation company soon. Grey, maybe I wronged you in your life more than once. But I tried to do what your father wanted. He wanted you to earn things. He knew that ultimately you would have everything given to you, and he wanted you to understand that wealth and power come with responsibility. And I wanted you not to fall for the first gold digger who batted his...or her... eyes at you. Ironic, right?"

Grey smiled. "You didn't wrong me. We're just different. I guess I thought that your problem with my lifestyle was just a design to separate me from Dad."

"Separate you from your father? That was impossible. He loved you more than anything in the world. Maybe that's where our problem started. I felt the same way about him."

Their eyes met momentarily, and Grey instantly felt regret for the years of anger and hatred she had aimed at this simple woman whose only two sins had been vanity and wanting her to share her father.

"Don't leave me, Grey. I know this sounds silly, but I don't want to die alone."

"I'm not going to leave again."

Just then, the door opened, and the nurse and Reggie returned to move Tawny and administer afternoon medications. Grey excused herself to unpack.

"Don't go too far, Grey," Tawny said. "We have a lot of work to do to get you ready to be CEO of a Fortune 500 company."

In her room, Grey turned on first her cellphone, then her laptop. She tried to resist the urge to comb her various social networks for any contact from Zoë, but she couldn't stop herself. She even googled Aimee R. Dupree for new posts. This was ludicrous, of course, as she had been gone only a few hours.

"I'm not doing this," she said out loud. Tawny needed her. Her father's company needed her. Fuck Zoë. If she didn't understand that what they had was rare and beautiful at her age, then fuck her. She could live her life out in a loveless marriage with a crazy cunt of a wife. And Emily would turn out either a bipolar bitch or a milquetoast author, living life in her fantasy-written world. As for Grey, she was going to become the hardest, richest, most successful CEO in Chicago. Fuck love.

It wasn't a switch she could just turn off. But she could reintroduce herself to something called reality. She snorted at herself in disgust. How long had she even known Zoë—a few months? How very stereotypical of her. They had kissed a couple of times. They had flirted. There had been inappropriate touching, a few gestures of longing. Grey decided part of her problem was that she'd crushed on Zoë for so long as a teenager it was simply inevitable that she would fall for her in person. And to see her idol trapped had simply stirred a sympathy within her. Right. She loved her because she felt sorry for her, and she had a cute kid.

It was lame and beneath her. She was a Chesterfield. She didn't need the alluring, sexy, haunted woman with so many complications in her life. She didn't need to fight through an age gap to find common ground somewhere in the middle of their decades apart.

Her chest hurt, and she laughed, running her fingers through her tangled hair, physically putting herself back together.

Relationships were hard enough. She didn't need this kind of baggage up front. She was about to rocket to the top of Chicago's social elite. She was young, single, and damned good-looking. She didn't need a child she hadn't chosen to have. She didn't need a moody author. She didn't need Rochester in her life. Not to mention that Bridgette would never relinquish her hold on Zoë so easily. She'd always somehow lurk in the shadows with her drama.

Grey told herself all this and tried her best to believe it. She tried to push Zoë and Emily out of her mind. She wasn't wanted anyway. She'd been thrown out like some piece of trash. She could be angry about that, and it was okay. Anger always did seem like a better choice when it came to giving in or charging out.

With great ceremony, Grey deleted every email and social media account Zoë knew. She blocked Zoë and Bridgette's numbers. She was going underground. She had to clean up her act anyway.

Chapter Twenty

The next few months passed quickly. Christmas, New Year's, Grey's birthday in January—all gone in rapid succession. There was only one day that caused a brief pang of regret. Grey would have liked to have spent Mardi Gras in New Orleans. But such is life.

Tawny seemed to get marginally better with Grey in the house. They spent quiet evenings watching television and talking trash about the women who had replaced Tawny in the Chicago social scene. No one had come to visit her, and Tawny refused to leave. Grey, for her part, spent hours a day buried in briefings on the inner workings of her father's company. Chesterfield Aeronautics was currently negotiating union contracts, Jonathan had told her. She would have the final call on approval.

This ordeal had been overwhelming at first, but even the board members were surprised at how quickly Grey picked up on the business, despite their initial objections and severe reluctance to have this "much too young" future CEO take over.

"Just like your dad," they finally admitted. She'd heard that at least a dozen times over the past week. Every single time, the statement made her smile.

It was a fine, crisp afternoon toward the end of March, the Friday before Grey would be officially tapped to head the company, and Grey found herself wishing, as strange as it seemed to her now, for Tawny to attend the event.

"Damn it, Tawny, you have to go," she said more firmly than intended. "Dad would want you to be there." She softened her voice just a little, her sparkling eyes giving her away as she teasingly begged. "Shit, I want you there. Are you happy? I said it. Come on... Please, please, pretty please?"

"Greyson, stop it. I'm not going. You must remember that I'm quite ill."

"Bullshit. You drink four cosmos a night. You can haul your skinny ass to the office one time." Grey sat next to her and took her small hand.

Tawny grew quiet and peered at Grey through heavy-lidded eyes. "I'm sure you will think this is vain, but I'm not letting those bitches who have replaced me see me looking like this." Tawny's left hand pulled the turban she had worn consistently from her head.

Grey gaped at the nearly bald head, eyeing the few patches of graying hair wearily. "Wow." Grey knew it wasn't even close to an acceptable response. She watched Tawny closely, and for the first time in her life, she saw a tear escape the older woman's eye.

"Oh, Grey," she cried in earnest. "I used to be the queen! You can't expect me to go out like this or with that damn turban. So, no, I'm sorry. Just *no*! Now go away, I'm tired." She dismissed her in a gesture so reminiscent of their earlier years that Grey backed out of the room without objection.

Grey dragged her feet down the hallway and into her own room, a small shudder—certainly not of disgust but rather pity—running down the length of her spine. She stepped in front of her dresser and stared into the mirror positioned there. Grey ran her hands through her long,

254

thick black hair. It had grown well past the middle of her back now, looking unruly and wild. Tawny had so far ignored it only because she kept it well hidden in braids or buns.

Grey hadn't had the energy or desire to cut it since before she left for New Orleans. She knew the long hair was one of her best features, even uncared for as of late. And yet... A plan was already forming in her mind. She picked up the house phone.

"Reggie, it's Grey. Go to Salon Nuvo and pick up Tony. Tell him to come here immediately. No is not an acceptable answer. He will be paid whatever is necessary. Please do it now."

It took two hours, but Reggie did his thing and convinced Tawny's hairdresser, Tony, of the importance of his requested presence in the Chesterfield home. Grey was seated in front of her bathroom vanity with Tony, who poised behind her with a pair of shears.

"Honey, are you sure?" he asked, holding up a chunk of hair over twelve inches long.

"Yep, can't be a lesbian CEO with girly hair, Tony. Do it."

And with that, Tony began to cut. It was terrifying and freeing. Grey clamped her eyes shut and hoped for the best. It was only hair, after all. The long black hair she still associated with Jacqueline and Rochester. Fuck it. Nobody was going to appreciate her hair more than the recipient.

When he was finished, Tony looked at Grey with a glorious smile. "Honey, if I do say so myself, you are fucking gorgeous." He stepped out of the way and let Grey see herself in the mirror. She was pleasantly shocked. She'd expected a buzz cut or an Annie Lennox at best.

"Did you take enough hair?" She touched the freshly cut ends.

"Plenty. She's going to be fabulous. I don't know if I can have it by tomorrow, though."

"You will. I'll give you a thousand-dollar tip if you have it for me at ten in the morning," Grey said, so sure of herself. It was amazing how quickly she fell back into issuing orders. But the amounts meant something now. A thousand dollars was about three weeks of wages in terms of her recent employment. Tony could make that much in a week easily. But she felt confident he would jump on it.

"Then at ten you shall have it," Tony smiled, exiting through the bathroom door.

Grey showered and went to bed, smiling to herself at how light she felt. The next day was going to be trying. It would be rewarding, too, but definitely challenging.

Early the next morning, Grey didn't bother to fix her hair, merely brushing the curly mess. She applied makeup sloppily, intentionally doing a poor job, not that she had ever been that great with makeup to begin with.

Keeping with this trend, she pulled out the ugliest suit she owned—bright lemon yellow. It was two sizes too big, an inadvertent disaster purchased by Jonathan on her eighteenth birthday. He hadn't seen her in a while and had clearly assumed she'd grown more. And bright colors had been a thing that year. She hadn't been able to bring herself to tell him just how hideous it was.

Dressed as such, Grey marched into Tawny's room, Tony trailing behind her trying to hide a grin, and opened the curtains around her stepmother's bed.

"I need your opinion," she snapped. "What do you think? Your faithful stylist and I are trying to get me ready for Monday."

Tawny pulled her sleep mask off weakly.

"Dear God, you are kidding me, right?" She groaned. "What do I think? I think you look like an enormous bag of lemons. And your hair and makeup?" She snorted indignantly. "Grey, what did you do to your gorgeous hair? Oh, my Lord, can't you talk to me before you make bad decisions? I mean, you might as well wear Doc Martens and a wallet chain."

Grey could no longer contain herself. Grinning, she pointed at Tony. "This is what I did to my hair, old woman." He had been hiding the black wig behind his back, nearly bouncing with eagerness to show off his work. Now he held the wig out to her—styled in short, cascading curls, soft and gentle, perfect for framing an emaciated face. With great reverence, he removed Tawny's turban and placed the wig on her head, adjusting it just so.

She gaped at Grey as Tony adjusted the wig. Tawny could barely keep tears from spilling over while he worked his magic on her face, adding a ton of very tasteful makeup. He chided her gently when he had to touch up her soft eyeliner.

Tawny looked like an older, thinner version of Grey—their eyes sparkling for different reasons, their cheekbones and lips very distinct, but their expressions and hair made them look related. Tawny was beautiful and sick. But still stunning.

Grey took the handheld mirror to Tawny and lay in the bed next to her. They both looked at their images together. In a gesture of affection, something Grey never dreamed she would share with Tawny, her stepmother leaned her head on Grey's shoulder.

"I look really quite beautiful as a brunette, don't you think?"

Grey smiled. "Yes, I think you do. Very beautiful."

"Thank you," Tawny whispered under her breath.

Then, as abruptly as ever, the bitch was back.

"Tony, level Grey's hair out in the back and give her shorter bangs," she barked. "This multilevel cut is bullshit. Give me Catherine Zeta-Jones in *Chicago*. I want black eyeliner with lavender base to bring out her green eyes. Now. And get Angela in here. I need to be dressed. My daughter is not taking the chair of Chesterfield Aeronautics in a lemon sack. Bring the limo around and call Neiman's. We're going to need all the stylists and the private room. And some Cristal, don't you think, Grey?"

"I can't possibly shop without champagne." Grey grinned.

"That's my girl." Tawny was already leaning to be helped out of bed.

Her attendants jumped into place, including Grey, struggling and succeeding to get her into her wheelchair. They retrieved the suit she demanded and slowly helped her into it.

"Fabulous," she said upon inspection in the mirror. "Not that I can say the same for you, darling. But you will be by the time we're finished."

Grey snorted in acknowledgment. "Just what I've always wanted."

"Sarcasm doesn't suit you. Has anyone ever told you that? I thought I had, but just in case, *cut the sarcasm, Greyson.*"

Grey cleared her throat. "I wasn't being sarcastic. I've always wanted to go shopping with you. No matter our differences, I knew you had good taste in clothing and accessories. So this should be fun, right?"

Tawny stared at her, caught off guard, then closed her mouth and nodded. "It's long overdue." Then she snapped her fingers. "Come on, Tony, Reggie! We don't have all day!"

258

"Yes, we do," Grey murmured. "Take your time."

Again, Tawny nodded. "Just this once."

Tony led Grey into the other room to deliver the "appropriate" haircut, muttering under his breath about demanding women, while Reggie prepped Tawny for the outing. Forty-five minutes later, they were all in the limo, headed off to Neiman's, where surely the crew was eagerly awaiting them.

They arrived at the private entrance where a gentleman named Gustav fawned and flustered over Tawny for the appropriate time as the ladies and their entourage were escorted to the private fitting rooms. Three, not one, bottles of chilled Cristal awaited them. When Tawny was finally enthroned in a large wingback chair, champagne in hand, the real show began.

Three stylists stood in matching black turtlenecks in front of the regal older woman.

"All right, listen up. We are looking for size four lesbian chic, boys. All couture designs, don't bring me any of that off-the-rack shit. I want to see the entire Brooks Brothers for women line. Fitted suits. Blues and jewel tones. I want Valentino booties and kitten heels only. My gay daughter does not wear hooker shoes. Gustav, a Chanel bag and briefcase, the matching set, please. One in black and one in red. Now go."

Lesbian chic? Grey snorted.

She was amazed at the speed and efficiency of the entire process. Over the next six hours, she was stripped, dressed in appropriate undergarments, and redressed in the most beautiful fitted suits and day wear she had ever seen. Black on black Brooks Brothers ladies cut suits, skinny-legged pants and cinched waist jackets. Black Cuban-heeled boots interchanged with short kitten-heeled Steve

Madden dress pumps. The jewelry was elegant, not overpowering. And none of this was overtly feminine. Tawny had managed to understand Grey's "style" better than she had herself.

Twenty thousand dollars and two bottles of champagne later, Grey found herself willingly sitting at the Chanel makeup counter as a very patient young woman explained how to apply makeup "appropriately" as per Tawny's direction. When she was done, Grey stood to face her stepmother.

Black fitted suit, black Valentino heels, and a red Chanel bag and briefcase. Her flapper hairdo offsetting her lavender eyeliner. She had to admit, she looked sophisticated and beautiful.

"Well?" Grey asked, her eyes sparkling.

"Perfect. Grey, you look beautiful and perfect." Tawny was beaming at her. "Let those bitches call my daughter names now. You are going to run this town."

Grey leaned down and kissed her cheek. "Yeah, your daughter is going to run this town."

A touch surprised, Grey realized that she absolutely believed it was true. If she wanted, if she applied herself, she could run this town. She had the resources. She had the right advisers. She had the right guts.

Nothing else needed to be said.

Chapter Twenty-one

Monday morning was crisp and bright. A perfect spring day in the Windy City. The home was abuzz with eager anticipation—they all knew this was Grey's big day. The board was meeting at nine o'clock sharp for the formality of swearing Grey in as Chesterfield Aeronautics' new CEO. Press would arrive soon, they knew, and a long day awaited the young Chesterfield, who sat patiently in her bathroom, allowing Tony to apply her makeup and style her hair.

She would have preferred a mimosa to the cup of coffee she held. Nerves were finally creeping up on her. Jonathan stood in the bathroom's entryway in his most dashing Armani suit, reviewing yet again her acceptance speech, giving pointers on tone and inflection. Thank goodness he had been so well-groomed by her father, she thought, since she hadn't been. Jonathan was going to make a great mentor over the next several years while she really learned the ropes. Sure, she'd call the shots. But she'd pretty much confer with Jonathan about everything and didn't plan to go against his advice unless absolutely necessary.

She eyed him in the mirror, watching him as he paused, his brows furrowed in concentration. "Perhaps we should change this part. The transition needs some work."

Their eyes met in the mirror, and he poked his tongue out at her. Grey grinned nervously.

She sighed and took another sip of coffee. Tony plucked the mug from her hand. "You'll mess up your lipstick, honey."

Grey resisted the urge to roll her eyes, a habit she was determined to break. There was something about eye-rolling that conjured up thoughts of insolent teenagers instead of CEOs.

It was eight o'clock. Tawny was parked in the kitchen, waiting patiently in her wheelchair. Grey emerged from the bathroom and took the arched eyebrow and smug smile as a good sign.

"That'll do," Tawny said. "Let's roll, Reggie."

Grey's palms were sweating slightly. She plucked a tissue from the convenient box rather than wipe her hands on her thousand-dollar suit. She took a deep breath and let it out slowly. Traffic was a bitch on Monday mornings, but they had plenty of time and not far to travel.

"Chin up, shoulders straight," Tawny barked, making her jump. "You are your father, Grey. You have his looks and his brains. You just haven't applied either to the most capacity yet. It'll come with ease once you practice. Today, I want you to remember where you just came from."

"Excuse me?"

"Look them in the eye and laugh. Think to yourself, 'That's right. I'm in charge of this whole shebang, and three months ago, I was a fucking nanny for a lunatic woman in New Orleans.' You tell yourself, 'I was cleaning up after a toddler, and now, you get to take my word on multimillion-dollar decisions.' You laugh at that. You take it and run with it. You remember who your father was and what he accomplished and that every last shithead on that board owes your father all they're worth. You smile at them like *you know* they only have that yacht because of your family, and you could crush them just the same."

Grey chuckled.

"That's what I do. I look at those bitches like, 'I know you think I'm a gold digger and don't deserve all of this, but it's mine, and you can't have it, so suck it.'" She touched her beautiful black wig, smoothing down the edges. "I think, 'How many of you have a daughter who would sacrifice such beautiful hair for this old wreck of a stepmother? None of you.'"

She took Grey's hand. "Oh, don't look at me all wide-eyed and sentimental. Toughen up, girl. You kill it in there today."

"Yes, ma'am," Grey murmured and squeezed the frail hand she held.

Jonathan watched them, a bemused and wistful expression twisting the corners of his lips. Grey could only imagine what he must be thinking—likely that it should be Bradley standing there in the Brooks Brothers suit, about to be swarmed by media. He would be right. It should have been Bradley. But it wasn't. Perhaps that was why Jonathan's bemused smile had a twist of wistfulness to it.

"Your brother would have been proud," he murmured.

"My brother would have been in my spot," Grey replied.

"It should have been Bradley," Tawny chimed in. "He would have done well. But you'll do better. So never mind this nonsense about what could have or should have been. This is your show now, sweetheart." The three passengers smiled at one another.

A few reporters were already hanging around the entrance to Chesterfield Aeronautics. They lingered on the stairs but darted forward, cameras ready, when the limo pulled up to the curb. Reggie strode around to curbside to open the door for them, first helping out Tawny, delivering her gingerly into her wheelchair, before extending a hand for Grey.

She took a long moment, staring at that hand. Several images flashed before her in rapid succession—her father's shining million-watt smile, the eager glint in Sarah's eye when she realized Zoë and Bridgette had money, Bridgette's sneer when she mentioned Grey's "unfortunate situation."

So much for those English literature studies not being worth a damn in this industry. So much for not having a skill set to be able to support herself. As Jonathan had explained, she merely had to be an ambassador of the brand. She had to be a diplomat. She was a pretty face to head the image of the company with a sharp head on her shoulders to back up her decisions. She had to protect her employees and please stakeholders.

Grey was young. Beautiful. Powerful. Rich. Smart—and very clever.

She gripped the offered hand and gracefully stepped out into the morning sun—exhaling the long breath she'd been holding, watching it escape her lips in a puff against the bitter cold Chicago winter air. She squared her shoulders, a carbon copy of her father's smile comfortably in place. She graced the reporters with that smile only briefly before turning toward the stairs and comfortably marching forward to claim her rightful inheritance.

I am a Chesterfield, she thought.

The entire process with its pomp and ceremony had taken very little time but was followed by hours of photos and interviews. Per Jonathan's directions, Grey took her time with each person she met. "Make them feel like they are the most important person in the room. Never check your phone. Never ask for the time. We will move you along as necessary. As far as you are concerned, you have all the time in the world. Listen more than you talk. Learn."

It was no wonder then that Grey hadn't noticed when Tawny had motioned for Reggie to take her home. She must have been exhausted. Grey was relieved and excited to finally be heading home as the sky darkened. She so wanted to tell Tawny about her day and rode up the elevator lost in her own thoughts. The ambulance out front had escaped her notice.

When she got to the condo, she burst into Tawny's room shouting a greeting. But Tawny wasn't there. Angela was waiting for her. The long downward look told her that fate had once again robbed her of an attachment.

"No," Grey nearly growled. "No, ma'am. This is not happening." She cast her gaze around the room— everything still seemed in place, just as they had left it in the morning. She grabbed Reggie, who had delivered her home from the office and stood to her back. "Reggie, no. It's not right. This *isn't fair*!" she shouted, struggling against his arms as he stepped forward and tried to hold her.

"Ms. Grey! I'm sorry, Ms. Grey! She just went to sleep and didn't wake up."

"There was no pain, ma'am." Angela nodded her assent.

Mascara was bleeding down Grey's face, dripping in black rivulets onto Reggie's suit. "I don't care!" Grey continued to shout. "What the hell is going on in my life? Can I not have one person?" Then a moment of panic. "Where is Jonathan?"

"I'm right here," he said. His arms clamped down around her waist as Grey collapsed. Her body simply slid out from under her, piling in a pathetic heap on Tawny's rug, from which she couldn't seem to move.

At some point, Beth appeared. She, Jonathan, and Reggie managed to maneuver Grey into her room. When she was scrubbed and in bed, they excused themselves to various guest rooms.

There were so many arrangements they would have to make the next day. Beth had assured her she would handle everything.

"There is nothing to handle," Grey had finally said, the first sentence in what felt like hours. "She wanted to be cremated and left with Dad. Just do it the way she wanted it, Beth. And make sure the wig goes with her. She was pretty adamant about that."

Beth had squeezed her shoulders and had reluctantly left.

Miserable didn't begin to describe the twisting of her guts. Grey felt so alone. If something happened to Beth or Jonathan, it would be the end of her. Her voice felt hoarse from shouting and crying. Her head throbbed with a dull ache behind her eyes. She felt such deep remorse for the relationship she could have had with her stepmother and which had lasted such a short time. Her life could have been very different. The past six months might never have happened the way they did.

Grey rolled over and glared at the Aimee R. Dupree novels on her bookshelf.

Loss.

Was all life loss? Tawny had been indignant on her behalf over what happened in New Orleans. "Her loss," she'd snorted, patting Grey's hand awkwardly. "Don't you give that woman a second thought."

Yet Grey did now, alone in the room with her regrets and her memories. She remembered Thanksgiving, when

Zoë had brought her a bottle of wine and a stuffed toy to comfort her. She remembered the playful teasing to lighten the mood. At least Zoë had sort of tried.

Grey didn't want to think about the upcoming funeral. Another fucking funeral, burying another parent.

She stared at the books. If she stared hard enough, she could almost hear jazz playing down the hallway. Etta James, *Fool That I Am*. She could almost smell the light roast of American Spirit cigarettes and taste the Rémy Martin cognac. She could taste tears on her lips, hear the desperately whispered "I love you."

"No," she halfheartedly resisted in the dark. But she knew her resistance was weak.

Three months of cold turkey, and she was breaking down. Love was not a light switch. She hadn't been able to turn it off. She had therefore buried it deep and set it aside, but it was surfacing in her vulnerable state of shock and disbelief.

Grey dragged herself out of bed and picked up her laptop. A rapid succession of keystrokes unlocked her temporarily disabled Yahoo account.

And there it was. The timing of it—at the top of a list of over a thousand junk messages, a single email caught her eye: ARDupree@ARDupree.net, no subject, having been delivered within the last ten minutes.

A single tear spilled down Grey's cheek. After all this time, all these months of no contact, she wondered what the message contained.

"I probably left something at the house," she mused, still unwilling to acknowledge her rapidly beating heart.

A mouse, a cursor, and a click later, she stopped breathing altogether. There was no message, just an attachment titled "Epilogue."

It was the final chapter.

267

The rush that nearly overwhelmed her was sickening in its intensity. The temptation to immediately open the attachment and disappear in the love affair between Alicia and Jacqueline pulled at her insides so hard it was painful.

Grey resisted with all that she had.

This was likely to be her last correspondence from the love of her life. She would wait until after the funeral, after she had done right by Tawny. Then she would open the chapter as though it were a gift and read it slowly and methodically, the only pain would be the pain between Grey and Zoë.

Grey snapped her laptop shut and stared at the ceiling in the dark until sleep overwhelmed her.

Five days and a whirlwind of activity later, Grey walked sedately into her bedroom, clad in the beautiful black Chanel overcoat Tawny had bought her. Her stepmother was now safely ensconced in the urn with her father. She peeled off her adult clothes and slipped into pink penguin pajama pants and a Wellesley sweatshirt. A glass of Malbec secured on her bedside table, Grey reverently opened the file she had stored on her computer. She didn't dare to hope or to build up expectations.

Epilogue

The last five days of Jacqueline's life were not really life at all. I could not supply her with enough vampire blood to dull the sensation of the cancer that now ravaged her beautiful body. She was too weak to change. It was just a matter of time. Strangely, as I watched my beloved labor to breathe each night, the time seemed to pass much too slowly and much too quickly, as well. And though I knew my innate ability to kill quickly could have alleviated her suffering, I did not have the strength to end her life, to let go of her. I found I did not want to surrender my humanity.

Three nights before her death, we lay in bed together laughing, simply holding each other. We shared the memories we had built together over the last months. We talked about the adventures we might have had, if there were more time. It was both terrible and wonderful.

On this night in particular, Jacqueline lay her head on my stomach and looked up at me from brilliant green eyes.

"I want to talk to you about something. But I want you to promise not to interrupt."

"Me interrupt?" I joked. "Preposterous."

Jacqueline smiled at me. "Stop, Alicia, please. I don't have the strength to do this and trade barbs with you." She took a difficult breath. The pain showed like fire on her forehead.

"Speak," I said, stroking her hair behind her ears.

"When I die, you have to promise that you will let me go. I know you. So noble, yet so unaccustomed to feeling loss. I want you to promise me that you will live another fifty years on this earth without me." She was searching my eyes.

"Don't be ridiculous. I'm immortal. Of course I will." I realized I was avoiding the promise. My intent was to not spend a second on this earth without her, watching my humanity such as it was slip away.

"Alicia," she said, grabbing my gaze with hers. "Here." From behind her back, Jacqueline pulled a rope of gold with a perfectly cut emerald hanging as a pendant. It was an emerald I had purchased for her in a ring on Royal Street at an antique shop. Our wedding ring, I called it. A pledge of my undying love for her.

"That's your ring, pet. What have you done?" I moved to put the emerald around her neck, but she stopped me.

269

"No, no. You wear it. Wear it and remember me. Remember us." She struggled to sit up, to hold my gaze with hers and her hands on my cheeks so I couldn't look away. "Alicia, if I was out there this whole time, and this, whatever we have, gave you back emotion, doesn't it make sense that there's another? I mean, that another woman can make you feel and love and live again?"

"Never," I hissed vehemently.

"Stop it. Stop being selfish. I'm giving my life for you. You owe me fifty years. And when you find her, and you will find her, please give her this and tell her about me. Please."

She could barely speak now, her breath was so hard.

"Tell her how much I loved you. Tell her to try, even just try to love you as much."

"Jacqueline," I whispered, kissing her lips for what would be the last time. "I promise."

And with that, she seemed to relax and sleep. She would not wake again.

Days blurred with my sorrow. I kept her as best I could. I hardly slept, hoping she would awaken so I could tell her I could not keep my promise. That it was all impossible. But she didn't. Human frailty, they called it.

She died as the sun rose on the third day from my promise. My love, my life, my everything took one long breath, and even as I stood there, I heard her say my name. Then there was nothing.

As quickly as she passed, my emotions flooded me, and my mind was overcome by a tidal wave of despair. I reached my hand to my face and felt tears, actual human tears streaking down. I took her in my arms, the emerald in my right hand clutched tight, and mounted the elevator to the door to the warehouse.

270

"Oh, Jacqueline, forgive me," I pleaded to her now cooling corpse. "Forgive me, it's too long."

I placed my love's body by the front door and put my hand on the iron face that led to imminent death. It felt warm. Warm and inviting, the Southern sun had already crested in the morning sky. It was a sun I had not seen for centuries. Surely, I would see it that day, then be consumed in fire with my Jacqueline in my arms.

As I reached down to pick her up, the emerald dropped from my hand and onto her heart, and I heard myself promise fifty years. Was there someone else like her? Was I so deserving of happiness with all my sins that this God that humans worshipped would gift me with this again? I could see no way to believe it. And yet...

I reached for the handle again and felt the warmth. I turned it gently, then I kissed her.

The End

"No!" Grey shouted and dropped her laptop on the bed. "No, goddamn it! What the fuck kind of ending is that?"

Her voice was raw with emotion, and she sounded gruff even to herself. Jonathan burst into the room, clearly alarmed by her shouting. He had not wanted to leave her completely alone, had volunteered to keep her company. Clearly, he was under the impression that she was losing it.

He sank to his knees at her bedside and clasped her hand in his.

Grey sniffled and didn't resist the tears. She was dead, or at least Jacqueline was. Zoë had killed her. She had known it was coming, and it didn't change how it made her feel—lost and empty and utterly alone.

"I know, I know," Jonathan soothed, wrapping his arms around her, stroking her back. But he didn't know.

271

"I have to go to New Orleans. Right now."

There was a very lengthy pause.

"Grey, we have meetings tomorrow. You have obligations. What on earth could possibly be so important that you have to drop everything and run off to New Orleans? Help me understand."

"Fuck meetings. They can give us a reprieve because Tawny is fucking dead. If they don't understand, then they can go fuck themselves." She sobbed. "She killed me, and she's going to kill herself. I have to know that she's okay."

"What are you talking about?"

So she told him. Everything. She implored him with big, round, sad eyes. Desperate eyes. She grabbed his shirt and tugged him within an inch of her face. "We are going. I can't do this alone."

He swallowed hard, struggling against responsibility. He stared at her.

"Jonathan, I feel about her the way you felt about Bradley."

His eyes widened, and he swallowed hard. He cleared his throat. "I'll call to tell them to get the jet ready. We can reschedule our meetings."

Grey nodded, relieved. "Thank you."

"Anything you need, Grey." He hesitated for just a moment. "This woman had better live up to my standards for you."

She snorted and hopped off the bed, already rifling in her closet for the appropriate outfit. Jonathan was on his cell, barking orders. He hung up and dialed another number.

"Grey and I have to jet to New Orleans." A pause. "Yes, it's urgent. A family emergency." Another pause. "Fine. We both owe you. We'll be back before Thursday." He eyed Grey, and she nodded her agreement. "Definitely

Thursday. Call me if you need anything, we can work this remotely." A pause. "Yes, of course. I understand. You got it. Goodbye."

"It's done," he said. "We can take off in forty-five minutes." He opened the door to her bedroom. "Reggie!" he hollered in an act so reminiscent of Tawny, it forced a smile to Grey's lips. Poor Reggie. It was getting late. She was about to suggest they catch a cab when Reggie came tromping down the hallway.

"Now that's dedication," she said, laughing.

"Yes," Jonathan said, all business. "Let's roll."

Chapter Twenty-two

An hour later, Grey and Jonathan were in the air, and her skin was abuzz with those same ants she felt before leaving New Orleans the last time. She had quickly called Antoine on his private cellphone and left a message that she was coming. She hadn't had time to wait for a response, but she could only hope that he would arrange for Zoë to meet her alone.

While the G6 hummed, Grey tried to think of what she would say. The cotton candy clouds, highlighted in bright pink and orange dusk, offered much beauty but little advice. Such a beautiful sky, and she couldn't appreciate it for all the nerves. She fidgeted constantly, picking at her cuticles, running her hands over her pants to smooth imaginary wrinkles.

How would she explain her sudden reappearance? What would she say to that horrible redhead? Fuck Bridgette. She wasn't a penniless teenage whore. She was the master of a fortune that exceeded even the great Aimee R. Dupree's. If there was one thing that crazy bitch understood, it was power.

"Well, you are about to get a fucking mouthful of that," she muttered, more than a little self-satisfied at the prospect of finally standing toe-to-toe with that woman, crazy and all.

As the plane descended into New Orleans, Grey went to the lavatory and checked herself. Even as unflattering as fluorescent lighting typically was, she could see the transformation for what it was. There was a new edge to her smile or smirk or even an attempted apathetic thin-lipped pursing. It was there in the eyes—knowledge and confidence. She was far from the doe-eyed, love-stricken nanny who had left New Orleans months before. Her hair, her wardrobe, her expression showed a level of sophistication that would be almost out of place in the Deep South.

Grey had remembered who she was. And she had come into her own. She was her father and her stepmother, her brother, her godmother, and herself. She had been humbled, and she was wiser for it.

"Bridgette, you have laughed at me for the last time," she muttered at her reflection. She would not back down. Where she had not been willing to wage war with the crazy before, she was determined now to end it. Driven. She was steeling herself for a confrontation she would have previously avoided at all cost.

"Grey! Grey! Grey!" A voice, underlying the timbre of the plane's engines, suddenly shattered her concentration. She knew that voice and the intimacy behind it. That voice pulled at places deep inside her and twisted her stomach. "Where are you, Grey? I need you, Grey. Grey!" It thrummed. The color drained from her face as she cocked her head to the side and listened to the echo of Zoë's voice.

"I'm coming," Grey whispered. "Wait for me." She listened a moment more, then reluctantly returned to her seat, her heart filling with dread and sickening anticipation.

She watched the familiar landscape loom into view. The twisting of her insides loosened momentarily as she watched the sparkling of the Crescent City grow larger with their descent. City lights glittered against the backdrop of pink dusk along the edge of Lake Pontchartrain. She imagined she could smell creole spices on the air. Honeysuckle riding a humid breeze. Crawdaddies boiling at the French Market. Tequila dressed with salt and lime.

Flying into New Orleans, she realized, felt more like coming home than Chicago did.

"Wait for me," she whispered again and with more urgency.

"We're nearly there," Jonathan interrupted her thoughts, startling her.

Grey dragged her gaze from the window and met his. There was something grim about the set of his mouth and jaw. Something had happened. Work, perhaps, or he was dreading their arrival on her behalf. She almost asked, "What?" then stopped herself.

Once they landed, Grey was relieved to find Antoine waiting for her with Zoë's car. She raced up to the big man and threw her arms around him, kissing his cheek. To her surprise, he picked her up and hugged her. He then opened the door to the car beckoning her inside.

"Well, look at Grey with her private jet!" He smiled.

"You don't have to drive us, Antoine. We have a limo, and we brought Reggie to drive." The two men nodded formally to each other.

"Why didn't she come?" she asked, staring into his dark brown eyes. "I thought if she knew I was coming, she would come."

"Grey, you need to ride with me. We need to talk. So many things have happened." Antoine looked serious, which frightened Grey a bit. She had never seen him look so nervous.

Jonathan nodded at her. He and Reggie would follow in an hour or so. He said he would text her. Grey couldn't shake the feeling that everyone knew something she didn't know. Her mind flashed to Jonathan furiously Googling on the plane and his grim expression.

"What's going on?" she demanded, but she got into the car. Instantly, Grey's mind was flooded with memories of their night together, of meeting the real Alicia at The Over Under Bar. She swallowed a bit of guilt with that.

"Grey, there are some things you need to know. A lot has happened since you left," Antoine said. Then, over the glass divider between the seats, he told Grey about the weeks after her departure from New Orleans.

"Zoë never got over you leaving. Things were never right. And Ms. Bridgette, she just got worse and worse. It was crazy. By the third week, she wasn't making sense. There were fights. Really, really violent fights. Zoë tried to protect Emily. But it was crazy, Grey. Just crazy."

"Oh, my God, Antoine," Grey said. She had no idea.

"We had the police out three times. Three times, she tried to attack Zoë with that hatchet. And finally, the state hospital was going to take her and try to force her back on her meds. And that was the night it happened."

Antoine finished this last sentence as the large black SUV rounded the corner to the mansion. But there was no mansion.

Grey stifled a shriek but just barely. The beautiful revival mansion she had called home for those few months was ruined—burned to the ground, the frame barely recognizable, caution tape providing a flimsy barrier. The gardens were gone, the trees blackened by what appeared to have been a raging fire. Her fingers were clamped hard over her mouth. She was shaking. She couldn't speak as Antoine pulled into the driveway.

The only structure that stood was the small garden cottage. The separate apartment bore some signs of damage, but it was at least intact.

"Antoine?" Grey finally managed in a weak voice, her face pale with nausea.

"It's all gone. She set the place on fire. She had threatened it many times, but none of us believed it would actually happen."

She wasn't ready to face the crazy bitch who burned down that beautiful house and put her love and child in danger. Surely, she would kill her, so strong was her sudden fury. She would not hide in her room. She would straight up punch that bitch out and be done with it.

"Zoë?" Grey whispered, desperate. "Emily?"

"The whole house was on fire. Zoë had gotten Emily out. She went back in after Bridgette. Zoë was already hurt, and we saw Bridgette framed in the grand staircase." He paused and lowered his eyes. "It collapsed. I've heard a lot in my time, but I have never heard a scream like the one that came from Zoë that night. She tried to go in after her. I was barely able to get Zoë out. Bridgette didn't make it."

Bridgette didn't make it. Bridgette set the house on fire. Zoë had tried to go after her, and Antoine was barely able to get her out. A hundred questions sprang to Grey's lips, and she opened her mouth, but Antoine very firmly said, "Go on now. Get out of the car and go knock on that door."

Grey could barely stand. She took a moment to run fingers through her hair, an old nervous habit. She was stalling, and she knew it. Jonathan had known, she realized—had Googled it, seen the story, and allowed her to walk into this mess without warning. Damn him, she thought furiously.

Her steps were slow and halting. But eventually, she stood in front of the less-than-formal door of the garden cottage. She raised her hand to knock, but it flew open before she could make contact.

Zoë stood there, in relaxed jeans, barefoot, white linen shirt—for all the world relaxed, like the day she had met her. But her face and arms, God, were a mess of burns in various states of healing—ribbons of thick, shiny red skin twisting along her forearms, slipping under the linen shirt to reappear along a collarbone, creeping along that beautiful neck and up over that firm jawbone.

Those deep, molasses brown eyes, which had sparkled with dark humor, now seemed flat and haunted.

And yet a small smile curled her lips, and she reached out and hesitantly touched the tips of Grey's shorter hair. "I see I'm not the only one with a new look."

Grey opened her mouth to say something, anything, and what came out was, "I have to know if she walked into the sun!"

"What do you think?" Zoë drawled, the statement sad and quiet.

A silence fell between them.

"Alicia has to live. She promised," Grey said indignantly, staring wide-eyed into those searching eyes, tears welling up.

Zoë dropped her searching gaze, staring at her bare feet, tears of her own dripping onto the door's threshold. "But she's half a person, Grey. Damaged." She sobbed. "She's half a person fighting for her child with nothing left to fight with. Look at me. Some of these will never heal. There will be scars."

"She has to live, Zoë. She promised. And she's not fighting with nothing. Everything I have is yours. My fortune, my life, my heart. She has to live." She paused. "Because I find I can't live without her."

And for the first time, Grey took control. She stepped forward and gently wrapped her arms around Zoë's neck, locking gazes with the woman she so desperately loved.

"You said you love me, and I believe you." She almost groaned at the much-needed contact, leaning into her. "I heard you on the wind. I heard you, and I'm here. I love you, Zoë. Let's help each other live again."

Chapter Twenty-three

Zoë stepped into the embrace. "I need you," she whispered, shameless in her vulnerability. Grey nearly stumbled with the intensity of that statement and all it implied. A weight settled squarely on her shoulders, and she took it willingly.

"I need you, too," she admitted on the edge of a whisper. "I've needed you all along."

They held each other fiercely, Zoë's face buried in her neck. "And Emily?" Grey finally dared to ask.

"At my parents'." Zoë said flatly. "I'm in no shape to care for her." She took a shuddering breath. "I will be, but not yet."

Grey turned and kissed her beloved's forehead, nuzzling her cheek. "Alicia does not walk into the light," she said firmly.

"Jacqueline lives forever in her soul," Zoë answered thickly.

Grey sighed and hugged Zoë closer—a fierce embrace that was not meant to be gentle, her fingers digging into skin without apology.

"Would you have left her if she hadn't died in the fire?" It was a question she had to ask. She needed to know.

There was a long pause. "I was going to come find you. I'm only sorry it took me as long as it did."

"Don't," Grey said. "Let's not apologize. It is what it is." She still hated the phrase, yet she better understood what it meant. What had happened had happened. It could not be changed. But it could be accepted. It could be welcomed as a path that led to this particular moment.

"You don't deserve this," Zoë whispered, her voice too hoarse to speak. "Find someone your own age, someone without this much baggage. Find…"

"No," Grey snapped. "You don't get to tell me what I deserve and what I need. You might be older, Rochester, but we are equals in our feelings and desire. I know what I'm doing. I know what I'm committing to." She gripped her harder. "I've lost a lot. I'm not a naïve child. This isn't some fan crush. I *love* you, damn it."

Grey eased up on her hold, pulling back so she could see Zoë's face. Those molasses eyes, swimming with tears, stared up at her without pretention, raw, full of need. Grey obliged without hesitation, dipping her head to capture those full lips.

The kiss was salty, just as she remembered. But this was no goodbye as it had been before. She was welcomed, the lips parting, Zoë moaning into her embrace like a drowning woman searching for air. Grey pushed forward, completely confident and sure of her actions' outcome.

Bridgette was gone. Zoë was hurt, but she'd heal for the most part. Emily was safe, and she vowed to get her from her grandparents. But not yet. She had unfinished business.

Grey's fingers trailed up into Zoë's short hair, grasping for a hold, tightening her grip. She crushed their lips together fiercely, not caring that they were going to have to breathe at some point. She poured all the longing, all her feelings into that kiss, needing the desperate response that followed, empowered by the hands that tore at her back, dug into her skin.

They broke the kiss, both gasping for air. Zoë seemed to have regained some amount of control. She pulled Grey from the door and slammed it shut, then shoved her up against the nearest wall. And they kissed again, the need building. But not the need for emotional support or healing. That was all finished when they both uttered the words "I love you" out loud. They kissed with the kind of raw physical need between two people destined to be together.

Zoë pinned Grey in place with one hand, as the other expertly fingered the buttons of Grey's expensive suit. One after another, buttons, zippers, and clasps all ceded to her experienced manipulation. They moaned into the embrace, the sounds swallowed under hungry mouths and tongues exploring. They were testing each other—pushing and giving, submission and dominance, struggling for control.

Grey's breasts were fully exposed now, her jacket and shirt pushed back, and Zoë's long thin fingers were trailing lines between her nipples and her navel. Grey moaned and thrust her hand between Zoë's legs, all denim but still so warm. Zoë unlocked the kiss and stared at Grey.

"Well, my, my, Ms. Grey," she whispered huskily. "What kind of a tawdry woman do you think I am?" Her fingers slipped into her own lips, moistening the tips, and she gingerly traced the curve or Grey's hardened nipples.

"Drop the act, Scarlett, and fuck me." They both chuckled and groaned. Zoë eased Grey's jacket and shirt off her shoulders, tracing gentle wet kisses along her collarbone, grazing the edges with her teeth. Grey pulled Zoë's linen shirt over her head. No bra, of course. Grey lowered her lips to the nipple of Zoë's left breast and inhaled it into her mouth gently, tiny bites eliciting gasps of pleasure. She reveled in each.

They stumbled to a small bed in the corner, both of them pulling angrily at their remaining clothes. They tore the offending items off, tossing them away like unwanted garbage. They flung themselves onto the bed, Zoë slipping her leg between Grey's soft thighs, the slickness of her desire overwhelming. Zoë descended on Grey's ear and whispered, "There's always time, pet."

Grey's eyes shot open, and she mouthed the word, "Alicia," but trapped the sound deep in her throat. "Fuck," she hissed aloud.

Zoë chuckled against her neck, teeth grazing along exposed skin, fingers working furiously lower, trailing through wiry dark locks moist with heat. Grey squirmed, arching her back, spreading her legs with abandon, encouraging her to delve deeper, faster.

She groaned, "I need you," echoing the words whispered so passionately earlier but with a different connotation. "I need to feel you inside me," she hissed as a finger trailed lower, grazing her slick and hardened clit.

"You will always be my Jacqueline. But I love you, Grey," Zoë whispered. "I'm going to make love to you. Then I'm going to fuck you."

"I will always need you." Grey moaned, writhing at the teasing touches. She wound her fingers into Zoë's hair and pulled her in for another crushing kiss just as Zoë's fingers slid inside her in one smooth thrust. Her scream was swallowed in the kiss, her hips rocking up to meet each thrust. But it wasn't enough, and she pushed with all her might, breaking their locked lips with an auditory pop.

She shoved at the top of Zoë's head. "Lick me," she demanded. Then added quietly, almost meekly, "Please."

Zoë laughed like a woman who knew she was going to get everything she needed. "Yes," she drawled, "my darling. Anything you want."

284

Her lips blazed a trail from Grey's throat, across hardened nipples, along her ribcage, teasingly down to her navel, skipping vital points of interest to sink teeth into a soft, quivering thigh. Grey groaned in anticipation.

"I want to hear it one more time," Zoë murmured.

"I love you," Grey groaned obediently. "And I will always need you."

She was rewarded with a tongue bathing her sex—running the length between her aching opening and her engorged clit. She cried out, unable to help herself, and ground her hips into that beautiful face. An arm wrapped around her restless hips and lips clamped down on her in earnest. Fingers thrust into her, satiating a need she'd never experienced quite so fiercely.

She was filling up inside—much too quickly, she realized. Her climax was going to hit hard and fast, much too soon. "Oh, Zoë, oh, God, I can't stop."

Zoë paused for only a second. "Don't stop, baby. I want this for you." As if to prove her point, she clamped her full lips down hard again and thrust deeper and harder into Grey.

Grey's back arched, and a thousand lights popped behind her eyes. For the first time, Grey heard herself cry out in pleasure as her orgasm shook not just her own body, but Zoë's, as well. Zoë bathed her in tiny kisses as her fingers continued to dance inside Grey in unison with each tiny spasm. They were lost in each other.

Zoë finally relinquished her hold and crawled the length of Grey's body. Grey captured those sensuous, kissable lips and tasted herself. The sensation brought tears to her eyes.

"Are those for me?" Zoë teased. "And for the right reason this time." She smiled.

Grey raised her hand and wiped her eyes. "Yes, but we aren't done yet." And with shivers of pleasure still rolling over her naked body, she rolled over on top of Zoë and said, "Oh, I will take you, whore."

Zoë roared with laughter at the reference to her own writing. "Yes, please, mistress."

For a split second, Grey hesitated, her confidence faltering a fraction. How could she please this woman with so much more worldly experience? She had decades on her, quite literally. By comparison, Grey was a novice.

Then she mentally shook herself. Experience didn't matter. She had inspired a novel. To this woman, she was love and humanity.

Grey tested the waters, teasingly running her fingers up Zoë's inner thigh and higher. She encountered slick heat that left little doubt.

"You are so wet," she groaned, excitement building in spite of her recent release.

"Mmm," Zoë agreed. "For you."

Grey lost all sense of inhibition, her need driving her forward. She rubbed the length of Zoë's clit, folding back the lips hiding her goal, teasing its length with her middle finger while she disengaged from Zoë's embrace, sliding lower.

Those hips began to dance into her strokes, and she smiled at her daring.

"So wet," she groaned again, marveling at Zoë's excitement.

She slid a finger into the slick opening, feeling the swollen folds. Then another. It wasn't enough to fill her. She thrust harder, trying to elicit a response.

"Fuck," Zoë hissed, giving her what she wanted.

Grey ached to be filled again as she was filling Zoë. She fucked her harder, sliding lower, her mouth descending

286

on the desired center. She coated her cheeks and lips in sweet slick sex, furiously working her hands, ripping noises from Zoë's throat that she had never even imagined.

She did not take her time. This was raw need—pent up over time and in urgent need of expulsion. This was a race to the finish line before a slower run could be had.

Zoë cried out, her muscles clamping down around fingers thrusting deep. "Fuck," she hissed over and over again, unable to control herself. Her hands clamped down on top of Grey's head, pushing harder, her thighs trapping her in place. "Right there," she demanded with all the urgency she could muster.

She came hard. Grey felt the muscles spasm around her fingers, felt her gush from her entrance. Sweat broke out along her spine from the effort to keep it going. Those strong hips came to a slow and steady rocking, then ceased all movement. Hands relinquished their hold on her head. She couldn't move. Grey grinned into her satiated cunt.

After a few minutes of silence, Zoë pulled Grey to her side. "See, I knew. It's you, Grey, it's always been you." They lay locked in each other's embrace for hours, each providing the other with comfort and at last a sense of home.

For three days, just like in the novel, they cleansed each other of demons with love, both physical and emotional. Tucked away in the charred garden cottage, rain pattering against the fading glass, they loved each other. Finally, on the dawn of the third day in that tiny shack, Grey believed she saw a clarity return to Zoë's eyes.

"I needed you, and here you are," she said as though she couldn't believe it. "I called for you."

"Somehow, I knew. Zoë, when I left, I hid everything about you from myself. I didn't want to see it. I stayed off the Internet. I stayed off my phone. I had no idea what had happened here."

"I thought you hated me."

"I could never hate you."

"It took everything in me not to chase after you," Zoë admitted. "Remorse is a terrible thing. It poisoned everything around me. But I knew that I couldn't come after you until I closed this chapter. I had to handle my shit first."

"I had to rebuild myself. It would not have been enough for you to show up in Chicago, looking for me. I would have run from you, I was so shattered and angry."

Zoë traced her jaw tenderly. "Look at us now, though. We found a way."

"Thank goodness."

Zoë sighed, then smiled. "Grey, do you know what I want to do today?" she asked, almost childlike.

"What, lover?" Grey smiled.

"Let's go get Emily."

Grey's heart swelled at the idea of reuniting their little family. She couldn't think of anything that would make her happier than seeing the tiny imp, preferably in pink unicorn pajamas like the night she had met her. She couldn't wait to chase after fairies in the garden under the New Orleans sun.

They would have to find another garden. Another home. There would be the inevitable argument over New Orleans versus Chicago. Work would somehow have to fit into their lives. So many changes were coming. It didn't matter. They had a foundation on which to build whatever world they wanted to imagine. Jacqueline and Alicia's love was forever. So was Grey and Zoë's.

The End

About the authors

It is particularly rare among writers to find someone with whom you can write with a complete lack of ego—to find a coauthor who can correct, add, conform, or criticize something you have just written, and you have absolutely no desire to reach across the table and smack the living crap out of her.

Both Caren Penland and Elizabeth Parmer were authors in their own right before attempting to write together. Likewise, both had attempted at previous times to write with other people without success.

That is not to say that either of these women were possessive of their work—ahem—okay, maybe they were. But together, each finally found another person who could cut, disregard, delete, or completely dissect her writing, and she would be forced to say, "Yeah, you're right, that sex scene was entirely too short," or, "Okay, I see your point, I should provide descriptive narrative of some sort there," — and all of this over a fantastic bottle of Moët!

Night after night, these two women simply handed the computer back and forth to each other and created what has been described as seamless plots and characters. After a while, they realized they didn't know where one writer's prose stopped and the other's began. Their characters began to build themselves. And that was when they both knew they'd met their match. In writing, at the very least.

Caren Penland is a former journalist who fell in love with the coffee shop scene and runs a busy store in downtown Fort Worth, Texas. Her best story ideas are spawned while running along the Trinity River trail or over a glass of red wine with her writing partner, Betsy.

Caren lives with her wife, Sarah, and pit bull, Zak, in a quiet neighborhood in the cultural district. She has previously published three novels under the pen name Kimberly LaFontaine.

Elizabeth Parmer is a practicing litigation attorney who escapes the monotony of the courtroom by writing erotic fiction with her coauthor, Caren. When she is not berating opposing counsel with stiff and organized constitutional arguments, she is drunkenly insisting that Caren add more moisture and folds to the most recent sex scene.

She lives with her husband, artist James, and daughter, singer Claire. She is the least talented of the family. She went to Yale, it was boring.

www.betsyandcaren.com
www.facebook.com/betsyandcaren
www.twitter.com/betsyandcaren
#ThePoisonofLife
#betsyandcaren

The next series installment to be released late 2016

Made in the USA
San Bernardino, CA
10 May 2016